He told J

what woke him. H

still ingrained aft

sound that, though hardly indistinguishable, warned his subconscious it was foreign. He lay in bed, his body taut, his ears straining to hear. After a minute he sat up, the top sheet and duvet falling from his chest. The beads of his necklace shifted position and the opposite side of the beads rolled and lay against his chest. When he thought about it afterwards, he supposed the air and the beads had been cold, but he wasn't aware of them then. He slid out of bed and tiptoed into the living room. A sound so faint as to be nearly inaudible came to him in the stillness between owl calls. It was the sound of breaking glass.

Accolades for Jo A. Hiestand

"A possible family reunion, a hit and run accident, an unexpected attack and a hunt for missing treasure take center stage in Jo A. Hiestand's *AN UNFOLDING TRAP*, the fifth book in the McLaren Mystery series. A well-developed hero, colorful secondary characters and a good mystery kept me turning the pages from start to finish."

~Queenofallshereads.blogspot.com review

~*~

"With hints of the 1940s movie *Laura*, Michael McLaren is drawn with haunting music into the intricate path of attraction for a dead woman. It is easy to get caught up in the wonderful descriptions written by author Jo Hiestand, and then suddenly realize she just gave us a clue. Jo leads us along, following twists and turns, making us guess who the murderer is. I was so sure I knew who did it, and in the end, I was so wrong! *Shadow in the Smoke* is an excellent mystery and well worth reading."

~Ann Collins, Librarian,
Webster Groves Public Library

No Known Address

by

Jo A. Hiestand

The McLaren Mysteries, Book 6

This is a work of fiction. Names, characters, places, and incidents are either the product of the author's imagination or are used fictitiously, and any resemblance to actual persons living or dead, business establishments, events, or locales, is entirely coincidental.

No Known Address

Contact Information: info@thewildrosepress.com

Cover Art by *Angela Anderson*

The Wild Rose Press, Inc.
PO Box 708
Adams Basin, NY 14410-0708
Visit us at www.thewildrosepress.com

Publishing History: Previously published as *Love Song* by Golden Harvest Press, 2014
First Crimson Rose Edition, 2016
Print ISBN 978-1-5092-1020-6
Digital ISBN 978-1-5092-1021-3

The McLaren Mysteries, Book 6
Published in the United States of America

Dedication

For Wilfred Bereswill,
Linda Houle,
and Paul Schmit.
Heaven is more beautiful with your presence.

Acknowledgments

My thanks to Detective-Superintendent David Doxey, Derbyshire Constabulary (ret.), for reading the manuscript and catching technical and grammatical mistakes; and to Paul Hornung, St. Louis-area Police Sergeant, for supplying some procedural details and for helping me sort out the end to the story.

Also, I'd like to thank the many readers who cheer McLaren on to the next case and who tell me I'm not writing fast enough. I appreciate each person, but I know only a few personally (the joys of e-mail and social media communication!). My new friends, flung far and wide: Kathy Johnson Allen, Ann Curtis Collins, Maureen Coyne, Don Keller, Marianne Kirk, and Melainey Walker, whom I thank again for the book. It did spark an idea, as she hoped, which I use in *No Known Address*. Everyone's enthusiasm for McLaren keeps me going.

Finally, thank you to publishing Senior Editor Lori Graham, for another McLaren mystery green light, and to my book editor, Cindy Davis, who I will also sorely miss.

Jo Hiestand
St. Louis, Missouri
June 2016

Author's Notes

The village of Crich and the old Wakebridge Engine House exist. I've used them in a fictitious way and added something to their immediate landscape.

No Known Address has a companion song. "Did You Not Hear My Lady" is available on a single-song CD recording, and is performed by Connor R. Scott, baritone, and Gabriel Maichel, piano. This Handel aria is available through the author's website www.johiestand.com

McLaren has his own website! Log on to learn about upcoming books, interesting places to visit in the UK, and a calendar of appearances by the author. www.mclaren-mysteries.com

Cast of Characters

Michael McLaren: former police detective, Staffordshire Constabulary

Jamie Kydd: McLaren's friend and police detective, Derbyshire Constabulary

Dena Ellison: McLaren's fiancée

Charlie Harvester: former colleague of McLaren's, now a detective in the Derbyshire Constabulary

Residents of the village of Langheath:

Luke Barber: talented amateur tennis player and musician

Gary Barber: Luke's father and local farmer/owner of Twin Beck Farm

Margaret Barber: Gary's wife

Ashley Fraser Fox: Luke's former fiancée

Callum Fox: Luke's doubles partner, Ashley's husband

Darren Fraser: Ashley's father

Sharon Fraser: Ashley's mother

Bethany Watson: Luke's singing partner

Nathan Watson: Bethany's husband

John Evans: Luke's music teacher

Doc Tipton: Luke's tennis coach

Philip Moss: friend of Luke's

Tom Yardley: friend of Luke's

Harry Rooney: friend of Luke's

Chapter One

The man seemed not to hear the continuous whine of the phone receiver lying on his lap. He sat upright, stiff-backed, in a wooden kitchen chair that, like the house, had seen better days. As *he* had also seen better days, he reminded himself, glancing at the calendar on the wall. A date circled in black ink smirked at him, the remaining days of the month X-ed out. As though he was counting down to something. But the dates were three years old.

The discrepancy didn't bother him. He had never flipped over the rest of the months, never crossed out the other dates, never looked at the color photographs illustrating the rest of the year. They didn't intrigue him; it didn't upset him that he had stared at January for more than a thousand days. If he flipped over the page it would signal that the search needed to continue into another month. And possibly another. And another. The consequence was too terrible to comprehend.

He'd have to mutely admit he realized it.

And realize his son could be anywhere. Or nowhere. He had no known address.

He sighed, his hand closing over the cold plastic of the phone receiver. The whine irritated him, cycling between a low and high tone. Enough to set one's teeth on edge. Or push one into action. He grunted. The action should've happened three years ago, should be continuing. Damned incompetence.

A tree branch scraped against the roof's gutter, pulling his attention to the window. The chair's hardness and the phone's voice faded under his son's face, a face barely nineteen years old. Brown eyes peered out of the night, the lips parted and smiling, as though wanting to speak. Tears flooded the man's eyes and spilled down his cheek but he made no effort to blot the wetness. He cried so seldom anymore. The emotion made him feel alive, yet simultaneously numbed him.

He stared at the imagined face beyond the window, the likeness blurred from the tears in his eyes. But he didn't need perfect sight to see his son: the boy's face was seared into his memory.

The wind slammed against the casement and he leaned forward, as though to touch the face behind the glass. The receiver crashed to the floor, pulling the base of the phone with it.

The man picked up the phone, recradled the receiver, and placed it on the table. A pelting of sleet filled the sudden silence and he stumbled to the window. The winter evening had descended early, the snow moving in from the Welsh border to the west. He'd never seen the Clwydian Range, the chain of hills in the northeast of the country. He'd heard they were beautiful, though. Maybe someday…

He ran his callused hands over his arms and shivered. The window glass held the coldness of the day and would only intensify over night.

Turning back to the table, he reached for the phone, then thought better of it. He'd already spoken to his friend. Who else did he expect would help him?

Especially after three years. Three years of meaningless sentences and broken promises.

He clicked off the table lamp and shuffled into the main room. Its framed photos and scrapbooks held the memories of those he loved. His wife had departed from his life twenty years ago and had never had to deal with the pain of their missing son. Now he was alone, but his love for her still lingered, still warmed him. He poked the fire into a feeble blaze and sank into the rocker. The flames threw indigo shadows across the rug, barely reaching the opposite wall. The shadows would deepen into black in an hour or so, when the sun set. But, then, the whole sky would be black. It hardly made any difference to him anymore.

He leaned back and closed his eyes. What did he expect that phone call to accomplish? Embarrass the chief constable? Prod a constable into writing up a report?

The snowfall deepened into drifts banked against the barn door as the man's breathing slowed, keeping time with the chant in his mind. He'll come back. Keep the faith. He'll come back. Keep the faith. He'll come back… He fell asleep praying this time the response to his phone call would be different.

****

"So, what you're really saying in a clumsy way is that the Derbyshire police have failed dismally, and after three years you want me to fix the cock-up and find your missing man." Michael McLaren glanced at the sheet of paper his friend waved in front of his face. It was too close for him to read.

"I would've phrased it differently, but I'll let it pass. I can't afford to antagonize you."

"If this is urgent, you're out of luck, Jamie. I've got a half dozen new jobs waiting for me, the Walker farm has a section of stone wall down and they've had to keep the horses elsewhere. I also have a wall repair job in Monyash, plus a repair outside Hognaston—"

"If you're trying to impress me that your skill, such as it is, is winning you fans, fame and fortune, I'll acknowledge it. But the stone wall work has to wait, Mike. This is important."

"And farmers' livestock isn't?"

"You know what I mean. Another week, give or take a day, probably won't make much difference to them."

"And how long has this case been cold?"

Jamie frowned, as though reluctant to admit there was no real urgency.

McLaren came to his friend's rescue. "And another week, give or take a day, after three years of no solution, probably won't make much difference to the hunt."

"If you spoke to the father, you'd not say that."

Sighing heavily, he frowned. "All right. Knowing you, I'll never get any peace until I read this thing."

"I would say something about your dismal lack of knowledge on a vast number of subjects, but I need your help. You *are* useful at times."

"That wasn't too painful for you to admit, was it?" McLaren grabbed the note and quickly read it, then shifted his gaze from the penciled scrawl to Jamie Kydd's face. It was slightly reddened from the wintry wind but it suited his light complexion. His thick, light brown hair was styled in a longer 'winter cut', yet the unruly lock of hair at his right temple still fell forward occasionally. He pushed the hair back into place and waited for McLaren's response.

"All right." McLaren nodded. He knew when he was licked. "Your lot couldn't come up with the lad, his trail, or a motive for his disappearance. What *did* you learn?"

Jamie allowed himself a smile before turning serious. He tapped the edge of the paper, as though it would kick the cold case into life. "The lad's name is Luke Barber. Nineteen years old at that time. He went missing on Friday, 20th January."

"What time?"

"No one knows exactly, but his absence was first noted around four-thirty that afternoon."

"Four-thirty in January is sunset." He looked at the night-wrapped land beyond the pub window. The sun had set nearly five hours ago. Lights from houses and the few shops still open in the village winked in the smothering darkness, giving the land definition. As did the smears of snow bordering the village's High Street and wallowing in the roof valleys. "It's begun to snow." His voice sounded thin, bouncing off the hard glass. "Wonder how much we'll get. I don't recall the weather forecast." A blast of laughter from a neighboring table brought McLaren's attention back to the paper. "I doubt anyone would've seen much if they'd gone out searching at that hour. Too dark to see anything useful. Especially if they were looking around the Peak District Dales." He paused again, imagining the English district of mountains, valleys, moors and rivers. A terribly difficult place to search at night. He cleared his voice. "They wait until morning?"

"For the most part, yes. Though a few people went

out with lanterns and determination right then."

"They came up empty handed, I assume."

Jamie took a swallow of beer before nodding.

"Who noticed him gone?"

"His singing partner, Bethany Watson."

"*Singing* partner? He was a professional, then?"

"Not really. More like serious amateur or semi-pro."

"Pubs and folks clubs and that sort of thing?"

"Yeah. They had a gig that evening at The Green Cat. He never arrived to pick her up."

"Did he ever do that before?"

"No. Which was what got her concerned and prompted her to ring up his house. His father said he thought Luke'd left for her place an hour ago."

"Too much to hope that there were footprints in the snow, I guess."

"If there had been, Mike, I wouldn't be asking you now to investigate."

Chapter Two

"So, if the Derbyshire Constabulary has shoved this into its unsolved case file, how'd you get ahold of it?" McLaren nudged his empty dinner plate back slightly and rested his forearms on the table. They were muscular, as were his shoulders. a product of lifting and shifting large stones in his dry stone wall work. He looked up, the light from the wall sconce catching the whitish streaks in his blond hair and casting a golden tint to his hazel eyes.

"A friend rang me up this evening and asked for help in locating his son."

"The nineteen year-old who's been missing all this time."

"Right. His father was content at the outset of the case to let the police handle it, but now that it's dragged on for three years, well…" He shrugged, as though to say it was McLaren's turn to take over.

"Did the boy…Luke?…live with his father?"

"Yes. In a small village. Langheath. You know it?"

"I've heard of it. It's between Wirksworth and Bakewell, isn't it?"

"Right. Off the B5057."

"Old lead mining country around Wirksworth." He paused, as though envisioning the mining town and a previous case he'd worked. He had the utmost respect for miners. They worked at a dangerous job and were shut off from the sunlight. He'd considered a mining career when he was nearing the end of his schooling, but he knew he'd quickly go insane underground. He needed sunlight, rain and open spaces, the emotional balm that kept his nightmare at bay. He glanced at his hands, large and calloused. In summer they, as well as his arms and shoulders, were usually tanned from hours working in fields. He reached for his glass but was content to let his fingertips tap lightly on its dimpled surface. "What happened during the original search, aside from the initial hunt by lantern light?"

"A handful of residents went out soon after Bethany Watson raised the alarm."

"Was she one of them?"

"No. She sat in the father's house, in case Luke phoned."

"Like he had car trouble or something?"

"I guess. Though they both live in the village, so I don't see what car trouble he could've had without any resident seeing him."

"Or without him walking home or to some shop."

"Right. They lived about a mile apart."

"Go on."

"There were four men who went out that evening. Luke's father, of course. That's Gary Barber."

"The friend who rang you tonight."

Jamie screwed up the corner of his mouth and sank back in his chair. "Why do I even bother?"

"It's just a logical assumption. Unless he was in hospital or away on business, the father would be looking for his son."

"I guess so."

"How do you know him? I've not seen him at our

poker nights or even heard his name before."

"He's a family friend," Jamie explained. "He and my uncle are best mates."

"So he's older than you by…oh, twenty years or so?"

"Twenty-two, if you want to get technical." He sounded like a woman begrudgingly admitting her true age. "My uncle talks about their adventures quite often. He says that during their school years, Gary used to practically live at my uncle's home. They did everything together, even got together on hols, Christmas and such. If marriage hadn't interfered for both of them…" He broke off, and McLaren wondered if there was some family history behind the statement.

"All right. We've got Gary Barber hunting." McLaren jotted the name in his notebook. Without looking up, he asked, "Who else?"

"Well, Callum Fox joined in. He volunteered immediately."

"Who's he?"

"Luke's tennis doubles partner. When they play doubles, that is. Mainly, Luke played in singles matches. But he and Callum entered a bunch of doubles matches. Especially when Luke was starting, which was when he was fifteen."

"Four years before he went missing. Awfully young."

"I guess those athletes have to start young if they want to turn pro. Look at those gymnasts, if you want any further proof. Don't they start before they're teens?"

"Is that what Luke wanted to do, turn tennis pro?"

Jamie shrugged and finished the last of his baked

halibut. In the interim, a blast of wind ushered an older couple into the pub. The breeze whipped around the corner and curled around Jamie's feet. "I heard some rumor about him wanting to go into music, but I don't know how serious he was about either. You'll have to ask around."

"At least he liked music as a sideline. I mean, if his singing partner and he were going to sing that night at a pub…" A phrase of the Michael Bublé song "Home" pushed over the hubbub of nearby conversation. McLaren listened to the words, hoping the lyrics weren't an omen of Luke's trouble. He shook the disturbing image from his mind and took a deep breath before continuing. "So far we have the father and tennis partner searching for Luke. Who else?"

"Two more. John Evans and Doc Tipton. John Evans was Luke's music teacher. He specializes in piano and guitar. Luke played guitar."

"Folk, I assume, since he and Bethany were on their way to a singing engagement at a pub."

"Yes, but John also teaches classical guitar, as well as jazz and folk. His mainstay for pupils, though, is the piano."

"And the other person, Doc Tipton. Family physician?"

"One would assume that. Doc is just a nickname. He's actually Albert Tipton."

"Albert. Don't hear that much anymore."

"His parents were enamored of Albert Schweitzer. Need I say more?"

McLaren eyed Jamie, trying to discern a joke. "You're serious, aren't you?"

"As serious as asking you to get the next round."

He shoved his empty beer glass toward McLaren. "Just got time, I think, before I have to leave."

"How fortunate some people are." McLaren walked over to the bar. The air near the front door smelled of cold and snow. The couple who just came in shivered slightly and rubbed their hands as they made their way to a table across the room. McLaren angled his body away from the chilling blast, paid for Jamie's pint, and returned to the table. "If you like your beer cold, like the Americans do, just leave it for a minute by the door."

"Cold, eh?"

"Cold *wind*, at least. If more snow doesn't blow in tonight, it's missing a good chance." He stamped his feet on the flagstone floor and set the beer on the table before he slid into the booth.

"You're not having one?" Jamie looked at the pint before him and at McLaren's half-filled coffee cup.

"I'm the designated driver." He watched Jamie take a sip. "Okay. You got your payment. Let's hear about Albert Schweitzer's namesake."

"Albert Doc Tipton is the local tennis coach."

"Tennis coach? You're joking."

"As serious as asking you to get—"

McLaren held up his hand. "You don't have to repeat it. I wouldn't have thought there'd be that much call for tennis coaches in a little village like Langheath."

"Surprised me, too. It's not exactly Manchester or London."

"Or even Buxton." He swallowed the last of his coffee before jotting Doc Tipton's name in his notebook. "So, how does this tennis coach make a living here? Was he famous? I assume he's retired from the game. A majority of coaches seem to be."

"I don't know particulars, since I wasn't assigned to Luke's case, but I believe he won some prestigious matches in Britain and overseas."

"So he's got his fame to pull in the learners. But surely there aren't that many around here who want or need tennis lessons."

"That's why he works in Chesterfield. Anyway, Luke Barber, the missing lad, was one of Doc's students on a regular basis."

"Like, every week?"

"Yeah. Luke's father, Gary, mentioned to me a few times how good Luke was and that he was debating between tennis and music as a profession."

"He was good at both, then."

"According to Gary. And Bethany."

"She's hardly unbiased."

"Might not be, but it does no good to lie about that. Either you're good enough for a music career and get a loyal fan base to support you, or you aren't. They had steady gigs on the weekends, so they evidently were good enough to draw in enough customers. But it's a lot different when you're trying to attain concerts or even open for some name group."

"Hell of a hard life, yes. How was he at tennis, did his father say?"

"Won several local matches—local meaning around Derbyshire, Yorkshire and Lancashire—both singles and doubles."

"Then his doubles partner, Callum Fox, isn't too bad, either."

Jamie shrugged and downed half his beer. "I have

no idea. But the point is, Mike, that Luke Barber had talent and could've taken either path."

"More to the point, perhaps, is that someone might've blocked that path."

"Chilling thought."

"Just these four men, then, were the only people who searched the evening he went missing? No police were brought in?"

"Gary—the father—rang up Clay Cross station. Officers arrived around six fifteen that night. Of course they couldn't do a proper search in the dark, so they took the information and told Gary they'd be back in the morning. Which they were. They turned the house, barn and sheds upside down, talked to residents, tried to pick up a trail, but nothing came of it. The ground was too frozen to retain footprints; the little snow that was on the ground produced nothing of interest. People had no idea where he'd gone."

"Except that he should've picked up Bethany and been at The Green Cat. Did he have a car? Did he usually drive to that pub? And where is that, by the way? Was the car at his home?"

Jamie held up his arms, crossing them in front of his face, and laughed. "You want me to answer these in the order you gave them, or am I free merely to talk as it occurs to me?"

"You're not cut out to be a comedian. Just give with the info."

"Luke was nineteen, as I said, and he drove. Had a driving license and his own car, a 2009 Mini Clubman—maroon color. He usually picked up Bethany at her home. She also lives here in Langheath. The Green Cat's in Youlgreave, about seven miles away. His car was at his dad's house, in the spot where he usually parked it—in the farmyard, on the south side of the house. His car key and house key were in his room. Nothing was missing. Well, at least as far as Gary could discern. Clothes all there. As was his guitar. His wallet wasn't, but most men shove it into their trousers or jeans pocket when they dress and don't take it out until bedtime. So I don't know what that means."

"Just that he didn't leave for Bethany's place or for the singing engagement. Something stopped him prior to four-thirty."

"So, what happened to him?"

Chapter Three

Good question, McLaren thought. He sat in the rear room of his house, his head against the back of the sofa, the room lights off. The darkness masked everything distracting, like his fiancée's framed photo on the wall. She had a stubborn habit of staring at him and whispering that he wasn't spending enough time with her, or reminding him he kept putting off setting the wedding date. And right now, McLaren hadn't the inclination to deal with it. Which, if he were truthful with himself, bothered him. If he loved Dena, and he didn't doubt that for an instant, why didn't he do something about it? Because I'm afraid I'm too independent? Because I don't want to give up my freedom?

His fingers toyed with the wooden beads strung on a leather thong around his neck. Like worry beads, he thought, feeling the smooth, round surfaces. Appropriate, too, for if I were honest with myself I'd admit my concern. I was ready to marry last year; why am I hesitant now?

The beads continued to hold his attention, focus his thoughts. He hummed a verse of Janet Ellis' song "Never Leave My Side" before he became aware of it. The choice surprised him. And bothered him. Did he still retain an admiration for the singer, still secretly wish he'd known her? The concession flooded him with guilt. He'd not known Janet, but he'd become enthralled with her song and her sultry beauty, become involved in solving her murder. But she was a phantom, never to be real to him. Why couldn't he find the same longing for Dena? Because Janet could be anything he dreamt, made no demands on him, expected nothing, would always be perfect?

He sighed heavily and got up. Maybe if he put some distance between him and the photo…

He stopped at the window overlooking the back field. The land stretched out dark and flat, rising gently until it met the hill to the west. Then the gradient steepened, and the ground changed from grazing pasture to rocky moor. Lines of stone walls trailed across the earth, like veins protruding from a hand, dividing the terrain into territories for sheep, horses and cattle, the life's blood of the farms in the vicinity. He didn't need to see the gray lines to know where they were; he had grown up in the house, spent more weekends than he'd wanted clearing the field or repairing the walls. So, the work, too, was in his blood. A different type of ancestry.

He pressed his palm against the window, knowing it would be January-cold, needing the frigid temperature to keep his mind focused. He leaned his forehead on the glass, staring at the sky. A bank of dark clouds crawled westward, nudged by the insistent wind. Moonlight periodically spilled through rifts in the black covering, pinpointing patches of frost and ice, and generally painting the land in silver light. Then, abruptly, the land plunged into darkness as a cloud obscured the light. It would go on like that for hours, he thought, giving the sky one last look. Snow or sleet would finish the dark hours and usher in the morning.

Shivering from the cold, he turned from the window and made his way across the unlit room. The mantel clock chimed eleven and McLaren flicked on the lamp beside the couch. He pulled out his notebook and sat down heavily, resigning himself to the investigation. Not that he didn't want to help Gary Barber find his son, but he had a horror of disappointing people. And he just might do that this time if he couldn't find Luke. Jamie evidently had sung his praises quite heavily to Gary. This was not the time for that praise to be false.

He spread the sketch of the village on the coffee table, noting the designated, labeled buildings. The Barber place, Twin Beck Farm, occupied the southern acreage from the High Street east toward the River Amber. Birch Brook cut through their land, forming a natural division of sheep pastures and wheat fields. Luke's singing partner, Bethany Watson, lived along Bridge Lane, in the northern area of the village. He would check driving distance tomorrow, but he imagined it wouldn't take Luke more than a few minutes to drive to her house. And his father had thought Luke had already left when Bethany phoned to ask after Luke. Had it been so dark that evening that Gary couldn't see Luke's car in the farm yard?

The local pub was too far away for its patrons to have seen anything at the farm, and the other nearest residence, Doc Tipton's, looked to be equally distant. More than walking or viewing distance, he thought as he envisioned the amount of land the farm must contain.

The other houses and shops meant nothing to him,

so he folded the map, jammed it into his jeans pocket, turned out the light, and went to bed. But sleep didn't come immediately: the nagging question of Luke's walking destination kept him up till two.

****

Friday morning began cold and, if it correctly followed the weather forecast, would end colder and with snow. McLaren finished the last of his coffee, filled his Thermos, and pulled on his sheepskin jacket. He had a feeling he'd need the extra warmth today. Tramping about the village would be frigid work.

Sleet sat thinly bunched between the wizened stalks of grass and in the seams of the flagstone walkway across his front lawn. The frozen pellets crunched beneath his boots and threw back the sunlight, turning the lawn and garden into thousands of tiny prisms. He pulled his muffler a bit closer to his neck and gazed at the sky. A smear of charcoal-hued stratus clouds loomed against the pale blue expanse.

After scraping the frost from his car's windscreen, he consulted his road map. Langheath lay to the east of Two Dales, a village tucked between the mountainous Hall and Sydnope dales. It looked to be approximately twenty-seven miles from his home in Somerley, to the north. Probably a forty-five-minute trip, he thought, considering the Friday traffic and the B-sized and smaller unclassified roads.

He got into his car, stowed the container of coffee in the cup holder, and laid the map on the passenger seat. The steering wheel was as cold as the air, and he exhaled sharply. His breath fogged up the interior of the windscreen, and he pulled on his leather gloves before starting the engine. He sat in his driveway for several seconds while the defroster cleared the glass, then cracked open the window, and headed down the tarmac.

The Dillards' song "The Old Home Place" quickly filled the car's interior as the CD started up from where it had finished playing last night. He blinked several times, startled by the song's subject. It was the second song about home he'd heard in less than twelve hours. He could almost believe it meant something.

Somerley, his home village, stirred awake in the early sunshine. Sparrows congregated on the pavement outside the bakery and greengrocer's, hoping for an easy breakfast. Frost encrusted the tops of the iron railings and copper gutters of the church and other buildings along the high street. Even the bench that sat in the small park between the bakery and gift shop was fringed with icicles. He squinted as he drove past the newsagent's, the sunlight glaring off the large front window.

He left the village, turning off the A625 and onto the B6049 heading south. The Dillards had launched into singing about Ebo Walker, a song McLaren felt his folk group, Woodstock Town, would sing well if they ever worked up an arrangement. Comprised of three men and one woman, his group held on to their acoustic sound in the hubbub of electrified instruments that seemed to increase each year. They had a steady and enthusiastic following who loved their spirited renditions of "The Blacksmith" and "Cold, Haily, Rainy Night." It was a tight-knit group and though they'd never make the status of The McCalmans or Union Station, still, they had fun. And wasn't that the major reason for singing?

He turned up the volume a bit and sang along with

Rodney Dillard, oblivious to the miles slipping beneath the car tires.

Traffic on the A6 out of Bakewell thinned, and McLaren made better time until he turned onto the B5057 at Two Dales. The road narrowed and turned sharply northeast, forcing him to reduce his speed. Patches of snow lay thick in the ditches on the verges of the road, sat heavy on lower boughs of the evergreens, the shade of the forest preventing the snow from melting. Ice rimmed a shallow puddle on the road and broke in a sharp retort as the tires cracked through the hardness. The fragrance of damp earth and chert flowed through the open window.

The village of Langheath emerged from a clump of dark Norway spruce, though the road shimmered ahead as it angled into the sunlight. Two houses sat opposite each other, the road between them and making room for more buildings as it widened at the junction of the high street.

McLaren glanced at his map, then turned right onto the High Street. Several minutes later he parked at the Barbers' farm house.

A dog barked inside the barn before a male voice called for it to be quiet. McLaren got out of his car, looked at the house as though considering going there, then headed for the barn as the large door slid open.

The dog, a collie, rushed out, barking loudly, but halted within several feet of McLaren. It looked back at the man who followed slowly, limping slightly on his left leg. He looked to be in his sixties, McLaren thought, with graying brown hair, clear brown eyes, and a ruddy complexion weathered by the sun and cold. Though of medium height, he appeared to be twenty or so pounds overweight. Of course, the bulk of the overalls and heavy canvas coat could add to the illusion.

The man stopped alongside his dog and slid his left hand to the dog's collar. The dog angled its head and licked the hand but the man didn't seem to notice. His eyes stared at McLaren, unwavering and assessing the man before him. When he spoke, his voice was rough and low, as though tinted by the wind and chill.

"Are ye lookin' for sumthin'? Can I be o' help?" He stayed beside the dog and neither moved nor extended his hand.

McLaren smiled and nodded. "Mr. Barber?"

"Aye. What would ye be wantin'?"

"I'm Michael McLaren. Your friend Jamie Kydd contacted me last night, told me about your son's disappearance." He paused, watching the older man's neck muscle tighten. Maybe the hurt still lingered, even if it wasn't evident until the subject was brought up. McLaren took a breath and went on. "I assume he told you about me, about my former…occupation." That described it well enough, he thought. There's no need to go into details.

Gary Barber nodded, the neck muscle relaxing. "Ye were a copper. A detective. One o' the best." He wiped his right hand on the front of his overalls and extended it.

McLaren took the man's hand and held it momentarily. The skin was leathery and callused, yet the grip was firm and warm. Like the people of the Dales—firm in their beliefs and warm in hospitality. McLaren flashed a grin. "That's nice to hear. I can't guarantee I'll have any better luck with the investigation than the police did, but I'm willing to try, if that meets with your approval."

The man squeezed McLaren's hand before releasing it. "I'd appreciate another brain and set o' eyes, lad. An' yers are bound to be better tha' most at seein' things. An' I hear tell from Jamie that ye're honest, ye keep the victim first and last. That means a lot to me."

You might change your opinion if you knew how close I came to killing a man last month, McLaren thought.

Gary looked at the sky and pulled the collar of his coat close to his throat. The wind had risen and the boughs of the Norway spruce bobbed beneath the buffeting. A low moan eased from the space between two loose fitting boards in the barn. In the grassy area of the yard several pieces of clothing pegged to a sagging clothesline were blowing in the wind. "Come," Gary said, gesturing ahead of them. "We'll talk inside the house. It's warmer an' we'll be out o' the wind." He released the dog and pointed to the house. The dog trotted ahead of them and sat on the slab of granite outside the kitchen door.

The house was typical of others of that type: gray stone two storey with a steeply pitched roof of darker gray slate. Black wooden trim encased the narrow windows, giving them the look of heavily mascaraed eyes. McLaren glanced at the nearest one. One of the curtains moved slightly. Was he being observed?

An exuberant rose bush near the door nodded in the breeze and McLaren's mind went back eighteen months to an incident involving another rose bush. He'd driven to his seventy-year-old friend's aid that night, wanting to help him through the maze of police procedure following a break-in at his pub. The friend had defended himself against the burglar, striking him with a fireplace poker. Now he found himself arrested for assault, and McLaren's anger at the injustice focused on the man responsible for it. The man in charge of the case. Detective-Inspector Charlie Harvester.

Years of personal animosity erupted that evening in a physical confrontation, and ended with McLaren throwing Harvester into a nearby rose bush. He'd quit his job quickly after that, fed up with the injustice of the event. Perhaps it had been inevitable, for he'd become less tolerant of incompetency in the workplace the previous year. Harvester merely personified it, the epitome of nepotism and unfairness. Whatever the catalyst, the outcome of McLaren's career would've been the same, whether a year or two or more in the future.

As he passed the Barbers' rose bush, he imagined Harvester in the mental ward he now occupied. Though the facility was in Manchester, it was still too close for McLaren's liking. Anything closer than Siberia was too near. Perhaps someone less personally acquainted with the man would've been more compassionate, but McLaren knew Harvester's wily tricks, the deceit he worked while he smiled. The man had no right being a police officer. With some good luck, maybe he'd be a resident of Cheadle Royal Hospital for many years.

"Just set yerself down in tha' chair." Gary indicated an overstuffed ottoman by the fireplace before going into the kitchen. His voice floated out from the room. "I'll just put the kettle on the boil and we'll ha' ourselves a cuppa while we talk."

McLaren nodded and took the offered chair. It blended well with the room's color scheme: hues of brown and blue in upholstery and carpets. Well worn furniture that conveyed use and comfort. A framed photo of a man in his teens sat on the mantel. McLaren got up and went over to the picture. Frank, brown eyes gazed at the viewer from beneath a mop of thick, brown hair. A slightly crooked grin seemed to envelop most of the boy's face. It was the kind of looks that women would warm to immediately, McLaren thought.

He turned, self conscious about his intrusion into Gary Barber's private life, when the man entered the room. McLaren quickly replaced the photo and cleared a magazine from the footstool. Gary set the tea tray on the stool and poured out a mug.

Handing it to McLaren, he nodded at the photo. "Tha's Luke. But I assume ye've figured tha' out." He sat down and stirred the milk into his tea.

"Yes, I did assume that." McLaren took a long sip of the hot liquid. "I didn't mean to intrude."

"Ye're not intrudin'. How are ye goin' to find out anythin' if ye don't ask questions? Now, what do ya need to know?"

A handful of sleet slammed against the window and McLaren looked up.

"Won't last long." Gary rested the mug on the arm of the chair, his fingers wrapped around the handle. "Just look a' the sky."

McLaren did. The thin line of clouds were nearly over the farm. A streak of blue already showed along the western horizon.

Gary settled into his chair as a log in the fireplace grate popped. "I'm grateful ye came and want to help find my son. There's no' many others tha' do." His eyes clouded, as though veiling his hurt from McLaren.

"Well, Mr. Barber—"

"Please call me Gary. If we're to be workin' together, I'd like Gary much better."

"You asked what I need to know. Did Luke seem at all agitated or angry or excited the day he went missing, or any days prior to that?"

"He seemed his usual self. Which is to say he was cheerful an' friendly. If he had a problem, he didn't tell me." He stared at his tea, as though he were reading the future in the tea leaves. "He was an only child, and I knew only children can be secretive. It's about no' havin' someone close to confide in, or somethin' like tha'. Anyway, whatever the reason, Luke wasn't like the majority. We were close. Maybe 'cause our family was just we two. But he'd tell me his ambitions and his problems and we'd have many a chat over our tea. I-I was proud he'd talk to me like that. 'Course, he still could've talked to one o' his mates, but at least he included me."

"Had he been in a fight with someone, or was there a feud he was involved in?"

"Ye're thinkin' someone dragged him off?"

"It's a possibility, no matter how far-fetched it might seem. I have to know about the people in his life. Was there anyone he particularly didn't get on with?"

"Don't we all have our little rubs wi' someone?"

"So no specific name comes to mind."

Gary shrugged and finished his tea. The dog came in from the kitchen and yawned before stretching out before the fire.

"So no one in the village here, or anywhere else,

had any ill feelings or anger with Luke. No overt feud, no simmering anger beneath the surface, no problems with a girlfriend."

"He never said if he had such problems. He did have a special girl, was engaged, even. But I never heard o' any trouble about tha'."

McLaren paused with his pen on the page of his notebook. "What's his fiancée's name?"

"Ashley Fraser. She's now married, though. Her last name is Fox."

"Fox? Would she be married to Callum Fox?"

"Ye know him?"

"Only the name. Do they live in the area?"

"Aye. Just north o' here. Still in the village, though. On Bridge Lane west o' Birch Brook. Fine house. Ye can't miss it."

McLaren jotted the information in his notebook. "I know Luke had a date set up to play at a pub in Youlgreave that evening. Did he play at The Green Cat prior to that engagement, or was this his first appearance there?"

Gary blinked, clearly surprised with the question. "He an' Bethany played there before. I don't know when their first performance was. Bethany might know. Or the publican."

"Was it a steady job?"

"Ye're wantin' to know if it were every Friday night or third Saturday o' the month?"

"Yes."

"Why does tha' matter?"

McLaren finished his tea and placed the mug on the small table near his chair. The collie lifted his head, cast a suspicious eye at McLaren, then settled down for a nap. McLaren patted the dog's head. "It establishes the frequency of him being there, the opportunity for pub customers to catch his act and form an emotional attachment to him."

Gary frowned and moved his tea to the tray before leaning forward. "Like he was bein' stalked by someone? He never said." The man's voice grew softer as he shook his head. "It's sick."

"I'm not saying it happened, just that it could have. People are odd. Some take a fancy to something or someone and become obsessed. You have only to hear the TV about film stars, sports celebrities and rock stars, or even royalty, to realize how enamored some people get. Seems like there's always someone in court who's given a non-molestation injunction or charged with stalking."

"I can't see tha' happenin' to Luke, Mr. McLaren. He wasn't famous."

"Doesn't matter. He's a good looking man. He's talented. Someone hearing him sing might emotionally build up a fantasy about being with him."

"An' tha' fantasy might lead to his kidnappin', is what ye're sayin'."

"Newspapers and magazines carry all sorts of those stories," McLaren said. "God forbid it happened to your son, and of course I'm going to talk to the pub owner, but I want to know about their events schedule so I'd get a hint if something like that could've happened."

Gary eased his pipe and tobacco pouch off the table. His hand shook slightly, betraying his concern, as he stuffed tobacco into the bowl of the pipe. He lit the tobacco, drawing heavily on the mouthpiece, and watched the blue smoke float over his head. His gaze was still on the fading smoke when he said, "Who can really be certain what goes on in folks' minds, even those ye think ye know."

"Had he ever said anything about someone causing a problem there?"

"No. I would've remembered if he had."

"What about in school? Did he have any problems with anyone?"

"Bullying, ye mean?"

"That, certainly, or infatuation that may have grown into obsession."

Gary shook his head, his gaze on the photo of his son. "I didn't think so."

"Did Luke ever mention anything like that?"

"No."

"Do you think something like that could've happened? I'm not talking about text messages exclusively. Physical bullying or infatuation is very frightening and intimidating. Sometimes it gets out of hand. Could Luke have been scared of someone?"

"He never said, but I would've known. We were close, bein' just the two o' us. I would've sensed if he had that sort o' problem. No, Mr. McLaren, that didn't happen."

"He's fond of music and tennis, I know, but what other interests did he have?"

Gary's eyes narrowed as he frowned, trying to divine the reason behind McLaren's question. A log settled in the grate, the soft sigh of shifting coals voicing the older man's acceptance of the on-going questions. "Oh, the usual things, I suspect. Sports, especially cricket. A bit o' woodworkin'. Nothin' like furniture makin'. I mean carvin' things, like animals."

"That takes a steady hand and eye."

"Aye, it does. He didn't do much o' that after he became serious about the music. I think he was fearful he could cut himself quite bad."

"Best to be careful."

Gary exhaled slowly, as though pulling up memories from his soul. "He did some photography for a year or so, but he gave that up."

"Did he say why?"

"Not to me. I figured he wasn't that keen on it when the music took root."

"So nothing competitive or with a group, other than the cricket."

"If ye're thinkin' that he made an enemy o' a teammate, I don't believe it. Oh, not that there wasn't a spark of envy, perhaps, in some o' the lads. There sometimes is when one lad is better at somethin' and gets a lot o' attention. But Luke wasn't an outstanding player. Yes, he was exceptional at tennis, but perhaps average with cricket. He enjoyed the game but it wasn't really what he loved. And that makes a difference, doesn't it?"

McLaren nodded. Passion often propelled a person to greater heights, no matter if it were music, sports, cooking or anything else. "So no one on the team harbored jealous toward Luke."

"No. Anyway, that was a year or two ago."

"It might not matter. If something triggered an old anger…" He let the thought die, knowing it sounded farfetched. But he'd known people who nursed a grudge for years. Gary, however, didn't need to worry about fictitious stalkers.

"I always thought his music might've been the

catalyst." Gary focused again on McLaren, his eyes steady as he spoke his hidden fears.

"Why is that?"

"As you said, Mr. McLaren—some people have fantasies they need to bring to life."

Chapter Four

"Were he or Bethany ever bothered by a fan?"

"He never said. But perhaps he didn't know. I guess it doesn't have to be blatant…the stalker, I mean. Still, I think he'd know if someone followed him home from the pub. The road into Langheath isn't exactly crowded at that time o' night."

"When he had a gig at The Green Cat, did he always leave home at the same time?"

"Aye. Well, near enough to be th' same time. Give or take a few minutes. Ye know how it is. Things get in yer way an' make ye late. A phone call, somethin' misplaced, late with yer shower or getting' dressed."

"What time did he usually leave? Approximately."

Gary angled the pipe stem to the corner of his mouth and scratched his chin. His gaze went to Luke's photo as he replied slowly, as if reliving that afternoon. "Oh, 'bout an hour ahead o' time. The drive's not long. Ye can see how close Langheath is to Youlgreave." He stared out the window, as though he could see the village from his chair. "They had to set up once they got there, so it wasn't just the time for the drive. There's a raised platform in the corner. That's where a' the musicians play. So it took a while to get their gear in order on the stage."

"I understand Bethany waited for him to get her and when he didn't arrive, she rang you up."

"Aye, that'll be right."

"That was at four-thirty, then."

Gary nodded and drew another lungful of smoke.

"Isn't that awfully early?"

"Early?"

"To arrive for a gig, which I assume they were doing. Pubs and folk clubs normally don't have entertainment till mid-evening. Early evenings can occur at clubs, perhaps around seven o'clock. A pub might have singers begin at seven or eight. Sometimes later. But I've never heard of anyone performing at five-thirty at a pub. I guess," he added after a moment of consideration, "The Green Cat could have its own schedule. It just seems the clientele wouldn't be there at five-thirty. Most people aren't home from their offices or finished in the fields at that time."

Gary shrugged. "I wouldn't know. I don't frequent such places."

"You don't patronize the local?"

"I'll grab a pint a few times a year, but I'm no regular, ye might say. I haven't the money or the time."

"Did you go to the pubs when your son performed?"

"No."

"You disapproved of his singing?"

"Goin' to a pub has no bearin' on whether I liked, approved of, or disliked his music. I hadn't the energy most evenin's. I work hard on my farm an' I'm usually in my bed by the time he's singin'. If I want to hear him, I can hear him right here, in our home. I don't need to waste my time, petrol or brass goin' to some other village." He puffed several clouds of smoke into the air, as if underscoring his statement.

A brief silence built between them before McLaren spoke again. The dog whimpered softly, a descant to the window rattling beneath the sleet slung at it. "Did he always pick up Bethany, did they always go over together?"

"I think so. Ye'd best ask her, though. I'm no' privy to such details."

"What besides Luke's wallet is missing?"

"His mobile. But he'd have both o' them with him. At least, he always did."

"And his keys are still here."

"Right where they should be."

McLaren stood up. The collie woke, hearing the chair springs squeak, and glanced from Gary to McLaren. As Gary rose to his feet, so did the dog. He trotted over to the man and sat down. McLaren asked if he could see Luke's room.

Gary nodded, drew on his pipe, and walked to the back of the house. "Here she be." He opened the door and gestured toward the room's dark interior before flipping on the overhead light.

McLaren stood in the open doorway, slowly gazing round the room. The bed was neatly made, a green and blue duvet pulled tautly over the blue top sheet. A guitar case and folded guitar stand occupied one of the room's corners, several tennis rackets, a metal can that presumably held tennis balls, and a pair of sneakers took up a second corner. A desk, wooden chair, wardrobe and bed occupied the remaining space. A small color poster announcing 'Luke and Bethany, Performing Tonight' hung next to an art deco style print of a men's match at Wimbledon. These seemed to serve as a sort of headboard for the bed. McLaren nodded to the print. "Luke was good at tennis, I hear."

Gary sagged against the door frame but didn't enter the room. "Don't know how good, but he played a bit."

"Jamie tells me Luke had a coach. He must've been fairly decent."

"Don't know. I expect money will pay for most anythin', includin' lessons."

"Did you watch him play?"

"Lot o' nonsense, sports. If he'd worked around the farm a bit more he might still be here. Clothes are in the wardrobe, there."

"What's that mean?" McLaren looked inside the closet. He didn't know what he was looking for, but he had to see if the clothes were still there.

"Just what it sounds like. This is a big place. It needs a lot o' work to keep it goin'. My son used to be dependable, used to work from sun up to sun down. Used to do the work o' a hired hand. Then he takes to tennis, then to music. He didn't work as much as he used to."

"You couldn't hire someone to help out? Surely there are men who would be glad of the work in these tough times."

"I didn't ask about or advertise. Money's too tight to waste."

"You might've asked around the village. Surely someone would know someone wanting a job."

"It's Luke's place to work here. This is his home. He needs to put his hand in to keep the roof above our heads. Instead, Doc Tipton an' John Evans fill his head wi' wild notions o' fame and fortune—on the tennis courts or on the stage. It's daft."

McLaren opened the metal can, shook the tennis

balls onto the bed, peered into the can, then replaced the balls. "But if your son's heart wasn't into farming, surely there's no harm—"

"There's harm if I say there's harm." Gary's voice took on a hard edge and he pushed away from the door frame. "He's too young for a' that. He needs the steady work o' the farm. What if he starts playin' in tennis games or tours the folk club scene an' he gets hurt an' he's laid up? How does he pay his bills? How does he save any money stayin' in hotels all over the country?" He turned and walked down the hall.

The guitar case was a hard shell variety, black leatherette covering the wood. McLaren laid the case on the bed, unsnapped the clasps, and opened the lid to reveal a Martin D-28 guitar. He picked up the instrument and set it beside the case. He raked his fingers through the matted royal blue plush of the interior, feeling strangely that it needed looking after. Nothing other than three sets of new strings, a small sponge in a little glass jar with a perforated metal lid, a tuner, and a pouch of plastic guitar picks filled the string box. He picked up the guitar and turned it over, shaking it slightly to dislodge anything that might be secreted in the hollow body. Nothing fell out or made a sound. He righted the instrument and peered into the sound hole, angling the guitar so he could see the immediate body area. No note or foreign object was taped to the guitar's interior. He ran his thumb across the strings; some had gone flat from their correct pitch. It needed to be played. He put the instrument back in its case, closed and locked the lid, and placed the case back in the corner of the room.

Next, McLaren opened the desk drawer, hoping for

a letter or map noting a meeting with someone. But kids didn't write these days. They texted on mobiles or emailed. And without Luke's mobile… He went to the door and called to Gary.

"Sure, ye can look a' his computer." Gary's voice floated down the hall. "Police did that. Nothin' gave a clue to them, but have a' it."

McLaren sat at the keyboard, turned on the computer monitor, and quickly opened the emails going back a month prior to the boy's disappearance. Chats from a few friends—Bethany Watson, Harry Rooney, Callum Fox, and Judy Lindauer—some singing requests, a reminder from Doc about an early tennis practice, and a music store's sale on guitar accessories were the only pertinent messages there. He closed them, saw there were no documents detailing an elopement or run-away or meeting, and turned off the computer.

The search of the desk held nothing of importance other than the keys for the house and car, guitar picks, a set of fiddle strings, a guitar capo, a packet of guitar strings, a book on orchestra instruments, a tin of tobacco and pipe, paper and pens, and a small engagement diary. He flipped through the pages, noting dates of singing engagements and tennis games. A night out with a friend was all too rare. McLaren closed the diary, disappointed. He turned off the room light and closed the door, reluctantly admitting it was a dead end.

When he reentered the sitting room Gary was standing by the fireplace. He knocked his pipe's bowl against the edge of the stone opening, watching the spent tobacco fall into the flames. When he straightened up, he looked at McLaren.

"Don't get the wrong idea, Mr. McLaren. I love my

son. He's the dearest thing in the world to me. But a man's got to be realistic in these times. Ye don't run off for a dream and leave behind solid, money-makin' work." He turned slightly from McLaren and wiped his eyes.

"I'll look for him if you still want me to, Mr. Barber."

Without shifting his gaze, Gary nodded. His arm muffled his voice. "Please. Move heaven and earth if ye have to, but find Luke."

McLaren closed the house door gently behind him, but wondered if Luke hadn't done just that. Maybe he *had* run off in pursuit of a dream. Or someone had kept him from doing it.

****

"Do you think Luke could've deliberately run away? Was he feeling any type of pressure?" McLaren sat on the sofa in Bethany Watson's living room, a modern collection of white and green furniture, brown hardwood floor, emphatic indoor plants, and silver framed photos on the walls. A small wooden framed photo of an infant occupied the end table near Bethany's chair. He declined a cup of tea and waited for Bethany to answer his question. The electric tea kettle in the nearby kitchen made faint ticking sounds as it cooled.

"What kind of pressure?"

"Oh, his future, or a girlfriend, or money." He paused, slightly embarrassed. "I know he was engaged to be married, but sometimes that's when a former girlfriend comes back into a guy's life." He swallowed, wondering if he had just described her.

"Ashley and I were the only women in his life.

Well, as far as I know."

"Ashley's his fiancée?"

"Yes." Bethany ran her fingers through her hair. It was blonde, cut in a short, spiky style. Sort of an odd look for a folk singer, he thought, but it seemed to suit the woman's personality. Lively and modern. Her blue eyes stared quite frankly at him, perhaps judging his credentials to hunt for Luke. "Ashley's short and thin, like me, though she's a brunette. Or is that irrelevant?"

"It probably is, but it helps me get a picture of her. I've not talked to her yet."

"Well, you've got a treat, then. She's a few years younger than I am. Probably twenty-one. I'm twenty-seven, if you're taking notes." She smiled as he pulled out his notebook.

"Luke would be what…twenty-two now?"

Bethany leaned forward and laughed. "You're not too subtle for a police officer, Mr. McLaren."

"I'm not one anymore, Mrs. Watson. Perhaps any subtle skill I had has eroded with time."

"You're sizing me up. You're thinking about the age difference between Luke and me. You're wondering if Luke and I were a couple either before Ashley stepped into the picture or during her occupation." She picked up her teacup and eyed him over its rim as she took a sip.

"I'll abandon my attempt at subtlety, then, and just ask you. Were you and Luke a romantically involved couple?"

Bethany put down the cup and folded her arms, leaning on the chair arm. "Sorry, we weren't. I don't know if that helps weed me out as a suspect, but our only involvement with each other was our music."

"How long had you been a duo?"

"Two years. Doesn't sound very long, but you have to remember Luke was nineteen when he disappeared. We started singing together when he was seventeen and I was twenty-two. I knew what I wanted to do with my life by that age, and Luke was still hunting. He had a real passion as well as talent for music and he thought he'd like to become a professional."

"Did you know each other prior to this, see each other in the village?"

"Yes. We're both locals. Of course, I always considered him a kid. I heard him play guitar one night in the church hall, during a show they put on. I thought he was very good for a young teenager."

"When did you two talk about teaming up?"

"Actually, about a year before our first gig."

"Did Luke's father raise any objections?"

"You're being subtle again about the age difference, Mr. McLaren. I think Gary may've been less than elated with our partnership, but he didn't stop Luke."

"Probably figured he'd let Luke get this out of his system."

"Could have done. Sometimes you can only know what a thing is like by trying it. Anyway, I had a fairly good insurance policy."

McLaren blinked. "Insurance… Pardon?"

Bethany laughed, clearly enjoying his confusion. "A deterrent against his over zealousness, if he considered that. I was a fairly safe companion for Luke." She held up her left hand and wiggled her ring finger.

"You were married at the time you and Luke were

singing together?"

"Before that, actually. Nathan, my husband, and I were already married for a year before Luke and I even discussed becoming a musical team." She stared at her ring, rubbing the back of the band with her thumb. "I realize this doesn't really mean anything, like guaranteeing there'd be no…well, it doesn't throw up a brick wall. But there's not much in life that's one hundred percent reliable. You just have to take a chance or else you'd stay in your room your entire life."

"How'd your husband take to all this?"

"The music or to Luke?"

"Both."

Bethany finished her tea and refilled her cup. She talked as she added the milk and sugar. "He was fine with it."

"With the music *and* with Luke?"

"Yes."

"He didn't complain about the hours in rehearsal or at venues?"

"He knew how important my music is to me. He didn't want to stand in my way. He loves me, wants me to be happy."

McLaren wrote a reminder in his notebook. "On the evening Luke went missing, what time was he supposed to pick you up? At your house, I assume."

Bethany pressed her lips together and took a deep breath. Three years, evidently, was not long enough to heal all wounds. "He said he'd be by at four o'clock. Yes," she said hurriedly, stopping McLaren's comment, "it's early for a seven o'clock gig, especially when the venue is a fifteen-minute drive away. But we were going to stop at a fiddle maker's shop. He lives in

Matlock. So we needed the extra hour or so on the front end of the evening."

"You wanted to buy a fiddle for your act?"

"Yes. I used to play. Oh, years ago. I thought the sound would go well with many songs we did and I wanted to take up the instrument again. I don't have a fiddle anymore, so we were going to look at this one, that this man makes."

"And you didn't get there. What's the man's name?"

Bethany paused slightly, her gaze shifting to a stack of music books on a chair in the adjoining room. "Uh, Allen."

"First name or last?"

"Pardon?"

His question jolted her attention back to him. "Oh, last. K.J. Allen. I don't know his first name. His initials are all I ever saw in print."

"You didn't talk to him on the phone, set up an appointment?"

"No. Luke took care of that."

"So, Luke was to pick you up at four o'clock to go to Matlock. But he never came. By four-thirty you were concerned enough to ring up his father, who phoned the police, correct?"

"Yes. I'd tried Luke's mobile number, but it just rang and went into his voice mail. That didn't bother me at first. If he's driving, he doesn't answer it."

"He wouldn't be coming from his house?" McLaren frowned. "It's commendable that he'd ignore it if he were in heavy traffic and needed to concentrate on his driving, but is there that much traffic in the village?"

"Of course not. But I didn't know for certain where he was coming from. He sometimes sees a friend in Bakewell. I couldn't know if he was coming from the farm."

McLaren agreed that it made sense. But there was the problem that he evidently wasn't driving; his car was at his house.

"Around four-twenty or so I really became concerned. I tried his mobile again but still got no answer. I rang up his house at four-thirty. His dad answered. He had no idea where Luke was, that he'd assumed Luke had already left to get me."

"He hadn't been outside, then?"

"Outside?" Bethany looked blank.

"Luke's car and keys were at his house. Gary wasn't aware of that?"

"I have no idea. When he's busy with the farm, he doesn't notice much else."

"Did you or Gary ring up any of his friends or people he knew?"

Bethany screwed up her face. "I rang up Ashley just before four-thirty. I thought he could be there."

"Logical assumption."

Bethany nodded. "Ashley was surprised Luke wasn't with me. She knew about our gig that night and assumed he and I were driving to The Green Cat at that time. When I told her I was looking for Luke, she became very worried and asked where I'd looked for him. When I told her I'd just been calling his mobile, she said she'd phone some other friends of his, speak to Doc Tipton."

"Did Luke have a tennis lesson that afternoon? Did Ashley think it ran long so that he was late picking you up?"

"I don't know what she thought, Mr. McLaren. I agreed that she should talk to whomever she wanted, and then I rang off. I didn't want to stay on the phone long in case Luke was trying to get me."

"She have any luck with Doc Tipton?"

"Evidently not. Doc helped hunt for Luke that evening. I never heard a thing from him about seeing Luke that day. And I know he would've said while we were at the farm that evening. Gary—We all were incredibly worried."

"Did you call anyone while the men went out to look?"

"No. I sat in the Barbers' kitchen, waiting for word from someone. I'd exhausted all my ideas of people to call. If he wasn't with Doc or John or Ashley, or if he wasn't at home, I didn't have a clue where he was. After all, as you said, his car was there."

"He ever take the bus or go somewhere with a mate of his?"

Bethany shook her head. "Always in his car. He'd worked a long time to save up for it. He loved driving it."

McLaren glanced at the teapot. "I think I'll change my mind about the tea. Is there any left?"

"Yes." She got a cup and saucer from the kitchen cupboard, poured out a cup of tea and handed it to him. "I don't know how hot it will be, however."

"Don't worry about that. I drink it all temperatures. Thanks." He took a long drink before setting the cup and saucer down in front of him. "Who were his close friends?"

"He didn't have many."

“Oh? Why is that?”

“He had mates in school. On the rugby team and in classes. But his dad kept him pretty much tied to the farm with doing chores.”

“Farming’s a hard life, that’s for certain. Long hours of work in the summer.”

“Besides his work there, he spent what time he had free with tennis and music lessons. The practice alone for either of those activities would’ve completely filled his off hours.”

“So, no time for fun with his mates.”

“He’d go to the cinema or to a football match or something, certainly, but it wasn’t a regular occurrence. Not because he didn’t like his friends, but because he was focused on his career.” She stared at McLaren’s notebook, perhaps envisioning what her life might’ve been like if Luke hadn’t disappeared. Her voice sounded far off when she spoke. “Successful people do that, you know. Have a goal and keep chipping away at obstacles until they attain it.”

Or die trying, McLaren silently added.

Chapter Five

McLaren stopped for lunch at the local fish and chips shop before driving to Ashley Fox's home. The house peeked out from the stand of pine and spruce hugging the corners of the two-storey dwelling, like hands pressed protectively against its walls. He parked at the top of the large circle driveway and soon sat in the living room, his back ramrod straight in the satin-covered chair.

"Luke's friends, for the most part, lived in the village." Ashley, a twenty-one-year-old brunette who looked fashion magazine ready, dabbed her eyes with a facial tissue. She apologized as she glanced at McLaren. "I'm sorry. I thought I was over this."

"Three years isn't much time if you really loved someone."

"I suppose you're right." She gave him an apologetic smile and crumpled the tissue in her hand.

"Do you recall his friends' names?"

"Harry Rooney was probably the closest of Luke's friends."

"Where does he live?"

"Do you know the village layout?"

"I've made a rough sketch of it." He pulled the paper from his pocket. "If you'd indicate…" He held the map toward Ashley.

She glanced at the drawing, then brought her

fingertip down between Twin Dales Road and Birch Brook. "Just here."

"Just up from the farm." McLaren drew a square on the paper where Ashley had pointed, then labeled it 'Harry Rooney.' "Any other friends about?"

"Well, he was friendly with his two teachers, or coaches. However, you want to refer to them. John Evans and Doc Tipton."

"Anyone his age, or near his age, that he particularly was close to or hung around with?"

Ashley looked thoughtful as she stirred her coffee. The cup rattled slightly on the saucer as she set it on the side table. "Tom Yardley, to some extent. They were the same age, so that helped."

"Sometimes, yes."

"Tom was fairly thick with Harry Rooney, so he, Harry and Luke became a sort of threesome at times."

"Why at times?"

"Well, you know…work and things. Luke would be singing on the weekends, which was when Tom was usually free to howl."

"What's Tom do?"

Ashley frowned and pursed her lips. "I'm not one hundred percent sure, but I think it's odd jobs and yard work. He just floats, picks up jobs when he needs money."

"Hasn't he any ambition, or does he have a medical condition that prohibits his work?"

"I wouldn't think so. He's healthy enough when he wants to ride his motorbike."

"That'd take a bit of money, yes."

"I don't particularly like Tom, but he's never really done anything to me to make me dislike him. You see him in a sleeveless T-shirt in the summer, torn jeans, and sitting around the village. I don't know what Luke saw in him."

"Were they at school together?"

"I believe so. Why?"

McLaren shrugged and moved forward slightly in the chair. "Many times it creates a bond when nothing else does."

"Complaining about school work and teachers."

"Some things are constant, yes."

"Well, I thought Luke should choose his friends with more care. Tom's a bit of a wide boy, and frankly, I believe that's where he gets a lot of his money."

"Selling things he's nicked?"

"Yes. I hate to speak ill of someone, but I doubt Tom works enough to afford some of the things I've seen him with."

"And Tom lives…where?" He held the sketch of the village out to Ashley and she placed an X next to Doc Tipton's place.

"Across the street from my parents. It's a nice area, really. I mean, Tom doesn't have a gang or anything. But I wish he'd move. I'm always nervous something will happen."

"Like the police raiding his house?"

Ashley smiled shyly and bowed her head. "Something like that."

"Is that the extent of people who associated with Luke, then?"

"When he wasn't working on the farm, he spent much of his time with my husband—my husband before we married, obviously. Callum Fox."

"Why was this? Had they known each other in

school?"

"They did, but they became rather close when they decided to partner up for doubles matches."

"For tennis?"

"Oh, yes." Ashley smiled apologetically. "Sorry. I'm so used to everyone here knowing about this that I forget others may not. Yes, tennis. They were quite good together, actually. It's a shame it ended." Her voice faded, as though she conjured up memories of the two men's tennis games. Or mourned over what might have been.

"So that's the extent of Luke's friends."

"Well, there's Bethany Watson, of course."

"Luke's singing partner. Did anyone ring you up the evening Luke went missing to see if Luke was here?"

"Several people. Bethany was the first, I think, because she was concerned he hadn't arrived at her place yet. None of us would've known he'd gone missing, of course, because we all assumed things were normal. Then Luke's dad phoned me. And I believe John Evans did, also. But at different times, you understand. Throughout the evening."

"Like, within an hour of each other? Or strung out further?"

"I'd say several hours. Bethany phoned me fairly close to four-thirty. Luke hadn't picked her up for their engagement at a pub in Youlgreave. She wanted to know if he was here." Ashley sighed heavily, as though she were reliving the trauma of that evening again. "Between you and me, Mr. McLaren, I don't believe she *really* thought that. But she was frantic, grasping at straws. She didn't know where else to try."

"Had you seen Luke that day? Had he mentioned anything to you about where he might be, or an appointment he may have had?"

"We had lunch together. That was at twelve-thirty."

"Did you eat here, or at a restaurant?"

She pulled in the corners of her lips, as though she disliked airing her personal life to a stranger. But when McLaren repeated the question she reluctantly answered. "At The Green Cat."

"Where he was to have performed that evening?"

"Yes. It's—I like the food. And the atmosphere. We go there often. Even when he's not got anything lined up."

"How did he seem?"

"What does that mean?"

"Was he relaxed? Was he nervous? Did he see someone there who disturbed him or—"

Ashley waved her hand for him to stop. "Luke was his usual self. Calm, cool and collected. It was too early to get performance jitters, and there was no one there who affected Luke either adversely or happily. We ordered lunch and sat in a quiet corner and talked. I wanted to set a wedding date but he said he needed another year to save up some more money before we could do that. I wasn't happy at hearing that because I loved him dreadfully and wanted to get married, but I didn't pressure him. That's no way to begin wedded life."

"Did he mention any personal problems he might have, anyone that was bothering him?"

"Besides his dad?"

"What about his father?"

"Oh, nothing that wouldn't be cured if Luke would stay in the village and work on the farm. Mr. McLaren, you need to know that Gary Barber kept a tight hand on his wife and on Luke when he was younger. Gary thinks farming should be in Luke's blood and I feared at times he would physically try to inject that feeling into Luke's veins. But he never got violent with Luke, at least as far as I knew. I know Gary was disappointed because the farm came down through their family, so he couldn't understand why Luke didn't have the same feeling for the place as Gary thought he should have. He tended to blame it on his wife's influence when she was alive. Margaret really shouldn't have been a farmer's wife."

McLaren shifted in his chair and watched Ashley wind a lock of her hair around her fingers. The tick of the grandfather clock boomed in the silence. "Why is that?"

"She liked the land and the animals well enough. I don't mean she despised the life. But I always thought her talents were not fully employed on the farm."

"Talents like art?"

"She sketched, yes. But she also had musical talent. She played piano. Gary bought her an upright for their tenth wedding anniversary. It must've set him back some, but he knew she loved to play. He still has it. He didn't sell it even after she…well, it's in his parlor. It was the last time I was over there. It was very loving of him to get the piano for her, but she didn't have the time to play except a few summer afternoons and then of course winter gave her more time. But I always thought it a shame she couldn't really do as much with music and drawing as she wanted. It was a waste."

McLaren let the clock ticking fill the room again before replying. “Luke got his talent, then, from his mother. Was Gary bothered by it?”

“By Luke’s talent?”

“No. By Margaret’s. Maybe not by the talent itself, but passing on the creative gene to her son. Some parents love their child so much they want to claim responsibility for that part they love most in the child. In this case, it could be music. If Gary loved Luke so fiercely and wanted Luke to emulate him, Gary might’ve been jealous of the greater talent passed on by Margaret.” He paused, letting Ashley think about it. “Make sense?”

“Yes.” She said it slowly, as though unsure. “But Margaret—Mrs. Barber—didn’t really seem concerned one way or the other with Luke’s musical ability. *Gary* had the problem, and that only showed itself when the pub dates and folk club performances got in the way of Luke doing his chores.”

McLaren nodded and wrote several sentences in his notebook. When he looked up again, Ashley’s gaze was on a photo of a young man. The silver frame looked at home among the formal tea service, silver candlesticks and etched bowls. “Was *Margaret* pleased with Luke’s musical ability?”

“She never heard him play. She died twenty years ago.”

“Which would make Luke twenty-two if he was still with us.”

Ashley nodded, the color coming to her cheeks.

“Still, he had his father and friends to appreciate his talent. Hopefully he had many around the area who complimented him.”

"Aside from the people we've already mentioned, I think any other friends he had in school have moved off."

"I assume the police talked to them."

Ashley nodded and picked up her coffee cup.

"Since you were engaged to Luke, I assume you knew any preference he had in regards to tennis and music." He paused as she took a sip of coffee, watching the fingers of her left hand as they found the handle and gripped it. The blood had rushed to the fingertips, leaving the knuckles white. A tremor of her hand, barely perceivable except for the faint clink of the china cup against the edge of the saucer, unnerved her, and she shifted her right hand to grasp the lip of the cup and the saucer. She set the china back on the table and pretended to cough.

She cleared her throat. "He showed talent in both areas, but I thought he had his best chance with tennis. He was hoping to become a pro, follow the circuit and play in some large, prestigious matches."

"He was that good, then."

"Oh yes. He had a terrific serve, always precise. He used to practice serving to a target Doc Tipton set up. Luke hit it every time, no matter where Doc placed it."

"Impressive."

"He began practicing tennis in earnest when he was fifteen. You have to begin anything like that when you're young."

"I can't see his father being too keen on the idea."

"He wasn't. But Luke soon was an adult, so there wasn't much his dad could do to stop him."

"Still, it would make for difficult life at home."

"I think his father had more or less resigned

himself to Luke's career choice. Though he'd have been over the moon if Luke had wanted to stay at the farm."

McLaren agreed that sometimes parents and their children didn't see eye to eye on many things. "When did you marry Callum?"

The abrupt change in topic startled her. She blinked and glanced at the grandfather clock in the corner. "Two and a half years ago."

"What does he do? Still part of the tennis world?"

"Yes. Well, in a way. He plays, but nothing on the scale he did when he and Luke partnered for doubles. We own a tennis equipment shop. Callum manages it." She pressed her lips together and glanced at him.

"Must be interesting. Is it in the village?"

Ashley crossed her legs and leaned back slightly in her chair. "No. There's not enough custom in a village this size. The shop's in Chesterfield. We were lucky to get such a good location. It gets a lot of foot traffic."

"I hope it's successful."

"Why, thank you." She glanced at her watch and rose from her chair. "I'm sorry, but I have to pick up my daughter from nursery school."

"You look incredibly young to be a mother."

"Uh, thank you." Her face flooded with warmth as she grabbed the car key.

"How old is your daughter?"

"I'm sorry. I really have to go." She headed toward the door, herding him outside as effectively as if she were a sheepdog and he a stray lamb.

He called after her as she walked toward her car, thanking her for her help, then left to talk to Tom.

****

Tom Yardley was walking down the front pathway of his house, tossing a key and catching it in his leather-gloved hand when McLaren parked and walked up the driveway. Tom stopped by his motorcycle and slipped the helmet out from beneath his arm. He held it and eyed McLaren as he strode up.

"Mr. Yardley?" McLaren smiled and extended his hand.

"Yeah. Who are you?"

"Michael McLaren. I understand you were a friend of Luke Barber."

"What of it?" He stood with his feet apart, leaning forward slightly, emulating a boxer ready for a confrontation. Of medium height and weight, with brown hair and eyes, there was nothing distinguishing about him except for the tattoo of a knife on his neck. Though McLaren couldn't see the knife's point—he presumed it was at the base of the boy's neck—the hilt was highly visible on Tom's right cheek. The left cheek sported a small grinning skull.

"I'm investigating his disappearance, that's what." McLaren's voice hardened slightly although his smile had not altered.

"Yeah, well, I don't know a thing about that. Now, hop it. I'm late already." He zipped up his black leather jacket and dug the gloves out of his jeans back pocket.

"This won't take long, Mr. Yardley. I just have a few questions."

"I told you, mate, I don't know a thing. I wasn't around. Now, like I said, I gotta go."

"You don't care about what happened to Luke, if he's found or not?"

Tom hung the helmet from one of the bike's

handlebars and sighed heavily. "Man, are you serious? That's ancient history. It was…what? Three years ago?" He pulled the remaining glove onto his left hand.

"I would've thought you'd like to help find Luke. If you were a friend, that would interest you. Even a stranger should be concerned about another human being."

"Yeah, you'd think that and you'd be wrong. He's gone, right? We've not seen him around, right? He's split. Gone to Manchester or London, most likely."

"You know that for a fact?"

Tom snorted and curled his lip. "What are you, some berk? Of course I don't *know*. If he ain't *here*, he's somewhere *else*. You that dumb that you can't figure that out?"

McLaren stepped forward until they were only inches apart. He stared down at Tom. "Are *you* such a clot that you're so insensitive to your friend's disappearance?"

"He did nothing for me, man. Nothing."

"What was he supposed to do for you?"

"Give me a job."

McLaren tilted his head and looked at Tom's attire. "And what kind of job did you have in mind? Or did you leave that up to Luke, too?"

"He said I could work for him."

"On the farm?"

Tom spat on the ground and rolled his eyes. "Get real. I'm talking about a tennis job. Or music." He shrugged and backed up a bit, putting more space between them. "Whatever he went into."

"Doing what?"

"Body guard. Driver. Check out the arrangements

of the venue. Whatever he needed."

"Sounds like you needed it more than Luke did. Had he agreed to giving you a job?"

"Not yet. But he was going to."

"You know that for certain?"

Tom hesitated, as though considering his answer. He ran the tip of his tongue over his bottom lip and took a breath. "Yeah. He was going to. He just hadn't got to it yet."

"What kept him?"

The fingers of Tom's right hand slowly curled into a fist and he glared at McLaren. "He left the village."

"And you don't want to find him, you don't want to know where he went so you can get that job?"

"Waste of time. He's gone. He ain't coming back."

"You know that for certain, do you?"

"Stands to reason. If it's been three years…" He shrugged and walked into McLaren. "Who cares anymore? What's the difference if you find him or not?" He put out his hand to shove McLaren aside. "I've given you enough time. I'm late already, man. Get out of my way."

"I'd sure like to thank you for your time and your overwhelming concern, Mr. Yardley. You certainly make the world a wonderful place."

"Shut it. Sky off!"

"What a brilliant way you have with words. Head of your class in Year Six, were you? Assuming you were smart enough to attain that grade."

Tom made a grab for McLaren's jacket but McLaren clamped his left hand over Tom's wrist and twisted it. As he pushed Tom's hand away, Tom swung at McLaren's jaw. McLaren blocked the punch with his forearm and pushed Tom to the side. Tom slipped on a patch of ice and fell to the tarmac, landing on his knee. He yelled in pain but rolled over and staggered to his feet. He lunged at McLaren and locked his fingers onto McLaren's trousers. McLaren bent to his right, grabbed the motorcycle, and jammed it against Tom's side. The man's fingers released and he crumpled to the ground. McLaren dusted off his jacket and trousers, and grabbed the collar of Tom's jacket. Pulling him partway into a sitting position, McLaren bent over Tom, smiling. "I'm going to find out what happened to Luke Barber, pal. You had better not be involved in his disappearance."

Tom tried to say something but only a groan escaped his lips.

McLaren continued. "You may not believe it, but I'm not always this friendly when I learn someone's been lying to me. You got it?" He flashed a wide grin, released Tom's jacket, and strolled back to his car.

****

McLaren spent the remainder of the afternoon talking to shop owners along the village's High Street. The publican of The Two Ramblers saw Luke in Callum's car, but that was late morning and hours before his disappearance. The green grocer thought he saw Luke late afternoon thumbing a ride south, but it could've been a different lad. Someone else recalled seeing Luke early afternoon walking down the High Street with Harry Rooney, or with John Evans, or with a woman who wasn't Bethany or Ashley. No one else remembered anything untoward that day. Everyone confirmed he appeared to be in good spirits, hadn't an enemy in the world, and would've been the next Björn

Borg or Andy Murray. Or Chieftains. Which might've been interesting to see, he thought, one man morphing into a group. But the comparison was apt, even if it wasn't precisely correct.

He met Jamie for dinner at The Split Oak in Somerley. The pub dated from the reign of Elizabeth I and, as such, drew history-seeking tourists like its variety of beers drew thirsty men. Discussion and committees had started two hundred years ago to entertain ideas about the sagging slate roof, but the start was also soon the end of it. General feeling held that as long as the oak beam ceiling stayed up no modifications were needed. Why fix it if it wasn't broken? Besides, modernization would chase off the tourists.

McLaren slid farther away from the casement window and rubbed his left shoulder. The seal around the metal frame gapped in a few places, letting in blasts of winter from the enthusiastic wind.

Jamie drained the last of his coffee and eyed his friend. "How'd the first day of inquiry go?" He loosened his dark green tie, a compliment to his light brown hair, and nudged McLaren's cup. "Should I find the waitress? You want a refill?"

"What?" He turned from the window and stared at Jamie.

"Your coffee. You want some more?"

"Oh. No, thanks. I was just thinking of Luke Barber."

The acoustic band was tuning up at the far end of the room, and Jamie leaned forward.

"What about Luke? You've got a lead already?"

McLaren laughed and settled back in his chair. "Hardly. Give me some time."

Jamie reached for his fork and angled the slice of apple crackle cake toward him. “So, what’s the dilemma?”

“What makes you think I’m stuck?”

“You wouldn’t be thinking about the case if you weren’t. Give.”

McLaren ran his hand through his short-cropped blond hair and sighed. “Luke’s mother died when he was two years old. His dad reared him single-handedly.”

“Commendable. Hard work, that.”

“I can understand how protective Gary became, fulfilling the role of both parents, making up for the maternal love Luke never got.”

“So, what’s the problem?”

“I know I’m an outsider, but it seems like that love smothered instead of nurtured him. Gary couldn’t let go. Oh, he made some excuse about the farm and how stable a way of life it is, but it’s not that way so much anymore with corporation take-overs. I think he couldn’t bear to give Luke up, didn’t have a strong enough love that would bend and give his child freedom.” He paused, his attention drawn by the musicians setting up their microphones and guitar stands. “You can hold on to those you love best if you let them go.”

Jamie paid his fork on his plate and nudged it to one side. He rested his forearms on the table and leaned forward. “Awfully philosophical this evening, Mike.”

“That’s the way I feel, Jamie.”

“Might be best if you thought about the case. By the way, I emailed you the information on the case.”

“What?” McLaren frowned in his astonishment. “If

you'd been caught—"

"Yeah, I know. I'd be in Big Trouble. But I wasn't caught. I glanced over it and typed what I recalled in the email…on my laptop while I sat in my car."

"I can't deny I'm grateful for the information."

"Just thought it'd save you some time, Mike. You know…all the pertinent facts at your disposal."

McLaren checked the email messages on his smartphone, then turned it off and repocketed it. "What you meant to say is that you won't have to answer so many of my phone calls for information."

"There's that, too." He angled his head slightly and stared at his friend. "Well?"

"Well, what?"

"The band must be louder than I thought. I haven't heard a thank you coming from your side of the table."

"Thanks, Jamie. I hope the risk is worth the information."

"It will be." He grinned and picked up his fork. "What we do for our friends and loved ones."

"You're back to Gary keeping Luke on a tight rein, you mean?"

"Yeah. A smothering love like that could've driven Luke away from his dad."

"I doubt if the absence or presence of motherly love has much to do with Luke's disappearance. Maybe if Margaret had died when Luke was older, and he left right after that, I'd say yes. But twenty years after the fact?"

McLaren nodded and pushed his coffee cup around in circles.

"Now, what besides Luke's childhood bothers you? I'm not flippant, Mike. That's a tough road for a kid.

But I'd like to know what else you discovered today."

"Probably the eye-opener for me is Gary Barber's attitude." He glanced at Jamie, unsure if he should continue. Jamie appeared interested, so McLaren told about looking around Luke's room.

"What's wrong with that? The police always do that. It gives us an idea of the victim's life. His interests, maybe an idea where he went, can sometimes break a case."

"Correct, but Gary didn't even ask why I wanted to look in Luke's room. He just took it as if I'd asked him to pass the box of breakfast cereal. He showed no emotion."

"Well, the police did all that three years ago, Mike. Gary remembers that, so he didn't question your request."

"I accept that, and I accept the supposition that three years won't bring out the emotions as strongly as when they were fresh. But the man just leaned against the door jamb and talked like it was any other activity. I mean, I was rooting through the remnants of his son's life! And he's opening the room's door and directing me inside like he was a tour guide. He tells me where the clothes are, as if I couldn't figure it out."

"Mike, the man's upset by it all. Even after all this time. Give him some slack."

"The slack I'll give him is that he was a little teary eyed when I left."

"See?"

"But does he really love his son? The whole thing seemed so cold hearted."

"Gary never was one to show his feelings, Mike. He's a hard working farmer, and he's trying to keep going. I'm certain he loves Luke. He just doesn't show sentiment. Especially to an outsider." He picked up his cup but didn't take a sip. The light from the wall sconce illuminated the cup's rim. "You okay with everything else?"

"I'll be okay when I find Luke…or what happened to him. But I know what you mean. Gary's close-mouthed, almost no help. Singing partner Bethany was reserved but forthcoming. Former fiancée clammed up on several topics and rushed into her marriage with Callum Fox."

"How rushed?"

"Six months after Luke went missing."

Jamie whistled softly and shook his head. "A shotgun affair, do you think?"

"If so, why'd Callum have to marry her? Luke was the intended groom."

"Mike, my babe in the woods, when does engagement to one preclude dalliance with another?"

McLaren frowned and swallowed the rest of his coffee. He toyed with the cup, scooting it in a circle when he set it on the table. "I don't need life lessons from you, Jamie. I'm well aware that…things happen. But it's a problem that needs resolution. Why not call off the engagement to Luke and take Callum's hand in marriage?"

"Could've been a one-nighter. A mistake they both regretted."

"If they regretted it, they wouldn't compound that regret by marrying each other."

Jamie agreed that didn't seem likely. "How old's the child? Do you know?"

"I can assume. Three years old."

"Why do you think that? Based on the hurried wedding?"

"Based on her parting comment. She needed to go get her child at nursery school."

"Nursery school. They accept kids only between the ages of three and five years."

McLaren nodded, flashing a smile at his friend. "See what I mean about the quickie trip to the altar?"

"I don't suppose it could be Callum's kid."

"Nothing rules that out, as far as I know."

"And I don't suppose there's a photo about, showing Ashley on her wedding day. When was it, by the way?"

"She didn't have a photo displayed in the room I was in, but that doesn't prohibit there being one."

"It'd be helpful if you could find one, Mike."

"It'd be more helpful if I could get a DNA test on the kid."

Chapter Six

McLaren woke early Saturday morning. He lay in bed, staring at the ceiling, listening to the wind at the window. The clock chimed seven as he rolled onto his side. The world outside the pane of glass looked as subdued as he felt: gray sky, black limbed trees, white patches of snow. A drab landscape that wouldn't improve his mood.

He showered, shaved and dressed, then had his breakfast at his computer. Overnight emails consisted of several stone wall job inquiries and an invitation from a former work colleague to attend a rugby game. He brought up the police report Jamie had emailed him and printed it out before reading it. After finishing his meal, he jotted some reminders into his notebook, grabbed his sheepskin jacket and keys, and left the house.

Frost rimmed the blades of grass and sprawled across the car's windscreen in geometric designs. McLaren unlocked his car, got the ice scraper from the glove compartment, and cleaned off the glass. Minutes later he was on the A625, heading for Langheath.

Morning was well established in the more open stretches of road and in the fields and moors. Sunlight spilled from the tops of the lower hills and flooded the valley in citron-colored light. A kestrel hovered near the junction with the B6001, and McLaren was reluctant to leave the bird. He slipped a CD into the car's player and sang along with his folk group doing "Leather-winged Bat."

The village of Langheath was up and into its Saturday routine by the time McLaren parked outside the Frasers' house. It sat on the southern leg of Twin Dales Road, caressed by a stand of trees, alone and in shadow.

McLaren walked up the flagstone path to the front door, wondering if the place was more welcoming in spring. Just now it seemed more the stuff of Grimms Brothers tales, with leafless tree limbs waving in the breeze and wrought iron fencing caked in snow.

The door opened at his knock, and the aroma of cigarette smoke and a strain of a Mendelssohn symphony greeted him. A pair of brown eyes surveyed McLaren's face and form, evidently saw nothing threatening, and retreated a few feet to let the door swing back. A middle-aged man wearing a paint-stained sweatshirt and an air of authority growled out a question. His hand went to the edge of the door and he stood in the opening, his irritation barely masked.

"Mr. Fraser?" McLaren smiled and extended his hand.

"Yes. And you are…?" His hand remained on the door.

"Michael McLaren. I'd like to talk to you for a few minutes, if this is a convenient time."

"Not particularly. I'm in the middle of painting." He tugged at the lower edge of his sweatshirt, as though emphasizing his activity.

"Oh. I hate to intrude. Would another time be better?"

"What do you want to talk about? You're not from

the village. I'd know you if you were."

"No, sir. Gary Barber asked me to investigate his son's disappearance. I live in Somerley, north of Buxton."

"Oh, yes? You'd best come in, then." He stood aside and indicated a chair in the living room. The door eased shut and McLaren took the offered seat.

"Does that bother you?"

"The Mendelssohn?" McLaren twisted around in the chair, trying to discern the source of the music. "No. It's quite nice."

"I'll turn it off if it bothers you. I like a bit of music when I'm working. Helps with the chore if it's boring." He sat down opposite McLaren, crossed his legs, and offered him a cigarette.

"No, thank you." McLaren looked around the room. A drop cloth covered the furniture and the bare floor along the far wall. A large can of paint, roller, tray and several brushes sat haphazardly near the ladder. "Your room's nice. Why are you painting it?"

"Just want a change. You know." He flashed a smile and arranged himself in the sofa. "Now, I don't mean to be rude, but you said you're here about Luke Barber?"

"Yes. I believe your daughter Ashley was engaged to Luke."

Darren Fraser flicked the ash from the end of his cigarette and held it loosely between his left index and middle fingers. He gazed at it periodically as he spoke. "That's correct. For one month."

"One month immediately before Luke went missing, I assume."

"Of course. What else could I mean?"

"Well, engagements have been called off, you know. The intended bride or groom gets cold feet, thinks better of the decision…that sort of thing."

Darren pushed himself straighter against the back of the sofa. The canvas cloth crinkled beneath his weight. "Well, nothing like that happened between Ashley and Luke. They loved each other. They have all the way through school. I felt their marriage was inevitable, but I didn't think it would be so soon after they left school. I thought they'd wait a bit before tying the knot. Perhaps see if Luke really had pro tennis ability, made a steady income." He took a puff of his cigarette and exhaled quickly. "You don't get anywhere in life by ignoring the important things like income, housing and the like."

"I agree. The first year of marriage is difficult enough without worrying about money to pay the bills."

"And I told both of them that very thing. That's why I wanted them to wait until Luke got firmly established in the tennis world. But they got engaged against my wishes, said they were both of age and knew what they were doing." He stared at this cigarette, then laid it in the ashtray. "Ashley's mother held my opinion, only stronger. She didn't want Ashley worried about finances. Tennis is a great life as long as you're on top and bringing in the money. But what happens when you get old and don't win matches any more? What happens to your life style?"

"Perhaps Ashley and Luke had plans for that."

Darren shrugged and looked at the photo of Ashley on the side table. "Perhaps. Don't get me wrong, McLaren. I liked the lad. I thought him talented and prayed he'd succeed. But a father wants what is best for his child. I wanted a secure future for her, and I thought that security could be obtained by Luke, no matter if he went in for tennis or music or something else. The lad was talented and had tremendous ambition. So I believed he'd get ahead in whatever field he chose. And I believed Luke was the best man for miles around. Best by far. He'd give my daughter a stable future."

"So, they became engaged in December, then."

"Yes." The word slipped out as though Darren were tired of discussing the topic. "It occurred at a formal party here on Christmas Eve. The gathering wasn't for the engagement. No one knew it was coming. Well, I mean we all assumed they'd get engaged at some time, but we didn't know it would be just then, that evening. It was family and close friends that night, for Christmas Eve, and Luke suddenly grabs Ashley's hand, bends down on one knee, and holds up the ring. Before anyone quite knew what was happening, he asks her to marry him." Daren grabbed his cigarette and took a puff. "She said yes almost before he'd finished asking."

"Was Gary Barber in attendance?"

"Yes, though that's not why he was invited. As I said, we'd not been expecting Luke to propose. Gary came because we had dinner and he and Luke were as near as family members as they could be, without any marriage bonds. It was a tradition between us, doing a bit of Christmas gift-giving and sharing dinner and a toast to the season."

"How did Gary take the proposal?"

"How did he take it?"

"Was he delighted? Was he angry?"

Darren blew a lungful of smoke into the air and

watched it disappear into the sunlight. "I don't know. Happy, I guess."

"You didn't know his thoughts about the upcoming marriage?"

"We didn't share confidences over a pint at the local, if that's what you mean. We weren't prospective fathers-in-law at that time."

"Perhaps not, but you said you knew Luke and Ashley would eventually marry. You and Gary hadn't talked about it?"

"No. I thought it way in the future. And Gary's too busy with his farm to spend an hour talking about an event that might or might not happen. There was time enough for a chat when the kids came up with a date."

McLaren leaned forward in his chair, his forearms resting on his thighs. The symphony's andante movement started up and McLaren lowered his voice level now that he didn't have to compete. "Was there anyone who was upset over the engagement?"

Darren's top leg began to jiggle. "Sharon, my wife, wasn't too keen on it."

"Due to the unpredictability of being a tennis champion or because she didn't like Luke?"

"She liked Luke well enough. As I said one minute ago, it was the uncertainty of that kind of life and the income they'd get. Sharon wanted a stable life for Ashley."

"And Luke might not necessarily have provided that."

"If you want to put it like that, yes."

"Is she here?" McLaren looked through the arched doorway, straining to hear sounds coming from another room of the house.

"Uh, no. 'Fraid not. Sorry. She's probably still doing the weekly shopping in Bakewell. I don't know when she'll be back, to be honest."

McLaren nodded, as though he could envision Saturday morning crowds. "Any friends, either at the dinner that night or just in general, who weren't over the moon with Luke and Ashley?"

"If there were, I didn't know about it. We didn't have that many people there. Just Luke and Gary, and me, Sharon and Ashley. And Callum Fox."

"Because he was Luke's tennis doubles partner?"

"Because he was Luke's and Ashley's good friend. I wasn't mixing business and yuletide festivities that evening. If I had, I'd have invited Bethany Watson and John Evans and Doc Tipton."

McLaren jotted the names in his notebook. "So, just the six of you were there."

"Yes. To celebrate Christmas. The engagement announcement was a complete surprise and, therefore, not the reason for the gathering."

"What was Callum's reaction to the big event?"

"He didn't leap for joy or gnash his teeth. He slapped Luke on the back and kissed Ashley. He looked genuinely glad for them."

"I doubt if Luke's marriage would ruin the doubles partnership, anyway."

Darren rose and stepped toward the front door. "I don't believe it would have, but it might have shattered a good friendship."

****

McLaren sat in his car outside the Fraser home, trying to make sense of Darren's obvious anxiety. The man had been jittery, his leg bouncing more rapidly the longer they had talked. And a five year-old couldn't see through the emphatic way he'd denied his wife's presence at the house. Was it merely that the man was nervous around the police, no matter how remotely removed McLaren was from his old job? Or did Darren know more about Luke Barber's disappearance than he wanted to tell?

He blew on his fingers and rubbed his hands together before he started the car and turned up the fan on the car's heater. The hot air felt good against his cold fingers, and he let the heat warm them before he drove back down the B5057, then turned right onto the A6. It was a straight shot, approximately six miles to Bakewell. He leaned back into the car seat, letting himself drown in Handel's *Water Music*. He was still whistling as he turned onto Granby Road, parked the car in the car park opposite the police station, and walked to Bats, Rackets and Clubs, a sporting equipment shop on Water Street.

Saturday afternoon shoppers crowded the modest shop interior. Displays of equipment and clothing for cricket, tennis and golf were well-defined, but tennis claimed the majority of floor space. McLaren wandered up to the checkout counter and waited for a teenaged boy to complete his transaction before asking the shop attendant if Callum Fox was working.

"Mr. Fox?" The twenty-year-old spoke the name as if he had no idea who the person was. He looked around, his eyes darting between the groups of customers, then refocused on McLaren. "I believe he's just finishing with those customers. There." He pointed to a red haired man not much older than himself.

McLaren thanked him and strolled over to the

tennis section. A woman nodded as the redhead handed a tennis racket to her and indicated the cash register. She made her way to the checkout counter as McLaren walked up to the man.

"Mr. Fox?"

The man turned slightly, smiled, and nodded. "Yes. May I assist you? Are you interested in tennis?"

"Well, I am, but not in the way you think. I'm Michael McLaren. I'm looking into Luke Barber's disappearance. I believe you and Luke were tennis partners."

Callum's eyes widened slightly and his hand went to the knot of his tie. "Yes. Sure, I knew Luke. We were best mates." He nodded toward the back of the main room. "We can talk in my office." He led the way through a curtained doorway into the rear of the shop. Stacks of boxes towered head-high in the open area. McLaren wondered how anyone could sell so much merchandise as he followed Callum into a small room at the rear of the space. He took the wooden chair near the door while Callum settled behind his desk.

"How much time did you and Luke spend together?"

Callum frowned and angled his chair toward McLaren. The springs protested the disturbance. "You mean daily? We practiced fairly constantly. But we had no set time, like ten to two, if that's what you mean."

"That's fine, but I really meant outside of tennis. Were you drinking buddies or go fishing together or share some other activity?"

"We'd have a pint. Not every night. Neither Luke nor I drank much. But some nights on the weekends we'd go to the pub. When Luke wasn't singing some place, that is. But other than that, no. Tennis was our only connection."

"How did you feel about Luke's engagement to Ashley?"

"Why, I-I was happy for them. My best mate getting married to a lovely girl…why shouldn't I be pleased?"

"And yet you and Ashley ended up marrying each other." McLaren studied Callum's face, noticing the quick swallow and the eye movement.

"What of it? Luke had gone missing. We did nothing wrong. We waited a decent period before our wedding."

"Six months. Seems like you rushed into it."

Callum's fingers gripped the arms of his chair, forcing the blood from them, leaving them pale. "I don't like your insinuation, McLaren. Luke had left. There was no word from him. It was a hell of a way to treat a woman, leaving her guessing where he was, what had happened. Ashley was sick with worry. She and I talked daily, she poured out her heart to me. It was only natural we drew close. Both of his closest friends commiserating with each other. Ashley needed my support and we grew to love each other." His grip relaxed somewhat and the knuckles returned to their normal hue. "Is it so wrong that we should marry?"

McLaren let the question go unanswered. He nodded toward the stacks of boxes outside the office. "Your business seems to be doing very well. When did you open?"

Callum followed McLaren's gaze and blinked, as though seeing the stock for the first time. "Oh, yes, we're doing fairly well. I—We've been in business for little over a year. I waited around for a year, expecting Luke to come back. I thought he'd run away for some reason. When it looked as though he was staying away for good, I sank what winnings I had into shop rental, advertising and equipment, and opened the shop."

"Had he talked about leaving the village? Was something bothering him, or was he frightened of someone?"

"Why ask that?"

McLaren snorted. "You're the one who brought up the subject. I assumed you knew something, heard him talk about it."

"No."

"Why did you give Luke a lift that morning?"

Callum snorted and shifted in his chair. "Are you daft?"

"Late morning."

"I didn't give him a ride that morning or any morning. You're round the twist."

"Where was Luke headed? What's south of the village that was important to Luke?"

"I don't know anything, south or any other direction, that he'd need to get to. I didn't drive him anywhere and I don't know anyone who would've. Besides, he had his own car. Why wouldn't he take that if he wanted to go somewhere?"

"So you didn't see him that day."

"His disappearance shocked me as much as it did everyone else. I thought his life was perfect, that nothing was wrong. He'd recently become engaged. He had a musical gig that night and was going to leave the next day for the singles match in London. His life was enchanted; he was going to reach the top of anything he reached for, whether it was music or tennis. If he had trouble with anything or anyone, he didn't tell me."

"Yet, he disappeared, either voluntarily or someone helped him."

Callum shook his head, his voice rising. "You can't believe that. Luke wouldn't leave Ashley. He loved her. He'd just become engaged. Besides, he wouldn't give up his tennis or music. He worked too hard to get where he was."

"Seems so, on the surface. Still, something may've been bothering him."

"I tell you, you're on the wrong trail. Even if he had some kind of problem with his career, he wouldn't have abandoned Ashley. They were inseparable."

"So inseparable that she married you six months after his disappearance?"

Callum opened his mouth, as though to retaliate, then shut it. He muttered, "You've no right to make a judgment. You weren't there. You don't know how much Ashley grieved."

McLaren scrunched up the corners of his mouth and nodded. "You're right. It just seemed as though you didn't give Luke a chance to show up."

"We waited. Like I said. How long should we have waited? What's the magic age? When Ashley turns seventy? When she's eighty-three?" He offered it as if it were an excuse.

The quiet wrapped around them as each man was busy with his own thoughts. Snippets of conversations from the shop wound back to them. The ringing phone jerked McLaren back to the present.

"And you offered the comforting shoulder." He held up his hand. "I don't intend for that to sound rude."

"I offered her more understanding and support than even her parents did, yes. I guess it was a natural thing for her love to manifest in me."

McLaren nodded, unsure of what to say.

"When I asked her to marry me it was from my heart, McLaren. I didn't do it out of pity."

Again the silence enveloped them. An image of Dena, his fiancée, welled in McLaren's mind and he wondered again why he was afraid of going through with their marriage. Because he was fearful of loving too much, of the pain that would smother him if something bad happened to her? He could emotionally hold her at arm's length, pretend he didn't care as deeply as he did. The wall created a barrier that would make the pain less poignant if she left him. And he assumed some day she would. Everyone else he had passionately loved had left him. So why not Dena?

But other people seemed able to make commitments, to see them through. Ashley and Luke had been engaged; Ashley and Callum had married. Most all of McLaren's mates had married and had stayed married, beating the divorce odds. If he needed an example, he need look no further than Jamie and his wife Paula. And yet, something stopped him from following the voice nudging him toward Dena. He mentally swore at himself. What was wrong with him?

He glanced at Callum. The man seemed not to have noticed McLaren's contemplation. He took a breath, trying to calm his racing heart. "You seem emphatic that Luke wouldn't have left Ashley of his own free will. That leaves an obvious alternative." He waited, watching Callum's emotions register in his face.

"I suppose so."

"Suppose what?"

"Luke was either abducted or murdered." He said it so quietly that McLaren nearly didn't near him.

"Is that so hard to admit?"

Callum shook his head. "Just hard to admit."

"Why? If you say he wouldn't have left Ashley, yet he has obviously left the village, there's no other alternative, is there?"

"No."

"So why are you reluctant to voice it?"

"I suppose it just makes it more real. You know, like you kid yourself into believing he just stepped out to run an errand and he'll be back."

"But you married his fiancée." McLaren leaned forward, wanting to find out why Callum was so reluctant to speak. "That's about as real as you can get."

"Yes."

"So you evidently suspected foul play, whether from an abduction or murder, or you wouldn't have wed Ashley so quickly." He hesitated, waiting for Callum's answer. "Well? What made you believe Luke wasn't coming back?"

"I don't know. Maybe I just hoped."

"You loved Ashley that much?"

"Yes." His eyes searched McLaren's, hoping for a sign of understanding. "But I didn't kill him. I didn't have anything to do with his disappearance. We were mates as well as tennis partners. I wouldn't wish anything bad to happen to him."

"You just took advantage of his absence."

"Yes. I-it makes me sound cold hearted and calculating, I know, but I'm not. We waited, like I said, but it seemed as though if Luke had left by himself, he would've told Ashley. And I can't believe he would've walked out on her. So he was abducted or killed." He stopped abruptly, as though speaking what he had always believed made the reality more horrible. He continued in a softer voice. "If I think of that I get sick. Physically sick. To think there are such people out there who would do that…to someone as nice as Luke, who never harmed anyone in his life…" He grimaced and turned in his chair.

"And you've no idea who might have killed or kidnapped Luke." McLaren pressed the question now that Callum was talking about it.

"None. I've thought and thought about this, and nothing makes sense. The whole event is beyond imagination."

"No one in the tennis world who had it in for Luke? A competitor, perhaps? Or did someone else love Ashley?"

"I considered that, McLaren, but I can't think of a single person. Sure, Luke stepped on a few toes to get to the top, but he didn't do it with malice. That's life. Sometimes you win, sometimes you lose. If you're going to get into professional sports, you have to expect that. There's always someone better than you. Luke played hard and won fair. If some opponent got his feelings hurt along the way, that's that chap's problem. Luke was a gracious winner and always had time for anyone who needed his help."

"And another man standing in the wings for Ashley?"

Callum shrugged and pulled in the corners of his mouth.

"Is that an answer for you don't know, or you don't care?"

"Of course I care!" The words erupted in a heat of anger. "I care if another man loves her, has his eye on her, perhaps wants me out of the way to move in on her."

"Could that have happened with Luke?"

Callum's face drained of color and he stared at McLaren with widening eyes. "You can't be serious."

"Something happened to Luke. You've admitted it. I'm investigating his disappearance because it's obvious. Did someone get rid of Luke to lessen the number of Ashley's suitors?"

"That's ridiculous."

"Why? Luke's gone, you stepped in. If the person who abducted or killed Luke is still interested in Ashley, why are you safe?"

Callum exhaled slowly and fidgeted with his shirt collar. "That sounds so…"

"Ridiculous? Calculating? Evil? Smart?"

"Calculating and evil, yes. No one around here would do that."

"You know for a fact it was someone around here? You just said a minute ago that you didn't believe Luke had any enemy. Which is it?"

"I-I'm afraid. Sorry."

"Afraid for yourself?"

"For Ashley. I don't want her to think someone's lurking around, waiting to nab her."

"Why should you think that?"

"Well, if Luke was kidnapped to make the road free for this bloke to marry Ashley…" He took a breath, trying to think.

"We're assuming that might be the reason. You've lost sight of the fact that Luke could've been abducted or killed for being Luke, whatever that entails."

"Like, a tennis or music connection?"

McLaren nodded and let the quiet well between them. After a bit, he said, "Why didn't you continue in tennis, Callum? You had to have been good if you and Luke played doubles matches, even in a semi-pro status."

Callum nudged a stack of papers back a bit on the desktop and leaned against the near edge. He seemed more relaxed with the conversation focused on something non-threatening like himself. "Oh, just a simple matter of no heart left for it. I was good, yes. When you play doubles each person has to be fairly equal. I could've developed my skill and gone on. Doc Tipton would've taken me on. But something went out of me with Luke's continued disappearance. It was like my will or fire had also disappeared." He shrugged, his fingers playing with the edge of the papers. "There's only so much a person can take before his soul is crushed."

****

McLaren finished up his interviews that day by speaking to the publican of The Green Cat. The man could offer no reason for Luke's disappearance, had no idea of any problems Luke might've had nor people with whom he might've had trouble.

He drove back to his home in Somerley as if in a daze, his mind on the case. As he passed The Split Oak, he hesitated briefly as he considered having a pint and ringing up Jamie to talk over the investigation. But the evening's cold settled into his bones and his own fire beckoned. He was home ten minutes later.

The day's mail held nothing more interesting than a grand opening special at a new computer store and a postcard from a former work colleague. He put the two pieces on his desk and heated up the leftover raspberry chicken and sautéed pears from last night's dinner. After making a quick tossed salad he brewed a cup of tea and took the meal into the dining room. He read over the case notes as he ate.

He'd just poured a second cup of tea when his mobile phone rang. He glanced at the caller ID display, then smiled as he flipped open the phone. "How's my favorite girl?"

"Tired." Dena's voice, flat and lifeless, betrayed her fatigue.

"Have a lot of people at the tiger sanctuary?"

"Enormous amount. I'd expect crowds if it was free admission, but it wasn't."

"Still, it's nice to have a full coffer for those cats. It saves on fund raisers, I'm sure."

"We're always raising money. Tigers like to eat, or haven't you heard?"

"I have that impression."

"What are you doing? I don't mean dinner. You working on a stone wall some place?"

"I should be." He glanced at his office. Somewhere on his desk was a list of repair jobs that waited for him. Repair jobs that passed as his nine-to-five job, but some weeks he'd never know it. His freelance work of working on cold cases took the majority of his time some weeks. He loved the investigation; it was as close to his former police detective job as he was likely to get. But it did cut into his bank account when he didn't get paid. He swallowed a mouthful of tea, then told Dena about Luke Barber's disappearance.

"Three years seems ages for a cold case. And no one's heard a thing from him?"

"Nothing. At least, no one's admitting it if they have."

"Why say that? Do you suspect Luke's communicating with someone?"

"I don't suspect anything right now. The investigation has just started. But not much surprises me anymore. Some people can easily say one thing to the police and not mean a word of it."

"You're not in the job anymore, Michael."

"I don't need reminding, thank you. I'm just making a statement about people's ability to lie."

"They must have strong feelings about the person or the situation if they risk lying. Is love or hate usually the contributing factor, do you know?"

McLaren shrugged, glancing at his notes. "Depends on the person, I guess. If the person is protecting someone, love's usually behind it. 'Course, he could lie out of hate, wanting someone to become a suspect or at least be inconvenienced by a police investigation. I've known it both ways."

"Still, it makes your job harder. It's a good thing you love what you're doing, to put up with that."

McLaren opened his mouth, about to ask her to set a wedding date, but the words caught in his throat. He imagined her brown eyes frowning as she listened to his complaining, her brunette hair satiny looking beneath the lamplight. He swallowed, trying to loosen his neck muscles. His fingertips played with his wooden bead necklace.

"You all right, Michael?"

"Yeah. Just swallowed my tea too quickly." He coughed again, feeling the heat flood his cheeks. Could Dena detect his lie?

"Got any interesting leads?" Her voice was low and soft, filled with concern for his emotional and mental well being. She didn't want him to fall back into the semi-hermit existence that had claimed him on leaving the police force. It had been all she and Jamie could do to interest him in life again.

"A few." He hesitated, debating if he should tell her anything. She'd involved herself in a case last year, very nearly dying as a result. But, he told himself, she'd tried to lift him out of his depression, make sure life interested him again. He nudged the notebook closer to him and mentally prayed he wasn't making a mistake. "There's a question of the parentage of an infant. It's easy to assume it would've been illegitimate if Ashley Fraser hadn't married Callum Fox."

"Meaning, you believe Luke Barber fathered the child."

"He's the most likely candidate. I get the impression that Ashley isn't the type of woman to have been wild in her youth—which was only three years ago—so it's difficult to imagine her name inked into all the village male's black books."

"Your instincts are right most of the time, Michael. Could the child be the current husband's? Was he married before?"

"That occurred to me. But I need to find out."

"I guess you can't come out and ask. That'd be a bit crass."

"So, I've got to sort through that. Then, there's the

problem of Luke's guitar."

"Something wrong with it?"

"On the contrary. It's a very fine instrument. Twin to my own." He glanced at his own guitar sprawled across two-thirds of the living room sofa. "Same make, same model. Dreadnought size. Perfect for folk or bluegrass music."

"He goes up in your estimation as a musician, then."

He opened his mouth to protest her suggestion that he played favorites with victims, but her laugh implied she was joking.

"So what's odd about the guitar, Michael? Don't tell me there's something stashed in it."

"As I said, the instrument is fine. But don't you think it's strange that he would vanish around four-thirty, presumably on his way to sing that night, and not have his guitar with him?"

Chapter Seven

"As long as you phrase it like that, yes." Dena's voice trailed off and McLaren could imagine her thinking through the possible reasons, perhaps her trim legs crossed and bouncing in her agitation. "Bit of a puzzle you've got."

"That's one way of phrasing it. Luke's father, Gary, is a riddle, too."

"In what way?"

"He's taking this whole thing as if he was taking out the rubbish. I get the impression it's just another day for him. He shows no emotion. None at all. No anger, no sadness, no grief."

"If it happened three years ago, he may have cried all he's going to. You can't grieve forever, Michael. A person has to get on with his life eventually, no matter how much he loves the missing person."

McLaren stretched and exhaled heavily, then ran his fingers through his hair. "I guess. He seems cold and uncaring, that's all I'm saying. After all, he *did* contact Jamie for help in locating his son."

"There you are. Mr. Barber does love his son. You know, Michael, not everyone has to rant and throw things to express emotion."

"I'll let that comment pass."

"At least I know what you're feeling, darling."

"Most people do. I make a lousy poker player."

Dena's laugh exploded in his left ear. "Remind me

to play against you, then."

"I'm serious, Dena. He also evaded a few of my questions. Now, wouldn't a father who's searching for his son be forthright and want to tell everything he knew, no matter how trivial, to the investigator? I felt he was playing dodge ball with my questions."

"Yes, I'd think he would tell everything, but maybe he's been burned. Maybe one of the investigating officers made light of something or belittled a statement Mr. Barber made. If he's a sensitive person he would be cautious of repeating that same mistake, even with you."

"Even though his friend, Jamie, recommended me. I don't know." He gave his scalp a final rub and leaned back in his chair. A fox yelped somewhere in the field behind his house.

"What does Jamie say about that? If he knows Mr. Barber, perhaps he knows if that's his usual response to this type of thing. Remember, Michael, you don't really know this man."

"I haven't asked Jamie yet. I just got through dinner when you phoned."

"Well, you need to find out. It'll help with your sleep, if nothing else. Speaking of which, I need to ring off. I've got a big day tomorrow."

"On Sunday?"

"It's one of our biggest attendance days. Part of the weekend. You know about weekends, don't you?" She meant it as a joke, but there was a weariness underlying the question.

"You normally don't work Sundays." He said it warily, as though something devious lay behind the change in her work schedule.

"I don't. But I've nothing special to do tomorrow, and two large groups are scheduled to come through. So I thought I'd help out." Her tone implied it was all the same to her whether she volunteered at the sanctuary or stayed at home alone.

McLaren locked his gaze on Dena's photograph in the next room. The lamplight gilded the edge of the metal frame. Was she staring at him? He took a deep breath, willing his wildly beating heart to slow its frantic beat. "Would you like something special to do with the rest of your life?"

"Like what? A concert or theater performance won't last that long, unless you've got season tickets to something. What do you mean?"

"I want to marry you, Dena. I want to set the date." He refrained from saying he'd considered asking many times, that he finally got his nerve up, that he ignored the feeling that everything, everyone he loved slipped away from him and he was scared as hell that he'd lose her, too. But he now knew that even if they shared one hour as husband and wife he would hold on to that memory with all his strength as long as he was sane.

Maybe I should've done this differently, he thought as he focused on Dena's eyes. Maybe I should've done it with a love song and a few dozen roses on a moonlit night. Maybe I should've been with her and asked in person, taken her into my arms…

The hesitation on the other end of the phone sounded deafening, as though a thousand cannons fired simultaneously. He waited for what seemed an eternity before she spoke.

"You're certain you want this?"

He frowned, confused. "Yes! I-I thought you did,

too. I thought you wanted to get married. I—We're engaged."

"We were engaged…before." She didn't mention the broken engagement that occurred after he quit his job with the Staffordshire Constabulary. "I know you were incredibly hurt emotionally, Michael, and I allowed for that. I gave you time. An entire year. It was one of the most difficult things I've ever done because I wanted to be with you. I loved you."

"Loved. Past tense?" He felt his heart turn over.

"I'm referring to last year, dear. I still love you. I just want you to be certain of your own heart. Have you honestly thought of what you'd be giving up if we married?"

"I'd be gaining so much more if we did marry. The rest doesn't matter."

Her warmth spilled over the phone. "If you're sure…"

"God, yes. I love you more than my life, Dena."

"Then I'll marry you, Michael." A hint of humor colored her words. "And how long have you been coming to this question?"

"I've not had a hell of a lot of practice. I don't make a habit of asking women to marry me each day."

"Thank God for that."

They settled on 31 December because, as Dena said, it was the threshold of a new year for them as a couple.

"It gives us nearly a year to make arrangements." She smiled and he heard it in her voice. "I can probably get my household items packed by then."

"Don't kid me. You started packing the day we met."

"Maybe I should think twice about marrying a detective. I can't keep any secrets from you."

"I hope not. I think that's part of the marriage vows."

They said good night, and McLaren hung up, feeling tremendously euphoric. He still felt the blood coursing through his veins when he turned out the lights an hour later and tried to sleep. But Dena's face danced before him and her voice echoed in his ears. He finally got up, brewed a cup of tea, and brought it back into the bedroom. He stood at his bedroom window, sipping it as the moon rose in a clear, black sky.

****

Dena quietly replaced the receiver and wrapped her arms around her shoulders in a slowly strengthening hug. She sank back into the pillows piled against her headboard and let out a yell. Her happiness bounced off the bedroom walls and swirled around her.

It had been a long time coming, over a year. Eighteen months ago, when McLaren had left the police force and cocooned himself away from the world, she'd given up on any possible wedding. He'd been filled with so much anger and disillusionment that she and his friends thought he'd never recover. But his saving grace had been investigating that first cold case. Fighting injustice was in his blood; it gave him purpose for his life. She prayed they continued to come his way. Without it, he was merely a shell. And she loved him too intently to want to see him slip into that again.

And now the marriage she had dreamed of would become a reality. She lay on her back, staring at the ceiling, mentally counting the days until the end of the year. Time might seem short to other women—

arranging for a caterer, church, honeymoon destination, flowers, reception—but she had begun planning her big day two years ago. She knew which friends she'd ask to be attendants, knew the color of their dresses, knew the caterer and the decorations she wanted. She was not one to sit around and waste time. All that she had lacked was the date.

She turned onto her side and stared at his photo sitting on her bedside cabinet. She'd never admitted it to anyone, but she was proud of the picture. Of course, she realized her subject matter contributed greatly to the superior quality of the snapshot: the slant of sunlight brightening his blond hair and his hazel eyes staring at her with such a warmth that even now her blood tingled. She admitted she no doubt viewed it in a prejudiced light, that her rose-colored glasses could affect her vision. But the lighting and angle were excellent, with an open window casing of a rock barn framing his face. She had caught many exceptional poses of him that day—sitting on a low stone wall, his arm laying across a tree limb, playing his guitar—but this framed one still was her favorite. And it was mainly due to the look he gave her.

Dena picked up the photograph and laid it on the pillow beside her. She curled up, her right hand beneath her head, her left arm stretched across the empty portion of the bed. By the end of the year he'd be there beside her. They'd be together. Nothing would ever separate them. She was as certain of that as anything she'd ever believed in. The proposal and the choice of a wedding date had been such a long time coming that he'd had enough time to overcome any misgivings. For him to ask her tonight, without waiting until he was with her, proved his decision. It was cast in concrete, as solid as a rock wall.

Of course, she would have scrubbed the elaborate plans and eloped with him if he had suggested they marry next weekend. Tomorrow, even. As much as she wanted a flower-filled church, she wanted him more. Receptions could be held later; an ardent McLaren should be grabbed as quickly as possible.

She slipped the CD of his folk group into her CD player alarm clock, hit the sleep button and set the wakeup time. His singing filled the room and she snuggled into the duvet, drawing it up to her chin. She'd wake to his voice, too. Would for the rest of her life. She fell asleep with his voice enveloping her.

****

He told Jamie later that he didn't know what woke him. Perhaps it was his copper's sixth sense, still ingrained after decades in the job. Perhaps it was a sound that, though hardly indistinguishable, warned his subconscious it was foreign. He lay in bed, his body taut, his ears straining to hear. After a minute he sat up, the top sheet and duvet falling from his chest. The beads of his necklace shifted position and the opposite side of the beads rolled and lay against his chest. When he thought about it afterwards, he supposed the air and the beads had been cold, but he wasn't aware of them then. He slid out of bed and tiptoed into the living room. A sound so faint as to be nearly inaudible came to him in the stillness between owl calls. It was the sound of breaking glass.

McLaren returned to the bedroom, slipped into his jeans, shirt and shoes, and snatched the torch from the top drawer of his bedside cabinet. As he passed through the living room he grabbed the fireplace poker, then slipped outside by the kitchen door.

The night air shocked him and he clenched his teeth to keep them from chattering. He remained on the step by the door, rooted beside the rose bush, waiting for his eyes to adjust to the darkness for, although he had kept all lights off inside the house, the blackness outdoors was deeper than he'd ever seen.

He focused on his car in the driveway. The dark shape of a person stood beside the passenger's side. He seemed to lay a crowbar on the grass, for he bent down briefly, then rose without the long object in his hand. He reached into the car and the faint click of the door catch releasing came to McLaren. The door opened and the interior light fell on the intruder's face.

McLaren moved away from the bush, eager to see the person's identity. He kept to the strip of grass beside the gravel drive and hugged the greenery embracing the house's foundation.

The intruder had dressed for the occasion, for he was clad in dark jacket, jeans, gloves and a knitted ski mask.

McLaren watched for several moments, curious as to the object of the man's search. He bent over the front seats, evidently looking beneath them and then in the glove box and the pockets in the doors. When nothing of consequence yielded to his search, he opened the hatch back door and looked through the back.

McLaren tiptoed down the length of grass until he came opposite the car's boot. As the intruder straightened up, McLaren grabbed the man's arm. The man gave a startled yell that quickly changed to anger. He twisted away from McLaren and fumbled in the grass for the crowbar. Seeing what the man wanted, McLaren lunged for the man's legs. He fell short and crashed to the ground. The fall knocked his torch from his hand and he watched it roll beneath his car. He lay there for several seconds, trying to clear his mind. The gravel bore into his chest with its cold and sharpness. He pushed away from it, wanting to distance himself from the ache and pain. As he got to his hands and knees, the man kicked him in his side, turned, and ran down the driveway into the night, leaving McLaren cold, hurting, and wondering what he had interrupted.

****

He got a late start Sunday morning, the effects of his sleepless night making him groggy. Several cups of coffee helped clear his head, but the bleary eyes staring back at him from the bathroom mirror made him feel worse. Despite just stepping out of the shower, he splashed more water on his face. Even if he didn't look better, at least the vigorous towel drying got his skin tingling.

His fingers gingerly touched his side where the burglar kicked him last night. No rib had been broken, he was certain, but the area was sore. He considered wrapping an elastic bandage around his chest, or at least taping strips of adhesive plaster over the tender area, but gave up the idea. It would be a cumbersome job. Best to just leave it alone.

He lingered over a breakfast of eggs, blueberries and toast, then answered several emails. He grabbed the calendar on his desk and turned the pages to December. The last date seemed to glow and he grabbed his pen and inked Wedding in the vacant square. Finished, he held the calendar in front of him, smiling. The year wouldn't pass fast enough for him. Now that he'd made the commitment, he felt incredibly calm and happy. Would he always feel this way when he and Dena were wed?

He set the calendar on the desk and turned the pages back to the current week. He'd shop for a ring in the next few days and give it to her this weekend. Maybe even Friday. He'd make it romantic, perhaps nestling it among the petals of a rose or among some of her favorite chocolates. He smiled, envisioning her surprise when she opened the box and saw the diamond winking at her. He got to his feet, too happy to sit still.

Or would she like his mother's engagement ring? It would be smaller than anything he'd buy Dena now, but it had sentimental value and would root her in his family in ways a new ring couldn't. She placed a great importance on family history. Yes, she might like that. Unless she thought he was too cheap to buy her a new ring…

He abandoned the ring debate and grabbed his notebook from the dining room table. Consulting the list of names, he decided to talk to Sharon Fraser. Provided he could get past Darren. He pulled on a heavy cable pullover, already feeling the sharp cold of the day, grabbed his keys and jacket, and went outside to look at his car.

The window on the passenger's side was broken, as he suspected last night, but the car's body hadn't been injured. He got a roll of plastic wrap and some duct tape from the house, then returned to his car. He opened the car door and tore off a long length of the plastic. He folded it lengthwise in thirds and laid the short end over the top of the doorframe. The plastic film caught snugly between the frame and the car body when he shut the door. He went around to the driver's side, leaned across the seat, and taped the bottom and sides of the film to the door's interior. He righted himself and looked at his handiwork. It wouldn't keep out the cold, but he could see through it, so he wouldn't be a hazard to himself or other drivers, which was his main objective. As he got out of the car, he glanced at the sky. It didn't look like rain or sleet, and he prayed he'd escape them before he got the window fixed.

He put the items on the back seat, thinking he'd probably have to replace his make-do window several times, then got into his car and drove off.

The plastic wrap bulged and sagged as the wind hit it, as though it breathed along with McLaren. He leaned over several times to press one of the duct tape strips more firmly against the door, then concentrated on the drive to Langheath.

He turned up the temperature on the car's heater, trying to combat the cold seeping through his makeshift window, and chided himself for not thinking of a cap. He promised himself he'd wear one tomorrow. He hit the BACK button on the CD player until the song "There Is a Time" came up, then let it play. For some reason the song's images of gray-hued woods and falling snow appealed to him. "The Whole World Round", the next song, added to the mood, and he added his voice to the Dillards as they sang about the fire's glow and the lonesome strains of the fiddle. He shivered and pulled his muffler around his neck.

The roads from Somerley to Bakewell were patterned with daubs of snow where it had fallen from overhanging tree boughs or been missed by snowplows.

But the route was passable and dry. He just had to contend with the cold.

As he crossed the gothic bridge into Bakewell he glanced at the River Wye. Small, icy patches settled among the clumps of dried cattails along the riverbank and fringed the rocks at the shoreline. A smear of snow where the riverbank mud met the grass held imprints of dozens of birds' feet. He didn't need to see them to know ducks, stock doves and sparrows would be numerous. But perhaps a mistle thrush or jackdaw had left its footprints behind. He almost turned into the car park, but he needed to get on with his day.

Traffic on the A6 into Langheath was light, the frosty morning finding most people still at home. McLaren parked at the Fraser house and debated whether he should go to the door and risk running into Darren or look for Sharon at the church. But he didn't know if she was a church-goer, and there was always the chance she might be absent this Sunday. He got out of his car, then hesitated beside the driver's door. Realizing locking it would make little sense, he jammed his key into his jacket pocket and strode up to the house.

The front door inched open to a shadow-filled hall, the security chain taut as the person on the other side assessed the caller. A female voice asked who he was.

"Michael McLaren. I'd like to speak to Sharon Fraser, if she's available."

"Why? What do you want?"

"I'm looking into the disappearance of Luke Barber."

"That happened three years ago." The voice sounded skeptical, as though he was trying to sell her

Big Ben.

"Gary Barber's aware of that, but he still wishes me to find his son. Is Sharon Fraser here?"

Either Gary's name or the topic persuaded the person to find out more, for the chain fell free of the slide and the door opened. A faded blonde with scrutinizing hazel eyes stood before him and asked him to come inside.

The door closed with a sigh, shutting out the biting wind, and he immediately felt warmer. The fireplace grate held no fire, he observed as he crossed the floor, but perhaps she was about to leave. It was a cheerless room, done in hues of blue, gray and white, everything blending together in serene understatement. Which was fine if you wanted to unwind at the end of the day, but it didn't do much to chase away January's chill. He glanced at an oversized painting of a wintry mountain range. It accented the color scheme, but it didn't do much to thaw his bones.

McLaren waited for Sharon to sit before he took the chair by the coffee table. Both pieces of furniture were painted white; the table had a pewter drawer pull and a bold blue and gray paisley print padded the chair. He sat forward, not completely at ease with the chair, the room or with Sharon. They all seemed well matched: cold and lifeless.

Sharon pulled the edges of her sleeves down, covering her wrists, and crossed her legs. Studying her in the sunlight he realized she was older than her voice had led him to believe. Mid-forties, he thought. Make-up concealed much of her wrinkles but couldn't hide the crow's feet or the backs of her dry hands. Small silver earrings winked in the light as she moved her head to readjust the cushion behind her. He thought she had chosen the jewelry well; it brought a bit of life to her dull features.

"I don't know what I can tell you about Luke." Sharon offered McLaren a cigarette from the pack on the side table, then lit one for herself. She drew a deep breath and exhaled slowly. "Why is Gary bringing this up again? Did someone find something or hear from Luke?"

"I'm not aware of anything." McLaren watched Sharon's foot tap on the floor. "I think there comes a time to anyone who's searching for a loved one to renew the search. Faith alone is good only so long. Action is needed, if for nothing more than to focus your energy and give your emotions an outlet."

"Oh. Too bad. I was hoping something of Luke's had been found."

"Did you see Luke that day, any time?"

Sharon averted her gaze from McLaren for an instant before coming back to him. "No. I don't think so. What day was it?"

"A Friday."

She nodded, as though recalling Luke's schedule or her own day. "He and Bethany played at The Green Cat on Friday evenings."

"Did you see him here in the village that morning or afternoon?"

"I can't say."

"Why can't you?"

Shrugging, she flicked the cigarette ash into the ashtray. "One day's like another. Unless there's some event or special appointment or trip, they all run together. I doubt if most folks would remember seeing a certain person on a specific day three years ago."

"You don't go into the village on Fridays to shop, might've seen him there?"

"I work on Fridays, Mr. McLaren." She said it rather haughtily, as if he should have known or her employer was someone awe-inspiring. "I work every week day. I do my shopping either in Chesterfield, where I am employed, or here in the village on Saturdays. So no, I didn't see Luke Barber that Friday morning or afternoon."

"I merely asked a question, Mrs. Fraser."

"Of course." She drew another drag from her cigarette before grounding it out in the tray. The dying tendrils of smoke drifted upward, then faded away.

"Where do you work?"

"In my husband's car dealership. That is, *our* dealership."

"In Chesterfield."

"I'm a receptionist." She glanced at her fingernails, perhaps making certain the manicure was still office quality. "It's important work. I'm the first voice the prospective buyer hears when he phones, and I'm the first person who greets him when he walks into the showroom. I'm the first impression of the business." She'd said it like a school child in a pageant, from rote and with a hint of self confidence.

"I have no doubt of it. First opinions are often the strongest."

"Darren—my husband—and I talked about it when we began considering the dealership. I was concerned that if we worked together it might injure our marriage. But he said I was overly cautious, that we weren't really working together since he'd be in his office and

I'd be at the desk near the front door. And he was right. We don't really see each other and we certainly aren't working side by side. Besides, it saves us one person's salary. Neither of us gets one. Well, not a formal pay packet. We just take living expenses out of the company fund."

McLaren let the quiet build between them before he asked about Ashley.

"What about her?" Sharon's voice took on an edge.

"She and Luke were engaged, then she married Callum Fox."

"Is that a crime?"

"Certainly not. I just wondered if your daughter and Callum had been close friends before their marriage."

"Obviously they were friends. You don't marry someone you dislike."

"Callum owns a sport equipment shop, I believe."

"Bats, Rackets and Clubs. In Bakewell."

"Too bad he didn't continue with his tennis matches. He must have been quite good."

"I understand he was. I'm no judge of that skill, but for Callum to have partnered with Luke…well, they were good enough."

"You don't sound exactly pleased with the tennis world, Mrs. Fraser. Don't you like it?"

"It's better than some."

"Did you object to your daughter's engagement to Luke, perhaps on these grounds?"

Sharon reached for her cigarette, realized she had finished it, then folded her hands in her lap. "Luke was a decent lad. I didn't object to him as a person."

"But you objected to his tennis playing?"

"Yes."

"Why? Didn't you believe he could make pro?"

"I believed he would. And that's what bothered me. I would've done anything to stop him."

Chapter Eight

The peal of church bells seeped into the room as McLaren fought to contain his surprise. "Why is that?"

Sharon fidgeted with the bangle bracelets on her left wrist and stared at the window. "I made no secret of my feelings. My husband and daughter knew of it. As did Luke. I wanted a secure future for Ashley. I wanted her to have a home, a normal life in a village or town where they could put down roots and rear a family. If Luke became so good that he would tour the country or world to play tournaments, he'd hardly ever be home. Ashley would have no husband around most days. All the work and house decisions would fall on her. What would happen if there was an emergency? She'd be alone to deal with it." Sharon searched McLaren's eyes to see if he understood. "It's hard enough rearing children or just taking care of a house when there are two of you. She doesn't deserve to do all that alone. Besides," she added, her voice low and faint. "You marry because you love each other and want to be together. A spouse that rings you up on your birthday or on your wedding anniversary isn't much better than no spouse."

A brief image of Dena sitting by the living room window, staring at the clock, flashed in his mind. That wasn't his ideal of married life with Dena. He wanted to be home every night, sharing the household chores and calamities, sitting by the fire on wintry evenings or relaxing in the shade on summer mornings. He wasn't marrying her because he needed a housekeeper; he was marrying her because he wanted to spend those evenings and days with her.

McLaren felt his throat thickening and he swallowed several times before asking if she would've had the same misgivings if Luke would've gone into music as a profession.

"I'm not sure. It would have depended if he would stay local or even just confine his engagements to Britain. Perhaps he wouldn't have been gone for such long stints of time as a tennis tournament would warrant." She smiled sadly, her mouth skewing at the corners. "Sad that we'll never know. But I never wished Luke any harm, like losing his matches or breaking his arm. I just wanted the best for my child."

McLaren rose and dug his car key from his jacket pocket. "Funny, but I think Gary Barber wanted the best for his child, too."

****

Doc Tipton lived in an aged cottage sitting cattycorner from the Frasers. A fresh coat of paint had been applied probably last autumn as protection against the onslaught of winter, McLaren thought. New gutters and roof added to the building's armor and upheld the well-kept look of the neighborhood. All that the cottage lacked was the picket fence and perennial garden.

McLaren left the car at the Frasers and crossed the road. As he walked beneath a grandfather oak, he glanced up. Its leafless person-thick limbs appeared to grasp the clouds. At its boulder-sized base, puddles of frozen water and lingering fingers of snow held fast to the depressions in the ground and along the northern edges of the trees and house. But the ground remained winter-firm where he trod. Spring still had a long time to wait.

McLaren had merely to mention his search for Luke Barber and Doc ushered him into the living room and to an overstuffed chair. He padded into the kitchen, still talking about what a shock the whole event had been, his voice floating back to McLaren. When he returned to the living room, he held a tray laden with mugs, spoons, sugar and milk.

"Water's coming to the boil. Won't be long." Doc offered a plate of biscuits to McLaren. "Only store bought, I'm afraid. I never was much of a baker."

"No apologies." McLaren accepted a chocolate biscuit and bit into it as he glanced at the room. It was not as elegant as the Frasers', but it had a lived-in feel that both warmed him with the reds, greens and earth tones and brightened his spirit. "Sensational scenery. Where is this?" He indicated a framed photo sitting on the table near him.

"Which one?" Doc stared at the photo of a fern-choked forest with a blood-red sunset silhouetting tall trees. He nodded, angling the photo toward him as though he contemplated the place or experience, the fingers of his left hand gliding over the mole at the left corner of his lips. "Half Moon Bay on Stewart Island. A family holiday. You ever been there?"

"I don't know where Stewart Island is. But it makes no difference because I've never been to *any* Stewart Island. Wish I had." He sighed slightly, looking covetous.

"That one's New Zealand. Their third largest island. We rented a house there for two months. We did that for years. It became a favorite spot of ours. A retreat from the world so my dad could unwind."

"It seems the perfect place for that."

"It was. Remote, yet so much to do. Well, no London nightlife type activities, but if you like any water sports or hiking or bird watching, you've come to the right place." The shrill whistle of the tea kettle cut into the conversation. "Ah. Water's ready. Won't be a tick." Doc excused himself, ambled into the kitchen, and minutes later returned with the teapot. "I guess I'm getting old. I feel the winter more each year. Settles right into my bones. But a nice cuppa helps displace all that." He handed McLaren a cup of tea, then poked up the fire.

"Are those all yours?" McLaren gestured toward the silver trophies, certificates and photos gracing the fireplace mantel and walls.

"What? These?" Doc Tipton craned his head and looked at the items. He replaced the poker and padded back to his chair. "Remnants of a few good years of tennis."

"More than a *few* good years, I expect."

"I've had fun, which is more important than all that. Still, it's a nice remembrance."

McLaren got up and walked over to the display. He read the inscriptions on the trophies and picked up a photograph. "This is you at Wimbledon."

"Yes. After winning the match. You might recognize my opponent." He smiled as McLaren whistled and set the photo back on the mantel. "Toward the end of my career, when I could still serve worth a damn."

"I can't believe you've lost that talent. Not from

what I hear about you from the folks around here."

"You'll pardon me if I say this—and I assume it will stay strictly between us—but the good people of Langheath wouldn't know a good tennis serve from a bloke swatting at a fly. Though I do exaggerate slightly. They know Luke Barber had an outstanding serve."

"Oh, yes? Did they attend some of his games?"

"May have done, but I'm referring to his little trick he did once."

"What was that?"

Doc refilled McLaren's cup, then settled back in his chair. "He drove a tennis ball into a hole in the old Wakebridge Engine House. I'm not talking about getting a ball through an open window. I mean he lobbed a ball into a hole in the brick face." He paused, letting McLaren picture the feat.

"You mean, one of the old Crich Cliff lead mines?"

"The very one. Southeast of Cromford. You know the place?"

McLaren nodded, the abandoned lead area sharp in his mind.

"Then you know that ruined section of the old building."

"Several bricks are missing, which gives the structure an odd appearance when viewed from the correct angle."

"This particular hole is toward the top. A few of the local lads—well, tearaways, actually—challenged Luke to serve a ball into the hole and make it stick. He took the challenge and did it. I don't know how long that ball stayed there. Close to a year, I think. Then the main hoodlum climbed up and pulled out the ball. Don't know why. Daft thing to do. The wall could've crumbled and come down on top of him. He was lucky he wasn't killed. Daft."

"Sounds like amazing skill. Luke's serve, not the hoodlum's climb."

Doc smiled and patted his hair into place. "Luke had great talent. I gave him lessons to develop it." He tapped his leg and sighed. "When you can't win matches anymore, you teach. At least I could help him that way."

"Did Luke want to turn professional? I ask because I heard he also had musical ability. I wonder if he had a difficult time choosing which path to follow."

"I heard Luke sing solo and with Bethany. He was very good. I'm no judge of the music world, but I thought he could make a decent living in the folk circuit."

"Did he have any serious leanings toward that?"

"I think he didn't know what he wanted. He worked hard at tennis and he worked hard at his music. He was well above average—even bordering brilliant—on both fronts. I gave him help, told him of the pro world and what to expect, and saw him play in dozens of matches, amateur to semi-pro. He played exceptionally well with Callum, too, but I don't know what Luke actually thought of going with tennis. Or with music, if it comes to that. He most likely would've made up his mind the year he disappeared."

"Did he have any trouble with anyone over his decision?"

Doc frowned and set down his cup. "What's that mean?"

"Was his dad pressuring him to go with tennis, for example, but Luke was more inclined to keep at his music? Anything like that?"

"Interesting question. Brings up visions of strong arm stuff and mobs."

"That wasn't particularly my intention, but that's basically the idea."

"I'd be more inclined to agree with that scenario if Luke had already turned pro in tennis. It's easy to throw a match, miss a lob or commit a foot fault. There are a lot of ways to lose and there is big money to line your pocket if the right muscle man intimidates you. Threats range from hurting loved ones to breaking your arm. 'Course, a lot of that went the way of the wooden racket." He shook his head and exhaled slowly. "I never heard anyone voice an opinion or suggestion which path he should follow. I'm sure Bethany wanted him to abandon tennis, and Ashley no doubt hoped he would give up his music. But other than that…" He shrugged and stared at his tea.

McLaren got up and went to a small table beneath the window. Sunlight fell across a large scrapbook and several framed photographs. He picked up the nearest photo and turned toward Doc. "You're a twin?"

"Yes. At least, I was. My brother, Alan. He died in a car crash in Australia. Twenty-five years ago next month."

"Sorry to hear that."

"Thank you. It's obviously been a long time ago, but it still bothers me occasionally. Particularly when I'm feeling sentimental."

"Did he share your love of tennis? Do twins have the same interests?"

"He liked the game but it was strictly hit-the-ball-against-the-garage-door stuff for him. He had no desire to go into anything like that. Alan was the academic of the family. He taught English Literature at the University of Manchester. Maybe I should've followed in his footsteps. I might not be so hunched over as I am." He eased out of his chair and shuffled over to the fireplace to add another log to the fire. When he uncurled he still retained a slight curve, as though he'd bent over a tennis racket too long.

"And this is your scrapbook." McLaren opened the tome and leafed through several pages. Newspaper articles, photographs, certificates, letters and other mementoes of a top quality professional life crammed the pages. "Very impressive. You must be very satisfied with your tennis career."

"It had its moments, although there are always matches or events at which you look back and think you should've done something different or can now analyze what you did wrong. Still, it's been fulfilling and I'm thankful."

"Did you see Luke any time on the day he went missing?"

"For a lesson, you mean?"

"A lesson or somewhere around the area. Perhaps running an errand or talking with someone on the street."

"He had a short lesson with me early that morning. Just at eight o'clock, I believe. After that—"

"Excuse me. Where was this?"

"At the tennis club in Chesterfield. I'm on the staff. I have several dozen students, but none with the quality or potential that Luke had."

"Thank you. Go on."

"Well…" Doc reclaimed his chair and picked up

his tea cup. "We worked on his backhand for most of the hour. We scheduled another lesson for Monday morning, at the same time, and Luke left."

"He left the club?"

"Left, as in hit the showers and dressed. He was hot and sweaty, obviously, so he showered off and got into his street clothes and left."

"Do you know where he went?"

"After his lesson?" Doc put down his cup and scratched his chin. A shower of sparks floated up the chimney as the log settled into the grate. "No. I just assumed he went home. He didn't work at the farm as often as he did in his years before he became serious about tennis or music, but he still had chores to do. He liked helping his dad and doing his bit. He called it payback for all his dad had done for him."

"Paying for tennis lessons, you mean?"

"Luke paid for his own. He used the money he earned from his music for the tennis. When I said payback I meant Luke felt an obligation to help around the farm as a thank you for the care his dad gave Luke growing up—food, clothing, schooling, first guitar. You know." He took a sip of tea and watched McLaren return to his chair.

"Seems a bit unusual. I've never heard of a child repaying his parents for that. It's an assumption, a given that those things are supplied as we grow up. Why did Luke feel he had to repay his dad?"

Doc stretched, leaning back into the chair. "He never said in so many words, but I assume it was due to his mother."

"How could he be responsible for her death?"

"It wasn't that. When Luke got older, he saw how

hard it was for Gary to tend to the farm, do the housework, and care for him. Just knowing the sort of lad Luke was nudges me into thinking that this is the reason behind the boy's feeling of obligation. He had uncommon empathy for anyone who worked hard in difficult circumstances."

"Where did Margaret Barber die? You said a car crash—around this area?"

"No. I don't know if it's better or not for her to have been away from home, but it was in Liverpool."

McLaren watched the flames throw shadows on the walls of the firebox. The room grew silent except for the occasional snap and pop of the burning wood. "Did Gary bring her body home for burial?"

"No. I believe she grew up around there—she may have even been home for a visit when it happened. I certainly didn't pry at the time. He needed his space and time to grieve. But I believe it's not where a person is laid to rest that is the utmost importance. It's how you cherish the memories and keep her in your heart that counts."

"That's a reassuring attitude if you can afford to have it."

"Sometimes that's all you have, McLaren."

"Getting back to Luke—did anyone ever tangle with him? Did he have any personal problems?"

"You believe he skipped of his own volition?"

"There's always that possibility if something really bothered him. How were his finances?"

Doc snorted and poured himself another cup of tea. He added milk and sugar while he talked. "You're assuming Luke confided in me, or at least let drop a tale of woe occasionally."

"Not so far-fetched. Some teachers and pupils become close."

"And you think we were." Doc set the spoon on the tray and grabbed the cup. "I was no father confessor to Luke."

"I didn't expect you to be. But an occasional solicitation of advice from a friend isn't irregular. I'd have expected a pupil who was passionate about acquiring the skill of his teacher would become a close friend, that's all."

"We were close. To a degree. Though he didn't tell me any tales of woe or ask avuncular advice on Ashley. I assume he wasn't in any dire financial straights. He had steady work on weekends with his singing, and from that he paid for tennis lessons, bought a car—even if it was used—and kept himself in guitar strings. He lived at home, so he had no bed and board payment issues." He took a long sip and eyed McLaren over the rim of the cup. "All in all, I'd say he was a lucky young man who could afford most things he wanted and was about to marry his love. Can't ask for much more from life."

"Except to decide on a profession."

"Well, yes. But as I said a bit ago, I had no qualms that he would do that very soon. Tennis tournaments and booking music gigs don't wait forever. He had to choose which way his life would go."

"What about personal conflicts? Did he have a history with anyone in the village?"

"History…as in on-going grudges or fights?"

"Yes." McLaren glanced at the trophies on the mantel. "Either someone who was jealous of Luke's talent or his engagement to Ashley. Assuming she was popular. Which I don't doubt she was. She's quite beautiful."

"You've seen her, then."

"Yes."

"Well, Philip Moss might not have been a professional hit man but he and Luke had their squabbles."

"Oh, yes? About what?"

Doc settled into his chair, as though getting ready for a long story. "Philip and Luke were two years apart in age. Philip was older. They didn't know each other from school—Philip lived then, as he does now, in Chesterfield. But Philip had and still has a mate who was friendly with Luke."

"And this mutual friend's name?"

"Harry Rooney. He lives in his family home. It's on the east end of the village. Just down the road, here." He gestured at the window. "Harry's parents gave it to him when they left Langheath for warmer climes."

"Lucky Harry."

"Yes, well, since Luke and Harry palled around, Luke got to know Philip. And from the little I knew about the association, Luke would've been happier if that was one acquaintance he'd never made."

"Why was that?"

"As I said, Philip's a bit of a tearaway. A semi thug, actually. He doesn't have a proper gang but he tries to believe he does."

"Harry follows Philip around?"

"Sometimes. It's not like he's a real gang member. Just a loose friendship. But Philip does have a wannabe thug who's more closely attached to his wallet. Tom Yardley."

"Is he decorated with tattoos and does he ride a motorcycle?"

"You've met the…lad?"

"Unfortunately." McLaren's hand went to his side.

"My condolences on your acquaintance. And unfortunately for me, he lives the next house but one to me. Tom's really not a bad lad, or he wouldn't be if he didn't hang around Philip Moss."

"What do they do? Steal garden gates?"

"Make light of it if you wish, McLaren, but they can be mean. Philip's a loud, egotistical bully who wants as much fun and money as he can grab. And he doesn't care whose toes he steps on to get it…or how he gets it."

"Which entails what?"

"I don't keep up with them. I'm not interested. But I think it's more serious than stealing apples. Luke asked my advice once on how to handle Philip."

"What was the problem?"

"Philip was pressuring Luke to get illegal drugs for him."

Chapter Nine

"How was Luke supposed to get his hands on drugs? Was he a user? Did he have a source? A friend who worked in a hospital or chemist's?"

"Luke knew no one like that, McLaren. He was a hard working, responsible lad with a tremendous dream. He wouldn't touch drugs. He knew what they could do to a body, and he trained too long and too diligently to throw that away."

"So, why did Philip approach Luke to pass drugs to him?"

"From the little Luke told me, Philip assumed Luke could get drugs any time he wished from athletes or musicians he met."

McLaren exhaled heavily and shook his head. "Not all athletes or musicians use drugs. That's a tragic myth. Anyway, haven't performance enhancing drugs pretty much been eliminated from professional play? Aren't they easily intercepted in drug checks?"

"I assume so. To tell the truth, I've been out of that aspect of the tennis world too long to say with any authority. But it does still exist, as you know from listening to the news on television. And as for musicians…" Doc shrugged and finished his tea.

"The music world's littered with users, too. I doubt if there's any segment of society where you couldn't find drugs if you knew where to look. But I guess this Philip character thinks the backstage music world has drugs laying about, ready for the taking. Thankfully, I don't think it's that bad." He drained his cup and declined the offer of a refill. "Do you know what Luke did about that? From what I'm learning of his character, I assume he didn't purchase drugs for Philip."

"I heard of the reference just that once. Luke told me of Philip's request. More nearly a demand, for he threatened Luke."

"With what?"

"I haven't the faintest. But a threat from Philip is something you don't laugh off, no matter what you think of the berk. I gave Luke my opinion, that he should ignore Philip. I realize that might be wishful thinking, that it wasn't realistic, that Philip could retaliate. But to go to the police didn't seem realistic, either. Luke had no proof of the request and I don't believe something verbal like that would be considered a crime. In addition, I assumed Philip would move on to bully someone else once he discovered Luke wasn't going to deliver."

"When was this? Near to Luke's disappearance?"

"You think Philip made good on his threat and killed Luke?"

"I'm considering everything, Mr. Tipton. You evidently saw or heard nothing about it."

"Never. Luke didn't say a thing after that and he didn't sport even a black eye, so I assumed Philip had dropped that idea."

"When did this happen?"

"I don't recall an exact date. Well, how was I to know it would be important later? But I believe Luke told me about it toward the end of December."

"And Luke's missing on the twentieth of January."

McLaren jotted Philip's and Harry's names in his notebook. "Couldn't Philip have been all mouth and no trousers?"

"If you want to know if there's a history behind his threat, yes, there is. Nothing to land him in prison for life, but he was linked to several severe beatings and robberies. GBH in a few of the cases. He has an explosive temper that doesn't take much to set it off. The few people I've heard of who crossed him ended up in hospital for months. So, Philip's request for drugs was more than a polite pretty-please. It was a veiled demand that carried with it the assurance of bodily harm if Luke didn't comply."

"And the police—"

"Couldn't really do a thing until something happened. And by then Philip either had an iron clad alibi or he was out of the area. Sure, he was arrested a few times and did a few short stretches in the nick, but it never amounted to much because the evidence was weak." Doc rubbed the corners of his eyes with his fingers, as though the subject exhausted him. "Makes you believe in a higher justice, doesn't it?"

"I believe you were one of the people who looked for Luke the evening he disappeared."

"That's correct."

"Who else was involved?"

"Not many of us. Gary Barber, obviously. Callum Fox and John Evans joined in. Bethany was there, but she didn't search. She stayed at the Barber farm, which we used as a command center."

"Bethany's husband didn't join you?"

"No."

"I would've thought she'd ask him to help, seeing

as how she and Luke were musical partners."

Doc shrugged and crossed his legs. "I don't know if he was busy or not available. He may have told her he was busy or he may have told her he didn't care. He may not have even known. I never heard. It was us four men and Bethany. That's all who were there that evening."

"This was before the police came?"

"Yes. Right after Bethany and Gary decided something had happened to Luke. He was to have picked her up that evening for their performance at the pub in Youlgreave, I think."

"Any specific reason why these people were chosen for the search?"

"Well, John Evans's family goes back generations. Lead miners and farmers in his family, so he grew up with the knowledge of the village and the area in his blood, I guess you could say. Gary wanted to go because Luke was his son and he was itching to find him, and because he knows the land well. Again, his family goes way back, though it's through farming. Callum probably did it more or less out of loyalty to Ashley, and him liking Ashley a little too much, in my opinion. Then, too, Callum was Luke's tennis double, so there was that incentive. Oh, Callum liked Luke—don't think there was no friendship motivating his search. But they weren't best mates or drinking buddies. Still, Callum searched readily enough and I'm sure did his utmost to find Luke."

"I know it was dark by that time, but did any of you find anything at all that was suggestive?"

Doc rubbed the back of his head and gazed at the fire. The wood snapped and split apart, falling into the bottom of the grate. "Luke's car sat in the farmyard, where he usually parked it. I thought it odd but if he hadn't left to get Bethany, it suggested he might be around the farm."

"You searched, I assume."

"Well, not me personally. Gary assigned areas for each of us. He and Callum looked around the village. John took the farm and fields. I searched along Birch Brook and the lower sections of the High Street that ran alongside the farm and the eastern stretch of Twin Dales Road."

McLaren looked up from his note taking. "I would've thought Gary would search his house and barn. He'd know the places Luke liked to frequent."

"He did, and that was why we decided he should look someplace else. You tend to skim over familiar territory, don't really see it because you know what it's supposed to look like."

"So, Gary might not notice a stack of hay that was moved or a missing horse and saddle."

"Correct. When you don't know the terrain or building, you look everywhere. I thought that advisable."

"How long did you look?"

"Not long. Maybe an hour. The police got there around six fifteen or six thirty. They took charge. Anyway, it was really useless, wasn't it, being so dark and us armed only with regular household-size torches. Kind of like hunting for the proverbial needle."

"Did Gary ask people in the village or did he just look around?"

Doc sighed, as though he were reliving the foot search. "Both. But no one had seen him recently and no one had any idea where he could be if he wasn't at his Friday evening gig. Gary said they were surprised he asked about Luke, for this had never happened before."

"Luke being so dependable, you mean?"

"Yes. John poked around the house and the barn and all the outbuildings. He took Gary's Land Rover and drove it through the fields and along the south stretch of the brook. I thought it another futile attempt, but we had to do something. I drove along the High Street, from just south of The Two Ramblers, to approximately five miles south of the farm. Then I looked around Twin Dales Road, as I said, concentrating east of the brook."

"Why east of the brook?"

"I didn't want to duplicate our efforts. I figured John would cover the north field lying along Twin Dales, it being part of the farm, so I concentrated on the road to the east of the property. I walked along the banks for a bit, going down one bank and coming back on the other, but I didn't see a thing. I thought it might be easy to search, winter having killed off the undergrowth and leaving the ground relatively bare. But I didn't think of all the leaf litter and downed branches and boulders. My search was laughable. The torch hardly dented the dark at all. I could've walked right past Luke and never known it if he'd been farther into the wood than the torch beam shone. So I gave up after an hour and came back to the farm. I was the last one to arrive and felt a fool for having found nothing."

"Neither of the others learned anything either, so why did you feel foolish?"

Doc frowned and pursed his lips. "Because I told Gary before we went out that Luke was probably at a friend's house and had just lost track of time."

"Did anyone check his friends' houses?"

"Bethany did. That was her job. She sat by the house phone and made calls to his mates. She sent out emails from Luke's computer, asking if Luke was at that person's house and if so remind him about the gig at The Green Cat. The look on her face when I got back to the farm…" Doc shook his head and wiped his eyes. "I thought her heart was going to break, her fear and love for Luke was that big." He repocketed his handkerchief and spoke in a slightly stronger voice. "So of course I felt like a right wally. Me rabbiting on about him being somewhere and yet we couldn't find him." He wiped his eyes again and blotted his hand on his trousers. "I should never have said anything."

"The police didn't do any better, Mr. Tipton."

"They didn't. But I shouldn't have got Gary's and Bethany's hopes up. It was just farther to crash when he never came back."

A car with a noisy exhaust silencer passed the house, then evidently turned north onto the High Street. McLaren let the quiet settle in once more before he spoke. "What's your honest opinion of all this?"

"About the search?"

"No. Your opinion of the danger Luke was in."

"About Philip following through with his threat, you mean?"

"That, and anything else you know about Luke and how he got along with people. I met Tom Yardley and, while he talked and tried to act tough, I imagine he could do some serious damage to someone who was weaker. What do you think about Tom doing something to Luke?"

Doc shrugged. “He could do, I suppose, but doesn’t it depend on motive? Tom didn’t ask for drugs, so why should he harm Luke?”

McLaren leaned forward, his pen tapping on the edge of his notebook. “How about jealousy, then? Was anyone opposed to his engagement with Ashley?”

Doc’s brown eyes darkened slightly and his voice hardened. “The only ones who had a problem with the upcoming marriage were Sharon Fraser and Bethany Watson.”

“I’ve spoken with both women. I understand Sharon’s reluctance to any sort of career that didn’t afford Ashley the stability of a nine-to-five paycheck. But why Bethany? Because she disliked him playing tennis? Did she know he was definitely abandoning their music? And even if she did, why would she be upset about his upcoming marriage? *She’s* married, isn’t she?”

“She is. And she was when she and Luke sang together.”

“Then what’s the problem?”

“I believe it was as simple as female jealousy.”

****

McLaren left soon after Doc’s statement, thinking he needed to get the truth from Bethany. He thanked Doc for the help and left the house, but he sat in his car at the curb for several minutes. Names jumped off the notebook page, and the tickling at the back of his neck suggested strongly that he follow that investigation first. Bethany could wait.

McLaren switched on the car motor, glanced once more at the house, then followed Twin Dales Road to the edge of the village. Harry Rooney’s house, a modest two story fronted by an equally understated front garden, sat on the north side of the road. McLaren parked several dozen yards from the house and walked up to the front door.

Snow had been pushed to the east side of the front pathway, creating a foot-high mound all along the length of the pavement. Fingers of ice where the snow had melted, only to refreeze last night, spread across the expanse of concrete. They caught the sunlight in a dazzling display, winking on and off as a sort of strange movie projector's light from the silent film era. McLaren averted his gaze as he made his way up the walk, the sunlight too brilliant to look at.

He stepped over a large patch of ice splayed across the concrete and butted against the base of the first step. The ice lay in deep shadow. It would probably remain there until the thaw in early spring. McLaren knocked on the door.

From the back of the house a dog yapped and a male voice called for it to be quiet. The yapping continued and suddenly increased in volume as a twenty-year-old man opened the door. He was dressed in a rumpled T-shirt and boxer shorts and seemed not to mind his state of undress. Running his hand through his already mussed blond hair, he asked what McLaren wanted. The dog sat at the man's feet, its teeth bared, but quiet.

McLaren eyed the Welsh Terrier, not certain if it would stay or charge, and introduced himself and the reason for calling on Harry,

Luke's name apparently worked magic, for Harry invited McLaren inside and offered him coffee before pulling on a pair of jeans and taking a chair opposite the sofa. “You caught me as I was getting up. I apologize for what I must look like.”

“No need. We’ve all probably been caught at one time or another in an embarrassing state.”

“Ta. Anyway, about Luke. I hoped someone would look into his disappearance.” Harry flashed a hesitant grin, then put his hand over his mouth as he coughed, as though he didn’t know how to react to McLaren’s presence.

“I understand you knew Luke fairly well.”

“Sure. We were chums. Had been since earliest school days.”

“Was that the extent of your association with each other?”

“You mean did we play sports or something together?”

“Yes. You don’t get much time in school to be so chummy.”

Harry snapped his fingers and the dog came to him and lay down at his feet. “We played on the same football and cricket teams. I got to know him better from our time with that. Well, you would, wouldn’t you? Teammates, and all that.”

“Did your time together extend to other things?”

“What do you want? A time table of what we did?” He leaned forward and patted the dog’s head.

“Just an idea of how matey you two were. Did you join in the search for him the Friday night he didn’t show up at Bethany’s house?”

“No.”

“Why not? If Luke was such a good friend—”

“I was doing something else.”

“You didn’t see him that day, either.”

"No."

McLaren tilted his head slightly and frowned. "You and he were seen walking down the High Street together."

"Impossible. I wasn't in the village that day."

"You weren't headed toward…oh, I don't know…Tom Yardley's house? He lives near the south end of the village."

"Of course not! Why would we go there?"

"I have no idea, but I'm not a threesome, as you evidently all are."

"Well, you're wrong about me and Luke together that day."

"So, I was misinformed, is what you're saying."

"Yes."

McLaren shrugged and wrote something in his notebook. "Thanks. Just trying to sort through all this."

"Besides, I didn't even know about him going missing until Saturday evening."

"So, you weren't at The Green Cat, waiting to hear him sing."

Harry's eyebrows rose slightly and he opened his mouth. He shook his head, mumbling that he had a prior engagement.

"Did you usually go to Luke's gigs?"

"Now and then. I didn't follow him around. I wasn't a fan like that. But he was good. Him *and* Bethany."

McLaren gazed back at Harry and looked hopeful. "I heard that one of their mutual acquaintances beat up Luke."

"What?"

"Philip Moss. I heard Luke was one of dozens

Philip Moss attacked. You know him?"

"Yeah, sure, but—"

"Why would he assault Luke? Did they have a history of bad blood between them?"

Harry leaned forward, his fingers gripping the chair arms. "You've got it wrong. Philip liked to project the tough image, sure. Especially when he was after certain things. That's how he got to where he is. He said it was the only way to get anything you really wanted. But he wouldn't have hurt Luke."

"Oh, yes? Why was Luke different from the others Philip beat and put in hospital?"

"Philip…" Harry paused, as though trying to think of something that sounded good.

"Go on. Why was Philip's threat a bluff? Was he a music lover and wanted Luke to be the next Cat Stevens? Did Philip harbor a passion for tennis and want Luke to win the Grand Slam?"

"He…"

"Yes? What?"

Harry exhaled loudly, shaking his head. "I think it was Nate. Nathan Watson."

"Bethany's husband? Why would Nathan Watson have any bearing on Philip's treatment of Luke?"

"I don't know for sure, but I think it was because Nathan was…" He took a breath, as though the explanation hurt to voice.

"Why?"

"Nathan's a personal trainer. He was back then and he is now. He's in super shape. Philip would never admit it, not even to Tom and me, but I think Nathan intimidated Philip. Oh, Philip can talk tough and can flex his muscle, but he's nowhere near as bulked up as

Nate. I-I think Philip's a bit of a coward when it comes down to follow through on some things."

"Like beating up certain people."

Harry nodded, looking sick.

"So the people Philip did put in hospital had no Nathan Watson standing in the wings, ready to run to the rescue or silently imply protection."

"I suppose." Harry's voice brightened a bit. "I'm not as matey with Philip as Tom is, Mr. McLaren. I don't understand or condone what he does."

"But you hang around."

"Guilty by association, you mean."

"Yes."

"That's true. But I've never participated in any beatings or robberies. I don't think that's the way to get anywhere in life."

"You have plans for your future?"

"Sure." Now that they had left the subject of Philip Moss, Harry seemed eager to talk. "I've got big plans. I want to own a nursery."

McLaren looked around the room. Plants occupied every available flat surface and sat on the floor. But the furniture caught his eye. The sofa, rocker and bookcases had seen better days. Better decades, even. They seemed to be either family hand-me-downs or purchases from charity shops. A dent, tear or stain marred each piece, and none of them were dusted. Was Harry saving every quid he earned for his business, or was the money going somewhere else? "You seem to have a knack for horticulture if you've tended these, Harry. They all look quite healthy."

"I learned about plants mostly by trial and error, though my mum gave me some pointers. Luke was one of the few people who knew my dream. I—I'd be ridiculed if Philip ever found out. He'd think I was a sissy or something." He pressed his lips together, forcing the blood from them, as if he'd said too much.

"Why would he do that? Doesn't he like plants?"

"He's a mechanic. He works at the Fraser's dealership, in the car repair shop. It's a macho thing for him, getting his hands and fingernails dirty, making engines run better. I think he likes the noise and the environment. You know—all male and one-upmanship about who slept with whom. At least with this bunch of blokes."

"Car repair isn't a bad career, and it should be steady work. Unless he feels his pay packet isn't large enough and he needs to supplement it." He eyed Harry, wondering about the boy. He seemed incredibly sensitive to be chummy with two known tearaways like Philip and Tom. "What are you doing to achieve *your* goal? Is that why you hang around with Phil, to use some of the money from robberies to buy your shop?"

Harry's hands curled into a fist and he glared at McLaren. "I'm not in that deep. I'm not one of Philip's dog's bodies. I hang around him occasionally, but I'm no yobo."

"Then why associate with him?"

"Because he's my brother."

McLaren's head jerked backwards. Nothing had prepared him for this bit of news. "But your surnames—"

"Are different. Yes. That's because we're actually half brothers."

"If you were reared here in Langheath, which I suspect if you and Luke attended the same school, did

Philip live here, too?"

"No. He lived with our grandmother in Chesterfield. She reared him and mum reared me. Philip's dad died before Philip was born. Mum remained a widow for three years before she and my dad married." He glanced at McLaren. "Mum wasn't well. She suffered from cardiomyopathy. You know what that is?"

"Yes. A disease of the heart muscle."

"She was always tired, or it seemed so to me. She hadn't the strength to care for Philip and me."

"She didn't have help or get medical care?"

"I was just a kid, of course, just starting school, but I don't remember any doctor visits. I doubt if she knew at the early state what she had. She could've just put it down to fatigue from housework, working a job, and caring for me. She worked as a shop assistant in the village. My dad and she divorced when I was around ten."

"Sorry to hear this."

Harry nodded, then sat up straight. His voice lowered. "Anyway, she eventually died of it. I guess her heart gave out or she overextended herself one day and couldn't get her breath. I just remember some talk of the cardiomyopathy. From the way the relatives murmured between themselves I knew it was bad and I never questioned anything related to mum's death." He shrugged and sagged back in the chair. "So that's why I keep in contact with Philip. I'm not one of his cronies in the gang sense. I just want to make sure we don't become separated. For better or for worse, he's the only family I have."

McLaren let the comment pass. His sister, Gwen,

wouldn't have been his first choice as a best friend. They rarely agreed on anything and their childhood spats followed them into the present. But the times they laughed together were probably some of the best moments in his life. The years of shared experiences certainly helped with their bond, but the strange link of ancestry forged something unbreakable. They could never escape that. Even if the depth of love wasn't as strong as he wished, the chain held them together. He appreciated Harry's situation. "So, you're younger than Philip, correct?"

"Four years younger. Phil's two years older than Tom, who is probably Philip's closest mate."

"And Tom…does he participate in the beatings and robberies?"

"Yeah." He said it like he wished it were otherwise.

****

McLaren stopped for lunch at the chippy in the village. The aroma of fried fish and fruit pies hit his senses when he entered the shop, and he chose a table near the order counter. The building squeezed itself between the butcher's and the local, and lacked the fresh air of the former and the coziness of the latter. Its color scheme seemed to be based on the decades that birthed the furniture crowding the room, for dark wooden chairs mingled with those of sleek chrome and leatherette. Nothing adorned the walls but menu suggestions and a faded poster of Whitby, Yorkshire. Perhaps it was more from practicality than lack of decorating expertise, McLaren thought. The grease from the deep-frying must go just about everywhere, making cleanup a headache. Still, how difficult was it to wash a green or yellow tabletop instead of a gray one?

As he waited for his food, he glanced through his notes and jotted his questions on a separate page in the notebook. For a moment he was tempted to ring up Jamie to ask for help, but he realized it wouldn't accomplish anything but lessen the length of the inquiry. And while that was commendable—he had a half dozen stone wall repair jobs waiting for him—he liked to do as much investigation as he could. Jamie was good at poking about, but he breathed Police more than McLaren did. And at times that wasn't so good.

He paused, remembering a section of Harry Rooney's interview from the police report Jamie had emailed him. McLaren hadn't tipped his hand with Harry, hadn't revealed that he knew about Philip's not-too-gentle request that Luke supply him with drugs. But he brought up the report on his tablet now and reread that part. The conversation between Harry and Officer Chapel held startling promise.

Chapel: Besides your houseplants, have you had any other experience that will help with your nursery business?

H. Rooney: Just yard work around the village. But I'm making money, and folks evidently like what I'm doing because I have a list of steady customers.

Chapel: The drugs Philip wanted from Luke…

H. Rooney: I told you he dropped that due to Nathan. He's in better physical condition than Philip would ever be. Just one frown or muscle flex from Nathan is enough to turn Philip away from any of his own strong-arm stuff. Not that his strong arm could surpass Nathan's.

Chapel: Right. Did Philip pursue that line with anyone else? And if so, is Philip a dealer?

H. Rooney: I'm fairly sure he still is involved with that. He asked Luke for drugs because he thought it'd be easy for him to lay his hands on some.

Chapel: The athletes and musicians.

H. Rooney: Yeah. Well, it's what you hear a lot. Of course Philip never took me into his confidence, us not really being that close, but I think the drug selling would've been just a means to making money. He wasn't a user because he saw what it did to people physically and how it messed up their lives. He was smart like that. But he saw a chance to make some easy, quick money if Luke could get a supply. And when Nathan started hanging around Luke and Bethany's music performances, well, Philip got cold feet. He's got a lot of faults but he's not dumb enough to tangle with Nathan.

Chapel: Does he go anywhere else to get drugs?

H. Rooney: I'm sure he does, but I don't know where. I heard he goes out regular, like. Certain days and certain times. I think Tom's involved, but I can't swear to it.

Chapel: What days and times? Where does he get the drugs? Do you know the place or the supplier?

H. Rooney: I'm not sure. You'll just have to watch him for a few days. He's regular as clockwork. You can find out, I guess.

Chapel: Do you think Luke would've told Bethany or Nathan what was happening…if he had been tempted to acquire drugs for Philip through some musicians?

H. Rooney: I don't know. He's gone. He can't tell us.

McLaren made a note about the interview, then sketched a map of the extended village area, labeling houses and points of interest. The Barbers' farm and Ashley's childhood home were conveniently close for Ashley and Luke to have known each other through school and to fall in love. Doc Tipton also lived close to the farm. Doc could have watched Luke try various sports and was also conveniently at hand to encourage tennis. As for Bethany and school chum Harry Rooney…they lived farther afield. Still, distance sometimes meant nothing if the friendship or goal was deep enough.

McLaren finished his lunch and decided Bethany could wait for another hour or so. He'd spoken to Doc Tipton, the tennis coach; it was time John Evans, the music teacher, got his turn.

****

A Beethoven concerto greeted McLaren as John Evans opened his front door. As McLaren told Jamie later, he didn't know exactly what to expect, but it wasn't the man who stood in the doorway. Tall, gaunt and with graying brown hair, John Evans seemed more suited to a profession of archbishop or majordomo than as a music teacher. His swept-back hair accented the high cheekbones and hawk-like nose, but it was the man's reserved air that reminded McLaren of the two professions that required dignity and grace. John Evans appeared to have both qualities in abundance.

"Luke's disappearance upset me greatly. It still does." John led McLaren toward the back of the house and indicated a chair at the dining room table. Then, evidently thinking better of its location, pulled out a chair that—though at the far end of the table—faced the opening of the kitchen. Two places were set for the meal. "We can still talk. The kitchen is small and has no proper table. I either eat in the dining room or in front of the telly. Are you all right there if I work in the kitchen? It's just on the other side of the archway, here. I hope you don't mind." He gestured, rather like a game show hostess, as he strolled into the kitchen. He called toward the hallway, "No, stay right there. It's just someone to talk to me." He pursed his lips and looked rather sheepish. "Sorry. Is the kitchen all right?"

"Fine. I can see you at the stove."

"Good. I'm in the middle of cooking and I hate to stop." He picked up a pair of eyeglasses, the lenses of which he wiped before putting on. "For reading or close work. I don't know why I don't wear them more often. Perhaps it's vanity. Or the realization that I'm becoming the old man of the village and I need them. Thank you for letting me continue. I'd like to get the soup on to simmer so I can have it for my tea."

"Not at all. It smells wonderful. What are you making?"

"Carrot and Leek Soup." He grabbed a large chef's knife and proceeded to chop the carrots into chunks. "I didn't think fifty-five was that old anymore, but no one told my eyes." He paused, his knife in his hand, and turned toward McLaren. "I don't mean to make light of Luke's situation. That *is* what you came to speak to me about, isn't it?"

"Yes."

"He was such an outstanding lad. Brilliant, talented in sports and music. A real hard worker. Not many lads would be able to complete his farm chores, take tennis lessons and play in matches, and sing in pubs on weekends. He had a very demanding schedule."

"That's what I understand. But I think many things are possible if you have the drive to do it."

"Precisely. Luke was one of those people." He paused, the knife blade sitting on a carrot, and frowned. "Hardly seems he's been gone three years. I still find myself thinking of a venue at which he should sing, or a contest he should enter."

McLaren nodded and glanced around the room. Navy blue cupboards and floor, and white worktop and appliances gave the room a crisp, clean feel. A row of glass canisters lined the back of one of the worktops and underscored the naval precision to the room. An antique-looking metal sign asked if the reader had had his morning cuppa. At the far end of the narrow room the front of the fridge held a few snaps, a sheet of paper, and magnetic advertisements for Frasers' Auto Dealership Repair Service, Walker's Car Hire, and Shellenbarger Insurance Agency. The red electric kettle was the only uncoordinated color item in the room.

The knife blade sliced through the carrot with a thud, drawing McLaren's attention back to John, who dropped the chunks into the stockpot. He reached for several leeks and trimmed off the leaves. "I was very close to Luke. I felt quite fatherly at times. I'd have been proud for him to have been my son."

"You have no children of your own?"

John turned away briefly. His voice was slightly muffled. "I had a son. He…he died in a car crash in Denmark, going to a musical venue he had."

"I'm sorry."

"You had no way of knowing. It happened thirty or so years ago. Anyway, I concentrated on Luke when he came to me. I like to believe he took my suggestions as it was intended."

"Wanting to help him with his music career."

"Precisely."

"He probably did."

"I tried not to be too heavy handed with the advice, but I knew what he faced. I used to be a professional musician, you know. Oh, not that I'm not a professional now, but my current profession is music lessons, not performing."

"Did you play with an orchestra or group?"

John lay down the knife and measured out a cup of light cream. "I might have sounded better if I'd gone that direction. I had an act with Margaret Barber's brother."

"Luke's mother?" McLaren's voice rose slightly.

"Yes. Her brother was a pianist, as was I. We met through Margaret, liked each other, and had the same aspirations for our music. We were a sort of Ferrante and Teicher, although where they did movie and show tunes and a few light classics, Rob and I concentrated on two-piano arrangements of standard classical works. We made quite a good living at it, toured the continent and America and Canada, until Rob decided he'd had enough traveling and settled down."

"Kind of hard on your act."

"I wasn't half pleased at first, but his quitting made me realize the road was getting to me, too. So I did a few years as a solo pianist, appearing as guest artist in community orchestras and in special concerts. I could've continued in that vein, but I wore out. Not physically, so much, as emotionally and spiritually. I finally came to my senses and came back here, to the village where I grew up." He mixed the cream into the chicken stock and tasted it. "I've done all right giving lessons. My pupils come from all over the area. I guess ex-concert pianist still has some draw or mystique."

"Not a bad way to earn a living, no. How was Luke as a student? Not temperament—I don't mean that—but had he any talent?"

John added the vegetables to the broth and put the lid on the pot. He washed his hands, his voice barely audible over the sound of the running water. "He was incredibly gifted. I thought he had an absolute flair for making arrangements to songs and for building harmony on the melody. A lot of young people starting out copy what they hear on recordings, which is fine, but you come to a point where you have to develop your own sound, style and arrangements. No one wants to hear a lukewarm version of Martin Carthy or Vladimir Horowitz. You'll get nowhere like that. I told Luke so when he first confessed he wanted to be a professional singer. Luckily, he developed his own style nearly from the start."

"What did you advise him to do with his music?"

"That's a sore point that still sticks in my conscience."

"Why? Didn't you think he could make a living with his music?"

"It wasn't that. I'd been on the road and I knew how tough the road could be. Not so much when you're young, but it devours you, saps the years from your life and wears you out long before you should need the rocker on the porch. The road eats into your soul and your spirit and your energy. You live out of your suitcase and only see your home and family a few times a year. If you're looking to establish a family or create a home, there are better ways to do it than living on the road."

"Did Luke listen to you?"

John turned down the gas flame under the stockpot and sat down at the table. "No. But not many youngsters do listen to the voice of experience. They think they're tougher, will be able to shed the back stage gossip of who's sleeping with whom and how so-and-so bombed on his last concert. They see only the love of twenty thousand appreciative fans and they're blind to the hours of travel and missed meals and sickness from stress."

"So, you advised Luke to forget music, then?"

"Certainly not! He had a gift that should be heard. I just tried to temper his enthusiasm and turn it in a different direction. I suggested he stay at home, or at least in the general area, and do local gigs at nights or on weekends. I hinted that a nine-to-five job was better for his health and any personal relationship he may develop. Most wives want their husbands at home overnight."

"How did Luke take your suggestion?"

John shook his head and glanced out the window. "Not well. He was determined to line up a road tour, with or without Bethany. I may as well have been talking to my cat."

"What did Bethany think of all this—the planned tour vs. weekend gigs only?"

"I really don't know. I wasn't involved with her. She was a musician before Luke ever started, but he surpassed her in skill and virtuosity. Her husband may have felt the same way—wanted her at home—but I don't know. I never spoke to either of them about it. Luke was my pupil and he was my concern. I could do only so much talking to him. He had to figure his life out for himself."

"Speaking of Bethany..." McLaren leaned forward, his forearms on the edge of the table. "I heard she was involved in the search for Luke that Friday night. Did she contact you personally to help?"

"No. Gary rang me up and asked me to help."

"When did he phone?"

John got up, lifted the lid from the stockpot and peered at the boiling soup. He replaced the lid and turned down the heat a bit more. "I guess around five o'clock. Bethany contacted Gary at four-thirty, but he waited a bit before doing anything about it. She may have convinced him something wasn't right—I don't know what went on prior to our arrival—but he called me around five."

"And he also phoned the police?"

"Yes. They got to the farm at approximately six-thirty, I believe."

"Did they call you in from the search?"

"No. We'd agreed to look until the police arrived. Bethany rang us up on our mobile phones to let us know they'd come. We wandered back to the farm at that time." He leaned against the edge of the table and frowned. "Though I think Doc may've come back to the farm earlier. I can't be certain. Still, it probably makes no difference, a few minutes one way or the other."

McLaren nodded and asked if Luke had tangled with anyone recently. "I realize you're not with him twenty-four hours a day, Mr. Evans, but you live in the same village."

"Which I'm to infer that I see or hear things."

"Certainly. There's a vast difference between sharing gossip and overhearing a remark while queuing up at the bakery, for example."

"Of course. Well, I don't recall any stray conversation. And you're correct about loose tongues. For all the glories of village life, gossip is one of the negative aspects."

"No one was on bad terms with Luke, then, to your knowledge."

"No one. I heard of a disagreement between Luke and Nathan Watson, but that's all. Unless you believe Luke's argument with his father has any weight."

"Luke and Gary didn't get along?"

"They didn't, though I suppose percentages don't matter if any conflict is violent enough. But Gary had his own ideas of what Luke should do, and he wasn't silent about them. Still…" John wandered back to the kitchen and tossed the carrot peelings and leek tops into the rubbish bin. "I can't believe it'd be worse than many parent-child disagreements."

"Was this an on-going problem, or specific to one day?"

"Oh, on-going, certainly. It began when Luke got his first job singing in a pub, which was two years before his disappearance. Gary didn't like the idea of Luke devoting time to what he considered should be a hobby, especially since he was also getting serious about his tennis. They argued constantly. Anyone in Langheath can confirm that." He held up his hand and leaned backward slightly. "Yes, dear, in a moment." He grimaced and apologized. "Such a racket. As if the earth will stop turning if I don't attend to it right this instant."

"Something the matter?" He frowned, not certain if he'd heard anyone call from the depths of the house.

"Tea's wanted, it seems. It can wait a bit."

"I don't mind you fixing tea."

"It's fine. Really. You were saying?"

"What about the Friday he went missing?"

"You mean, did they argue that day?" John wiped the worktop down with a damp sponge, rubbing at a stubborn dried spot, then filled the electric kettle. "Yes. That morning. It was a bit more vocal than most."

"How do you know they argued? Did Luke mention it?"

"Just in passing. Physically, not as an aside. We saw each other on the High Street. I'd just come out of my house and was nearing the news agent's, on my way to the green grocer's, and Luke was leaving the bakery." He paused to see if McLaren was familiar with the location of the two shops. Getting a nod, John went on. "I continued south on the street and Luke walked north. We met each other outside the fish and chips and paused for a minute or two to chat. I could see something upset him, so I asked if I could help in any way. Luke said no, that it was nothing new. He said he'd just had a row with his dad and needed some breathing space. I said I was sorry. Then he mentioned that evening's job at The Green Cat. I wished him and Bethany luck—not that they needed it—and we continued on our separate ways. I turned into the green grocer's and saw Luke turn right at the junction."

"If Luke walked north…" McLaren drew the map of the village from his jacket pocket and folded it on the table. His finger landed on the lone residence on the eastern end of Bridge Lane. He looked at John, wanting to see his reaction.

"The only residence down that stretch of Bridge Lane is Ashley and Callum Fox's. Not that there aren't any more houses, but people whom Luke knows, I mean."

"Doesn't Bethany live on Bridge Lane?"

"She does. But Luke would've turned left, not right, at the intersection if he were going to her place." John washed his hands, dried them on a towel, and leaned against the worktop. "What do you think it means?"

Chapter Ten

Dusk had a firm grip on the village by the time McLaren ended his day. He had driven most of the length of Bridge Lane, eastward and westward, and had talked to the people who lived there. They had known Luke and knew of his disappearance, but other than that no one had any connection to the lad. At least none that McLaren could yet discern.

He parked outside The Split Oak in Somerley and gazed around the car park as he opened his mobile phone. He had a few minutes before he was to meet Jamie, so he punched in Dena's phone number. She answered his call almost immediately.

"Are you home?" Her voice sounded optimistic, and he smiled.

"No. But I'm close. I'll be home in about an hour, if you're in the area."

"I wouldn't dream of disturbing you at the local. I know how involved you and Jamie get in your discussions."

"Will you still be this accommodating when you're an old married lady?"

"If I know what's good for me, I wouldn't be anything else. Accommodating, that is. Besides, I know better than to come between you two."

"Have as many people at the tiger sanctuary today as you predicted?"

"Ghastly crowds."

"What…rowdy?"

"No. We broke the attendance record for January. You'd think we were running a sale."

"So there's no dancing for you tonight."

"Not with my feet aching so dreadfully right now. Ask me when I've had a day off."

"When's that?"

"Next week some time. I think Friday."

"Set aside your dancing shoes, then, if you have nothing on your calendar."

"With an invitation like that, how can I resist?"

"I'm actually on bended knee."

"Snap a photo with your phone and send it to me, Michael."

"Sorry. The camera's broken."

"You always seem to have such rotten luck." Her laugh trickled into his ear and he felt his heart leap. "Aside from phone problems, how was your day? Getting any closer to finding Luke?"

"I probably am. I believe so."

"You don't sound too sure."

"I have a lot of notes to go through. And some things to check out. It'll take a bit of time to sort through all this." Silence seeped between them and McLaren struggled for something to say to stop it. "How about giving me the first dance on our wedding day?"

"I think that's customary, Michael."

"I'm taking nothing for granted. I-I've come across so much misery while I was in the job, as well as now, that…well, I just don't want to assume anything. Not ever."

"I'll always be here for you, Michael. You don't

have to worry."

"I'm not worried about you, dear. It's just that life—"

"What's happened?"

"Nothing." His voice rose in astonishment that she should think that.

"*Something* has. This is such an odd topic. And to come in the middle of our conversation—"

McLaren screwed up his mouth, berating himself that he'd said anything. This wasn't exactly the sort of talk to whisper in her ear. "Oh, just that I learned about Luke's mother quite recently."

"Dare I ask?"

"Oh, it's not gruesome. Not blood and guts, I mean. It's just that she died when Luke was very young."

"Poor boy. Does he go to her grave?"

"That I don't know. Margaret's buried in Liverpool."

Dena murmured that fifty miles was a long distance when the journey wasn't pleasant. Then, feeling she should change the subject, asked, "Have you found out about that child's parentage? Ashley Fox's daughter, I mean."

"I haven't even started looking. I wanted to interview everyone at least once before I go into that sort of thing. Then I might know where the discrepancies are and who's lying."

"Any hunches yet?"

"Something's poking my brain but I'm trying to ignore it. That's one thing that can sink your investigation quicker than you can imagine, ignoring all the information and zeroing in on one person."

They finished their conversation with Dena saying she'd retrieve her ball gown from the mothballs and see if Turkish slippers were still in vogue.

McLaren closed his mobile phone as Jamie eased his car into a parking space. He called to Jamie as he shut his car door and jogged up to him. "Another minute and I would've started without you."

Jamie didn't bother looking at his watch, but fell in step alongside his friend. "That's what happens when you've got no proper work to do. You have no conception of time."

They pushed open the pub door and strode inside.

The Split Oak harbored the niceties of a bygone era without suffering too much from modernization. The slate roof still sagged against the oak beams stretched across the white-washed ceiling. Aged metal-framed casement windows still rattled under a strong wintry buffeting, and probably had since its birth hundreds of years ago. But a blazing fire in the oxen-sized hearth and space heaters around the room's perimeters kept the interior comfortable. The addition of electricity in the 1960s did not, as some locals had feared, turn the building into a neon-lit horror. The pub retained its solace, history and ghosts.

"So, what's going on, then?" Jamie eyed McLaren and returned his menu to the waitress after she'd taken his order. "You on to anything since we talked Friday? You've had two days." His voice had a suggestion of humor in it, but his face remained as unreadable as a magistrate's.

"Funny lad." He took a long drink of beer and looked around the room. "Sparse attendance tonight."

"It's Sunday. Most folks have to get up early in the

morning."

"Doesn't mean they have to drink themselves into oblivion." He eyed Jamie's pint. "You're not."

"Stop avoiding my question. Where are you in your investigation?"

McLaren related what he'd learned about the people connected with Luke, ending with "It's definitely odd. Either Gary Barber or John Evans is lying."

"About what in particular?"

"When I spoke with Gary on Friday, he told me that on the day Luke went missing he was cheerful all day. But today John says Gary and Luke argued." He accepted his plate of salmon and cider-baked potatoes from the waitress and watched Jamie cut into his beef pie before continuing. "Granted, I have both men's words only on this, but why such differing accounts? You know Gary. He's a friend of yours. Is he truthful?"

"Sure, I know him, but I'm not bosom buddies with him, Mike. I don't know if he would lie when he thinks it matters. Could it just be a matter of embarrassment or pride with him?"

"Like, he doesn't want the whole world to know he and his son couldn't get along?"

"Yeah. Or he wants to leave a glowing memory of Luke."

McLaren lifted a forkful of fish to his mouth, then set it back on the plate.

"What's the matter, Mike? You need to send it back?"

"What you just said, Jamie."

"About the fish?" He looked around for their waitress.

"No. About the glowing memory."

"What about it? What father wouldn't want to remember his son in a positive light?"

"Most all, but none so much as a father who's already had a family tragedy."

"You mean Gary had another son?"

"No. But Margaret, his wife, died in a car crash. And although that wasn't his fault, I bet it still fueled the village tongues for a bit."

Jamie wrapped his hands around his pint, his fingertips pressed against the thick glass. He nodded slowly as his voice lowered in pitch. "Not that he's a killer, but it stands to reason that he might not welcome another 'poor me' episode. I don't know about Langheath, obviously, but some village gossip can be hurtful and go on for years." He downed a good portion of his beer, and set the mug on the coaster. It made a dull thud. "So what's that give you, assuming Gary lied?"

"Ignoring the gossip theory for the moment, I can only assume John Evans is correct about the morning argument. And if so, it raises the question of what was said that would be so embarrassing or suggestive about the argument topic."

"Could it have anything to do with the drugs Philip Moss wanted from Luke?"

"I doubt that Luke would've told his dad about that. Wouldn't that just be adding more problems on the home front?"

"Just a thought, Mike." He snapped his fingers.

"What?"

"It wouldn't be the tennis or music problem. That's an on-going thing and the entire village knows about it.

So what's to keep quiet or save face about?"

"Right. Therefore, the topic is more sensitive." McLaren sank back against the settle and shook his head. "Hell if I know."

"Which is probably why they're keeping it a secret."

"Jamie, you're priceless. Are you like this in the job?"

"Sure. How do you think I made detective?"

"God help your cohorts."

They finished their meal, then lingered over their coffee. The band—a concertina, guitar and mandolin—ended their last set with "The Drunken Sailor" and began packing up their instruments.

McLaren glanced at his watch. "Eleven o'clock." But he made no move to get up. "How did Gary Barber get his limp?"

"He still have it?"

"Yeah. Though it's not too prominent."

"I guess it was more than fifteen years ago. After Luke was born and not very long after Margaret died. He was out in one of his fields tending to one of his sheep. He was in a hurry to get back to the house and caught his foot in a rabbit hole. Unfortunately, he broke his leg and it never healed quite right."

"That's tough. That area around Wirksworth, Matlock and Elton has enough of a bad press, pockmarked with old boreholes and chutes and wells. How'd he manage with the housework and tend to Luke if he was laid up and on his own?"

"Sharon Fraser came in once a day to help. She was newly married and very pregnant."

"Must've been a strain on her. How'd Darren like

that, her tending to another man?"

"I wouldn't know, but if it were me, I'd probably not be over the moon. Still, you make allowances to help a neighbor."

"I hope her health didn't suffer for it."

"From the little I know of her, which isn't much more than you know, I doubt it. She didn't do any housecleaning or laundry. She cooked a main meal at home, brought it over in the evening for Gary's and Luke's tea."

"Every evening? That's a lot of meals."

"I don't believe so. Every other night. For next day's lunch they either could have sandwiches and soup or some easy make-it-yourself meal. Or the leftovers from the previous tea. I believe Gary had hired help once a week to do the cleaning and laundry. From some temp agency out of Matlock. John Evans, despite living at the other end of the village, arrived weekly to do whatever needed doing. You know. Handyman things, dog to the vet. Whatever."

"He could spare the time? His wife didn't mind?"

"He wasn't married then. Still isn't. He's a bit of a loner, from what I hear from Gary. 'Course, Gary is too, come to think of it."

"Were John and Gary close? Is that why John helped out?"

"I doubt if they were more than nodding friendly, if you get my meaning. Not best mates, certainly. Probably just a neighborly thing on John's part."

"We should all have such neighbors."

Jamie let the comment pass. "John was there for about a month, I believe Gary said, while he was on holiday from his music performances. That's how Luke got to know John. Luke may have latched on to him emotionally at that time, too. His mother had recently died and with her the only music in his life also dies. John may have grown to symbolize that music, maybe the lost love of his parents." Jamie exhaled deeply and shook his head. "I don't know. I'm no psychologist. But you hear of transfer of affection, don't you?"

"Seems perfectly logical, yes."

"Either Gary or John sensed that Luke needed more attention than Gary could give him at that point, so John started coming over every night for a bit. John would play the piano and they'd have singing. He would tell stories of his life on the road, of some of his performances. Luke seemed fascinated and begged his father for music lessons."

"Which he probably denied."

"Yes. Money wasn't plentiful on the farm at the best of times, and now he had the added expense of the hired help. Plus, he lost a good portion of his wheat crop because he couldn't harvest all of it."

McLaren grimaced. "Ouch. That had to cut into the family income."

"Don't you know it. Luke taught himself to play. Not all that great, but he achieved a higher level of success than most kids probably would. He got a cheap guitar at some point—I don't know how or when—and he learned the rudiments. But when music became more important he began lessons."

"How'd he pay for them?"

Jamie said he'd not heard but he guessed Luke did some odd jobs for John, such as weeding and looking after his house when he was on tour.

McLaren nodded. "I did pretty much the same

thing as a kid. I was lucky. One of my neighbors played guitar professionally and he had a very large garden." He smiled and looked at his hands.

"Anyway, that's how Luke became attached to John. Some chaps from a neighboring farm fed Gary's livestock, but they had to let the crops go and pray for the best. After all, there's only so much they could do. He has a lot of acreage." Jamie stretched and glanced around the room. They were the last patrons at the tables; three people sat at the bar. "Anyway, Gary struggled along with a cast on his leg that allowed him to walk. He did all right. He had to let a lot of things slide, such as attendance at Luke's school plays and church, but he came out of it fairly well, considering. I realize at the time he probably didn't think so. It must've been hell to watch his crops still standing in the fields while his neighbor harvested his."

"I take it this was in the summer or autumn."

"Yeah. September."

"Harvest time, as you said. Thankfully he didn't have to worry about sheep shearing."

"A small consolation, but yes."

"Did all this bother Luke, do you know?"

Jamie frowned, looking at his friend as though he'd jumped onto the table and started dancing. "Why ask that?"

"I just wondered how it affected him…if it did. He was a young lad. His mother had died. Now his dad had a broken leg and appeared quite helpless to Luke. Gary couldn't cook, couldn't clean the house, couldn't take care of the farm. That must have scared Luke. He might have wondered if his dad was going to die, or at least go to hospital, and he'd be left alone."

Jamie shrugged and stood up. "I don't know. I wasn't that frequent of a visitor to their house. But it mustn't have been too bad. I mean," he added as he grabbed his jacket, "Luke was an incredibly thoughtful, talented, intelligent young man."

"Granted, but who's to know about the scars beneath that thoughtful, talented and intelligent exterior?"

"You can't be serious if you think this has something to do with his disappearance, Mike. Anyway, all that was ages ago."

"I'm not ruling anything out right now, Jamie. We don't always know how or when a trauma manifests itself. Or if something else quite recently brought all that to the surface, panicking him, and he ran away."

****

Jamie bid McLaren good night outside the pub door and suggested he get a good night's rest, that it would help his wild imagination.

McLaren said a few choice words and stepped into the darkness beyond the pub's exterior lighting. The temperature had dropped while they'd been inside, turning the air sharp with cold. A breath of wind stirred the boughs of the hemlocks hugging the side of the building, reminding him of childhood phantoms waving threatening arms. At least there was no moon, he thought. Witches riding across the face of the moon would've been his undoing. He had enough difficulty battling childhood boogies at night without the help of a full moon.

Few cars remained in the car park at this hour; those that did belonged to the musicians and the pub staff. Jamie's car sat close to the road, under a street lamp and a glare of light. Jamie's footsteps tapped sharply on the tarmac and brittle patches of ice, and McLaren could track his friend's trek to the car.

The yellow pools of light fell behind McLaren as he crossed the asphalt. His car sat several dozen yards ahead, near a large sandwich sign advertising the day's specials.

Forgetting that he'd not locked his car, McLaren clicked his remote car lock and the headlights blinked at him. As he reached for the door handle, a dark figure lunged at him from the rear of his car.

The impact of the assault knocked the breath from his lungs, and he fell to the ground without time to brace himself. He slammed into the asphalt as his attacker grabbed his legs. McLaren shook his head, determined to remain conscious, yet the pain from his ribs washed over him. He could see nothing but the dark figure, hear nothing but the scrape of his feet as he fought to right himself, and the labored breathing of his opponent.

As his assailant reached for McLaren's arms, McLaren seized the man's wrist and pivoted the hand backward. A satisfying 'crack' shot into the night, followed by a yelp. The man released his grip of McLaren's forearm and rolled over, taking McLaren with him. McLaren felt the man's chest on top of him, felt the firm muscles and the warm breath against his face. Determined to gain the advantage, McLaren pulled up his strength from somewhere within him and rolled to his side while pushing the man off. McLaren grabbed the car door handle and pulled himself to his feet. But his assailant regained his balance quicker, and he lurched at McLaren. In the darkness he misjudged the distance; he recoiled off the side of the car and staggered around to its rear, his hand groping the slick metal surface for support.

McLaren turned toward the shape and reached for anything solid in that nebulous, black world. His fingers latched onto an edge of the man's sleeve, and he pulled it toward him with what little strength he had left. He felt the man's stumbling steps as he drew the body toward him, then he stepped back slightly and kicked.

His mark went wide and he felt his shoe slide down the man's leg. A fist slammed into McLaren's shoulder, missing his jaw by inches. The fingers uncurled and groped for McLaren's jacket, intent on steadying his target.

McLaren slipped on an icy patch and he lost his balance. In that unprotected second he felt a cable slip over the back of his neck. Another second later he felt the hands draw forward and across his throat, and the wire bit into his skin.

His fingertips clutched at the restraint, trying to slip beneath it and lessen the grip. Waves of blackness washed over him and threatened to engulf him forever. He strained his neck muscles, desperate to break the suffocation and bring air into his lungs. But the cable merely tightened and the breath he felt wasn't his.

As he felt his world slipping, a sound behind him filtered into his last moments of consciousness. With the greatest effort, he moved his head slightly. The slap of running shoes on asphalt and a shrill yell filled the night. The pressure on the cable slackened and the hands left his body. McLaren slumped against his car, gasping for air and clawing at the ligature.

Jamie shouted into the darkness, the roar bouncing

off the walls of the pub and chasing the fleeing footsteps. He stopped on the far side of the car, the light from his torch and his eyes searching the darkness, his chest heaving. When the quiet descended once more, he jogged back to McLaren, who was doubled over and holding his neck.

"What the hell happened?" Jamie stooped and looked into his friend's face. "Where'd he come from?"

"Out of the night." McLaren's voice was little more than a whisper and he drew in a lungful of air before straightening up. He sagged against his car and rubbed his throat. "Bloody hell."

"It probably is, Mike. Here. Let me look at it." Jamie angled the torchlight at McLaren's neck.

A ragged line showed angry and red against his otherwise smooth skin. Jamie let out a slow whistle and shook his head.

McLaren frowned and gingerly patted his fingertips over his throat and neck. "Is it as bad as it feels?"

"Since I don't know how it feels, I can't honestly say. But my opinion is yes. You've got a hell of a mark. Does it hurt?"

"Only when I laugh."

"Then it doesn't hurt. This is no laughing matter, Mike." Jamie shone the beam of his torch around the area and followed the direction of the man's escape for a bit. When he returned, he played the light over McLaren's torso and hands. "Anything else hurt?"

"Besides my pride?" McLaren pushed the torch aside. "Quit playing doctor and play detective instead. Nothing around here, I suppose."

"We may find something in the morning, when I

can see." He yanked his mobile from his trousers pocket. "I'm calling Silverlands," he added, referring to the police station from which he worked. "The scene needs to be preserved for a daylight search and your car needs to be taken in."

"You're not taking my car."

"Mike, you know the drill. Your car—"

"Yeah, I know the drill. Put the car somewhere to dry, then examine it for fingerprints."

"What's wrong with that? Don't you want to see if we can find your attacker?"

"Sure, but I'll be surprised if there are any fingerprints. He concentrated on *me*, remember? On my neck, if you want to get specific. So leave my car alone."

"He could've touched the car when he sneaked up to you."

"I doubt if he needed any steadying, Jamie. He seemed like an uncoiling spring."

"Why you don't want us to hunt for fingerprints is beyond me."

"I think it'd be best to let me drive home, let it sit outside overnight, and see who shows up. He might not be so sure he didn't leave any prints. If so, he'll want to have a look."

Jamie shook his head. "You're not going to play decoy."

"*I'm* not the bloody decoy. The *car* is!"

"Mike—"

"You're not getting the car, Jamie. You can cordon the car park, if you want to channel your energy into something, but I'm taking my car. I'll be fine."

"And I'll be reprimanded." He sighed, and his

voice eased a bit in its tone. "I know better than to argue with you. I can use one of the excuses I have stockpiled when the Super asks me, in not too friendly a tone, why we don't have your car." He winced, as though hearing the volume of his boss' anger. "Fine. Play detective, but I'm at least going to have the lads seal off the area." He phoned the police station and was told officers would be there within the hour. He put the phone away and turned back to McLaren. A slight breeze whipped over the tarmac, bringing a breath of moisture. "You think the assailant was after you?" He looked around, trying to see into the darkness. "Where'd he come from…besides the night?"

"I suppose behind my car. Nothing else would've concealed him."

"Well, it's got to be someone involved in Luke Barber's disappearance. Or have you been generally stepping on toes again during your investigation?"

"I've not been working long enough to step on toes. And anyway, everyone was cooperative."

"Meaning you didn't have to flex your muscles. Don't look at me like that, Mike. I know how you can get."

"Right now I'd like to get this berk and get home. Damn, I'm sore."

Jamie grabbed McLaren's car key, then stopped as he stared at the car. "What's with the plastic wrap? How'd you break your window?"

"I didn't break it. Someone thought I needed air conditioning in my car."

"Cut the comedy, Mike. You're assaulted, you've got a prime example of vehicle interference—"

"No theft occurred with it, actually."

"What the bloody hell difference. What's going on?"

McLaren related the car incident.

"That's super that you got a look at the bloke. Do you think tonight's attacker is also your car friend?"

"In the car instance, his face was covered by a knitted ski mask, so no, I really didn't get an ID look. In tonight's attack—"

"It was too dark to see anything. I know. Of all the—" He opened the car door and pushed McLaren onto the passenger seat. "Stay put. I'll be right back." He jogged back to the pub and pounded on the door.

A voice inside yelled that they were closed.

"I'm a police officer. I've got an injured man outside here. I'd like a glass of water, please."

The door squeaked open as far as the metal chain would allow and a light snapped on behind the door. The exterior light above the door shone on Jamie's face and his police warrant card.

"If you're uneasy," Jamie went on, pocketing his card, "you can ring up the Constabulary and they'll identify me. Or you can just pass me the glass and I won't come in." He stepped back to emphasize his statement.

"Never mind. Just a minute." The voice retreated into the building, leaving the door open but chained. A minute later a burly hand slid the chain free of the catch, the door opened fully, and the husky form of the publican emerged from behind the slab of wood. He held the glass of water in his left hand, and a stout iron-headed cane in his right hand. "I know you. One of my regulars. That's fine. Here you are. Do you need to call an ambulance? What happened?" He craned his neck to see into the blackness.

"Just a little accident. Thanks." He took the water and hurried into the darkness, leaving the publican scratching his head.

McLaren looked up at the sound of footsteps and asked if it was friend or foe.

"Well, I'm not Charlie Harvester, if that's got you worried. Take a sip or two, if you can." He handed McLaren the glass and eyed him critically as McLaren took several swallows.

"Damn, it's impossible to swallow." McLaren shoved the glass into Jamie's hand.

"Is that all?" He peered at the liquid. "You didn't drink very much."

"You're right. I didn't. You try swallowing with a broken neck."

Jamie set the glass on the bonnet of McLaren's car. "When the lads arrive we can make a search of the area. We might find something. What do you think?"

"I think he's long gone, got an alibi as solid as iron, and has already thought up a story to cover any injuries he may have sustained from my weak defense. But thanks for the gesture, Jamie."

"You through with this, then?" He picked up the glass and, at McLaren's nod, walked back to the pub door and handed it to the publican. By the time Jamie had returned, McLaren sat in the driver's seat but the passenger door was open.

"You in a rush to get home?" McLaren gestured toward the vacant seat when Jamie said no.

"Why?" Jamie sat down and stared at his friend. "You want to talk about something?"

"I'm just trying to sift through this. It seems to be

something other than a random assault attempt."

"So you *do* think it's connected with the car incident. I do, too. They're too close together to be coincidental, Mike. If it hadn't been for the event at your place, I'd have said the usual."

"I'm alone, it's dark, there are no witnesses about."

"Right. Standard crime stuff. That bloke, whoever he is, didn't find what he wanted to at your place."

"There could be another reason for this, Jamie, and it wasn't assault."

"What do you think it is, then?"

"A murder attempt."

Chapter Eleven

It took Jamie several seconds to catch his breath. "You think he was trying to kill you? But why? Have you scared someone in the case so badly that he needs to stop you? That's awfully drastic."

"He had the ligature with him, Jamie. He didn't have to undo his belt or pull the tie off his neck—"

"You know he was wearing a tie?"

McLaren exhaled heavily. "No. It's just a figure of speech. I'm trying to tell you that my friend had the wire *with* him. There was no let-up in the fight. He had it in his pocket and all he had to do was pull it out and loop it around my neck." He paused, letting the implication sink in.

Jamie leaned forward, his voice lowered in his concern. "My God, Mike! Who the hell is after you?"

"That's what I'd like to talk about, for a few minutes. I know it's late…"

"The hour be damned." Jamie swore and angled in his seat to face his friend. "We've got to nab this git. You have any suspicions as to who it is?"

"Yes." McLaren touched his neck, feeling the raw flesh where the wire had dug in. He swallowed slowly, testing his muscles. "He was incredibly strong. I sensed that not only in his muscular arms but also in his chest. Very taut. This is important because I doubt if the average person is that strong."

"So, who do you suspect? Farm workers tend to be

strong. You ever try heaving a bale of hay?"

"No one at Gary's farm has a connection to Luke. Neither do other farms in the district."

"All right. What are you thinking?"

"My immediate suspicions lie with Nathan Watson."

"The husband of Luke's singing partner? Why would Nathan be after you?"

"I'm not sure right now. I haven't met him yet, but I thought of him because he's a physical trainer. I've heard that he's in top condition."

"Biceps like boulders. Right."

"Or there's Callum Fox."

"Luke's doubles tennis partner."

"He may not be a professional athlete now but he still works out. He may still get back into the game, too. He's not that old."

"Wouldn't win many matches if he was a ninety-pound weakling, no."

"Then, there's Darren Fraser. While he's not especially strong, he did seem a bit uneasy. I don't know if fear would compensate for lack of strength, but he bears watching. He dodged some questions I put to him and was decidedly happy when I left his house."

"Maybe he paid one of his car mechanics to take you down."

"Possible." McLaren turned on the car's interior light and grabbed a bottle of water from the back of the center console. He unscrewed the lid and took a long sip, grimacing as he swallowed, then recapped it. He balanced the bottle on his thigh, his fingers digging into the plastic neck. The bottle crackled loudly as the shape distorted. "If he has something to hide and is frightened

I'll find out about it, he might do that. And hiring someone, even for a nasty job like committing murder or beating a man to a pulp…" He broke off, imagining his fate if Jamie hadn't been there.

"We'll put friend Darren and Callum on the B list. Anyone else?"

"I don't know the man, but from what I have heard he fits the profile very snuggly. Philip Moss."

"Leader of the three-piece ensemble."

"Faith, hope and charity they're not."

"Pity."

"I've not talked to him, so I don't see why he'd be bent on attacking me."

"You just said it not a minute ago, Mike. He could've been hired."

"By whom? Why? Again, the only connection to Luke *is* Luke. Philip had nothing to do with any of the other people I've talked to. Unless it was faithful follower Tom Yardley." He recounted the run-in with Tom.

"I bet he wasn't half upset that you bested him."

"He no doubt prides himself on being Phil's, or his own, strong arm." His hand went to his throat as he tried to shake his head. "No. This is too nebulous. People don't assault people unless there's a big payoff. The chance of getting caught is too great so the reward has to be quite substantial, worth the risk."

"So we're asking ourselves the original question, Mike. Who had a motive to do this, either do it himself or hire someone?"

McLaren ran his fingers through his hair and leaned against the headrest. He didn't know what part of him hurt the most. "Hell if I know, but I'm getting stiffer by the minute."

Jamie, caught up in the significance of the case, rushed on. "Do you remember anything about tonight's man, Mike? Anything that might identify him?"

"You're going to think I'm daft."

"Probably not any more than you are. Give."

"He had an aroma to him."

"Aroma…what, like sweat?"

"No. Something pleasant."

"Aftershave, you mean?"

McLaren closed his eyes, trying to recall his attacker. He spoke slowly as the senses bombarded him. "I'm trying to remember it all… I have the impression he is of medium height. I didn't see his features or hair color or anything like that, but he stood close to me during the attack. Of course we were both moving, but I think he came to just under my nose."

"Which puts him around five foot eight, give or take a couple of inches. You're six foot three, right?"

"Yeah. At least we've got a figure to go on."

"That's a tremendous help, Mike. I can't believe you had the presence of mind to retain that."

"Presence of mind is rare with me during an attack. It all happens so quickly." He glanced at Jamie, aware that he mimicked the same statements given by robbery victims. He went on. "His hair must've been dark, or at least not blond or white. It would've caught the light from the street lamps."

"Unless he wore a hood."

"He didn't. I felt his face and his breath. Nothing obstructed that."

"Okay. Darkish hair. What about his aroma?"

McLaren shut his eyes again and took several

moments to get back into the setting. "It wasn't aftershave, as I said. Not that spicy or tangy. More like…" He frowned, willing his mind to latch on to the elusive scent. "More like freshly dried clothes."

Jamie left him at that point, telling his friend he needed to get home and rest. For once, McLaren didn't object. Jamie walked back to his car but sat there watching McLaren's car until it turned the corner. The night closed in around him and he wondered if they would ever find the attacker. Chances were slim without fingerprint examination of the car, but they at least had a vague physical description.

Jamie started his car's engine, their parting sentences drowning out the roar of the motor.

"Oh, Jamie?"

"Yeah?"

"Thanks for saving my life."

****

McLaren sat on the edge of his bed Monday morning, his slippers ignored on the floor, his bathrobe wadded up on the seat of a chair. He had no intention of looking at a mirror, not wanting to confirm his suspicions of his physical condition. He knew he'd feel worse if he saw his reflection.

The cold, sharp light of January seeped through the slits in the Venetian blinds, throwing strange pale stripes on the wall. Normally he would go to the window and open the slats, gaze at the world outside and see about the weather, eager to get to his stone wall work or his breakfast. But today hadn't the feel of normality. His whole body ached as though he'd been hit by a freight train. And his throat…

He groaned and eased off the mattress. Unfolding

his body was agony, a million pins pricking his muscles. As he shuffled past the chair, he grabbed his robe and shrugged into it.

Someone must have moved the kitchen during the night. He couldn't remember the room being so far away.

He padded through the living room and into the dining room. The kitchen was a dozen steps ahead and offered the refuge of freshly brewed coffee.

The phone rang and he grabbed the receiver, willing the irritating noise to be silent. He mumbled "Hello" into the mouthpiece and was greeted by a cheery "Rise and shine, Mike" on the other end.

McLaren groaned. "I'm going to contact my constituency and see if Parliament can pass a law banning cheerfulness in the morning."

"You feeling that bad, then?"

"Worse." He sank into a kitchen chair and leaned against the table. "My only consolation is that *he* might not feel much better."

"How's your throat?"

"What do you think?"

"At least you can speak, though you do sound hoarse."

"That's about the bloody hell all." He flexed his shoulder and groaned.

"What happened?"

"Nothing important. I just took a physical inventory. What are you doing today?"

"On my way to the station. Do you need me to do anything? Take you to hospital or get you groceries?"

"I'm not an invalid yet, Jamie. Save your good deeds to when I'm flat on my back."

"Speaking of which, I'm going back to the car park. I thought maybe I'd find something significant in the daylight. Of course, I wasn't bargaining on the snow."

"What snow?"

"You just get up?"

McLaren stretched, stifling his yawn. "Not so as you'd notice. I've just been busy and haven't glanced outside yet. It snowed during the night, I take it."

"An inch or so in most areas, from what I hear on the radio."

"It won't help with your hunt, though."

"What else is new? The lads from the station cordoned off the car park—"

"I can imagine the publican is thrilled about that."

"—made a thorough search, but didn't find anything."

"It's tough to see anything outside at night, even with the police work lamps."

"Which is why I'm going back now to take a proper look around."

"Trying to make points with the Super?"

"You know what I mean, Mike. If anything like paper got dislodged somewhere and blew onto the tarmac, it could be buried in that stuff. And then it won't be a lot of use as a clue if it sits there all day."

"Probably not, but it won't be a first time."

"Any more words of comfort, Mike?"

"If I may echo *your* words, Jamie, I thought of something last night that may or may not be significant."

Jamie gripped the car's steering wheel tighter. "I knew you just needed to let your mind perk. What is it?"

"During the attack, the guy fell against my car. He leaned against it as he pushed off." He waited for Jamie to make the mental jump.

"He left his palm and fingerprints." He said it slowly, with a great deal of satisfaction coloring his tone.

"I hope to hell he did, and if he did, that they're not smudged. There's just one thing that will destroy my ebullient feelings this morning."

"Dare I ask?"

"Unless the berk has a criminal record, which means his prints are on file—"

"Yeah. Having his fingerprints won't help us at all."

Jamie rang off and promised he would search the pub's car park with a magnifying glass.

McLaren slouched against the edge of the worktop, drinking his coffee and thinking over his day. He knew he could take the day off to recuperate, but he didn't want to disappoint Gary. Also, now that he had some momentum going and had evidently rattled someone's cage bars, he didn't want to lose the advantage.

He grabbed a light gray and cranberry pullover, and his gray Dockers, and padded into the bathroom. He hesitated at the door, his hand just over the light switch. If he turned on the light, he'd see his face and the aftermath of last night's struggle, and he'd either get angry all over again or he'd vow to find the attacker. If he kept the light off, pretended he could see in the half light, pretended the beating hadn't hurt anything other than his pride, he would be spared the humiliation of knowing he'd almost been killed.

But running away had never worked. A year and a half ago he'd tried to ignore the other anger that had consumed him: the arrest of his seventy-year-old friend for defending his wife, his business and himself against a burglar. The injustice of it had overwhelmed him, and it had worsened during his confrontation with the police officer in charge of the case. Charlie Harvester and McLaren had a long history of rivalry that stretched back to their police school days. McLaren had never been the blue-eyed boy, but he had continually bested Harvester in grades, case solutions and promotions. Never mind that Harvester's daddy was in the upper echelon of the Force and gave his son a few hand-ups and undeserved accolades. The conflict had been forged and the jealousy was deep, ripening over the ensuing years.

All that had ignited the night of the burglary, becoming the deciding factor for McLaren to quit the job he loved. A year of cocooning himself away from Jamie, Dena, and his friends nearly cost him his sanity and Dena's love. The struggle back to life had been too difficult for him to sink back into it.

Taking a deep breath, he turned on the wall switch. The room flooded with light and he looked at the mirror.

His neck was slightly swollen and the abrasions where the wire had cut were red. His right eye stared back at him, the white now crimson and filled with blood.

He turned from the mirror and leaned against the sink. Should he just go back to bed, or at least do some computer research? There was the question of Ashley's child. And he could look up some other things.

Wouldn't it be better for his health if he just wrote off the day and tended to his wounds?

But if he took the day off, he'd feel better if he did something with Dena. A picnic in front of the fire wouldn't be strenuous. Or they could tour one of the grand houses she loved.

He showered, shaved and dressed, then had a second cup of coffee and phoned Dena.

Her home phone rang a half dozen times before the ansaphone clicked on. Halfway through her recording he decided not to leave a message, and hung up. He had better luck with her mobile phone: she answered on the second ring.

"You're out early." He sank against the sofa cushions and repositioned the phone against his ear. "Hot date?"

"Unless you consider the post office counter clerk, the caterer, the photographer and the grocer as hot dates, no."

"They could be. I haven't seen them."

"I wouldn't know either. I've given all that up, or haven't you heard?"

McLaren laughed, then quickly regretted it. His hand went to his throat and he massaged it.

"You sound dreadfully hoarse, Michael. You catching a cold?"

"I've caught something but not to worry, it's not contagious. I'm sure I'll get over it soon. So, what's with the caterer, photographer and the rest?"

"Just errands. I'm interviewing the two you mentioned to see if they'd work out for a fund raiser the sanctuary is planning in April."

"Fine. What about the post office clerk and

grocer?"

"Relax. Don't strain your muscles. They're strictly my personal errands. A girl has to post a package and eat sometimes. Say, do you need anything for your throat? I know you never want to admit you're ever ill, but you could be coming down with bronchitis."

"I'll be fine, thanks. It's really nothing to worry about. I've got medicines that any chemist would envy."

"Oh! The chemist's. I need to stop at Boots. And at a book store to get my father a birthday gift. Thanks for reminding me."

McLaren sighed as his day's plan went up in flames.

"Are you still talking to people about that boy's disappearance? I never heard that you had found him, so I assume you're still working it."

"I'm still on the case, yes." He hesitated, wanting to ask her out for the day.

"Anything interesting on that infant's parentage? I'm not prying, Michael. I'm just concerned about your work load. All that research you have to do takes time, never mind talking to people."

"I haven't got to that yet. I wanted to do a preliminary query of all the principle people in the case. That way, I have something on which to base the research information."

"Like knowing if someone's lying because you know what really happened."

"Something like that." He hesitated, debating how to ask her. "So you've got the day off, then."

"And it didn't come too soon, either. I've got to get this done today, if not sooner."

He mumbled something about good luck occasionally happening at the right time.

"Sorry. What did you say? I can't hear too well in this car park."

"Nothing. Just wishing you happy shopping. You want to have dinner tonight?"

"Oh, Michael, I'd love to, but I promised Maureen I'd help her decide which of her paintings to submit to the Buxton art contest. You don't mind, do you? I thought you'd be working on your case, so I said I'd help her."

"No. That's fine. You go ahead. We'll make it later in the week. You said you have the day off Friday?"

"Yes. I'm inking the date on my calendar." She said something but a car horn blared over her speech. "—set. I'll see you then. Love." She rang off, leaving him with the oddest sensation that he'd just escaped the Inquisition if she'd seen his face.

****

Dena turned off the A619 and parked on the ground floor of a multi storey car park near the Chesterfield Central Library. A snowplow had cleaned off most of the concrete drive but several trailings of snow and ice showed the plow's path. They crunched as her car tires ran over and flattened them. She found a parking spot in the sunshine near the entrance. The structure was incredibly cold, its concrete shell holding the wintry chill, and she hurriedly slammed and locked her car door. The sound bounced off the hard walls around her with a startling loudness.

She hadn't really lied to Michael, she told herself as she walked to the building. She stepped around the patches of snow on the street and pavement and dodged a slushy spray from a bus groaning up the road. The air held the odors of diesel exhaust and wet earth. If he was suspicious, she'd show him 'library research' written on her errand list. She just hadn't mentioned it when she named the day's activities, or that she felt like he had too much to do. She kept repeating that as she approached the building and opened the main door.

The glass and brick structure sat imposingly on New Beetwell Street, in a connect-the-dots arrangement with Queens Park on the south end and the Parish Church of Our Lady and All Saints on the north. The interior was bright, spacious and harbored a local studies department, free lunchtime Saturday concerts, and a café. As tempted as she was to get a pastry and cup of tea, she headed for the reference section.

The librarian suggested several websites Dena might try to locate the information she needed, and also suggested a few tomes of Official Information if the Internet search wasn't useful.

She found a chair at a table, and turned on one of the library's research computers. The monitor blinked away and she typed in her subject in the search bar. Several websites looked promising, and she opened them in succession. Eventually she found the marriage date she needed. Seventh of July, two and a half years ago. After making a note of it, she brought up birth certificate listings, looking for the birth record of a baby born to Ashley and Callum Fox three years ago.

After an hour of glancing at records, she felt her eyes glazing over. Of course she could have stayed home, using the Internet on her desk computer. Or she could have gone to the Buxton Library, which would have been closer to her house. But if she needed to dive into the tomes shelved in the library, or needed to ask the staff for assistance, she'd have to come here anyway. Besides, two of the errands on her list were in Chesterfield. Nothing like uncovering two parents with one computer search.

She rubbed her eyes, the strain tempting to stop for a cup of tea. There was no reason why she couldn't take her own laptop to the café—it was in the boot of her car—but she wanted to finish the job. She flexed her neck and shoulder muscles and did some isometric exercises, then brought up another file. The pages of scanned certificates threatened to blur into one indistinguishable blur, so she slowed the click of the mouse and forced herself to read the names.

Ashley Fox's name jumped from the computer screen fifteen minutes into her search.

Dena read over the page, then read it again and jotted down names, dates and place. With a satisfying smile, she closed the file.

She was about to log off when an idea hit her, so she opened up a file pertaining to death certificates. She typed the last name into the computer's search bar but came up with nothing. She tried several other websites but each search produced the same results: nothing.

She sat back in her chair, chewing on the end of her pencil. She reread the notes she'd jotted down after talking to Michael, and checked the subject of the Internet file she'd called up. No mistake there. So why couldn't she find what she needed?

What would Michael do, she asked herself, setting the pencil on the table. What did he always say? If you've pursued the avenues you think are correct, vary one of the components and see what that gives you.

The name would not be different; the person had lived in the village and was known to too many people. No records existed of the death, either in Derbyshire, Cheshire or Merseyside. So what else could be wrong? She glanced at her watch, then hurriedly brought up Gary Barber's name. Again, nothing pertinent to her search showed itself. So she delved into editions of the *Derbyshire Standard* for the same time period. A search for Gary's name brought up several articles. One variance appeared in the last one.

She stared at the photo, unsure if she were reading it correctly. The names were ones she knew, having heard them from McLaren. She read the caption. "Gary Barber presides over Langheath's annual Wakes Week festivities by presenting the Volunteer Recognition Award to internationally acclaimed tennis champion Albert Tipton. His brother, Alan Tipton, head of the well dressing committee, looks on."

Dena took a photo of the article, thinking to email it to McLaren, then for good measure jotted down the website address and printed a copy of the newspaper page. Before abandoning the website she made a note of the twenty-five year old newspaper's caption and the date in case the copy or emailed image wouldn't be legible.

She spent nearly thirty minutes clicking on and reading other related articles and photographs. When she finally looked up from the screen, her mind was whirling.

She logged off, gathered up her notes, and headed for her car, determined to talk to McLaren before she tackled the rest of her errands.

Dena followed the A632 south out of Chesterfield

as far as the Red Lion Inn. She turned right onto the B5057 and soon arrived at Langheath.

She parked opposite the green grocers on the High Street and sat for a minute in her car. Shoppers, business people and farmers streamed along the street, and Dena wondered if her idea would work. She had a cursory knowledge of the village, knew its small size. As such, she had decided that she could easily spot McLaren on one of Langheath's three roads. Even if she didn't see him, surely his car would pinpoint him. How many red Peugeots would be here?

But, that aside, she still hesitated. Last year's miserable attempt at helping him had ended in her near death. And all because she had wanted to help him. As she was trying to do now. She laid her head against the headrest, staring ahead, seeing nothing but his face before her. What would've happened to her if he hadn't rescued her? What would he have become if she had died? She blinked rapidly, suddenly cold, and rubbed her arms. Nothing would happen, she scolded herself. This was an entirely different situation. She wasn't playing detective now. She had merely discovered some information for him. No personal confrontations would take place to place her in jeopardy.

Feeling better, Dena got out and locked her car. She stood on the pavement, her eyes on the faces coming toward her. It was a daft idea. She had no idea where he was.

She pulled her mobile out of her purse, opened it, and punched in McLaren's number. The phone went immediately to voice mail. She closed her phone without leaving a message.

She walked along the street, alternately gazing at

the shop windows and the street. There was still no sign of McLaren or his car, so she sat on the wooden bench outside the school yard fence. She counted slowly to five hundred, then rang him again. His phone clicked over to voice message again. She rang off, exhaling heavily.

The aroma of hot fish and chips sailed downwind to her, reminding her she was hungry. She walked into the chippie, ordered a piece of plaice and chips, then took them outside to the same bench. Fifteen minutes later, she tossed the greased paper into the rubbish bin. The hot food warmed her interior but did nothing for her externally. She blew on her fingers, stamped her feet and pulled her cap over her ears. She'd be lucky if she hadn't caught her death, sitting outside in this weather. Still, it was a better vantage point to look for McLaren if he walked along the High Street.

She flexed her fingers and tried calling him again.

Still no answer.

She flipped the phone closed, then thought better of it, and sat down. Two elderly women and a middle-aged man occupied the bench next to hers. She angled her back toward them and rang up Jamie.

"Dena! What gives?" Jamie's cheery greeting eased her anxiety.

"Jamie, do you happen to know where Michael is, or know his plans for today?"

"Not really. I just know he's still working on the Luke Barber case. Why? Is something wrong? Where are you?"

Dena leaned forward, wrapping her coat about her as a gust of wind sailed down the street. A chunk of congealed slush on the undercarriage of a car knocked loosed and splattered onto the tarmac. "I'm sitting on a bench in Langheath."

"Langheath? Why are you there?"

"I thought maybe I could find Michael, but I haven't been able to locate him."

Jamie exhaled sharply, puffing out his cheeks. "I repeat. Is something wrong? Must be, if you've driven to the village."

"No, nothing's wrong. Not in the way you mean." She hesitated, rethinking the situation. Maybe the information wasn't that urgent. Maybe she was making a fool of herself and over-reacting—which wouldn't be the first time. Jamie's voice urged her to answer him.

"Well, then…"

She explained her morning research in the library, telling him she'd seen a photo of Albert and Alan Tipton, one being a tennis champion and the other working his farm. "I also learned about Ashley Fox's child."

"What about it?"

"The birth date, and her and Callum's wedding date."

"You *have* been busy. And these are pertinent to the case, then."

"Well, I don't know, of course, but I suspect he'd like to know. *If* he hasn't learned this already."

"Anything else?"

"Yes." She glanced at the three people on the next bench. They seemed more interested in the newspapers they were reading than in listening to her. She bent forward, bringing her chin closer to her chest in an effort not to be overheard. "I couldn't find out everything this morning, but I think there's something odd about Luke's father."

Jamie coughed and drew in his breath. "Odd? In what way? I've known him for years, Dena. If you mean he was arrested for something and is keeping it quiet—"

"No. It has to do with his wife, Margaret. I-I'm not sure, but I don't think she's buried where everyone believes her to be."

"Did Mike mention this to you?"

"Not in so many words."

"But you put two and two together and came up with this foreboding."

"Well…"

Jamie was silent, and Dena could imagine him thinking she was playing detective again. And the last time she'd done that… She ran her fist over her forehead, trying to dull the throbbing that had just started. "Plus, there's a villager who is highly thought of here and doesn't deserve it. Michael needs to know that, Jamie."

"Look, Dena. Mike and I both appreciate you wanting to help. He's in this thing alone and it's a big case to investigate. But he likes it like that. He even thrives on it. Sure, I help him occasionally, but only when he specifically asks, and it's usually official police stuff. I don't do things behind his back. That's the surest way to alienate him. And I value our friendship too much to do that."

"But if I found out something he should know—"

"It's tempting to help, but he's done this before, Dena. He knows what he's doing."

"You just said you help him." She sniffed, feeling shut out.

"I also said I do it when he requests my help. I don't jump in as if he can't work through the investigation. Besides, there's another big difference between you and me."

She waited, afraid of what she might hear.

"I do this as my career. I've had years of experience. So has Mike. And you, while you have the best intentions in the world—"

"I'm an amateur and I could stir up a hornet's nest if I'm not careful. Does that about sum it up?"

"I'll let Mike know you have the information, if you want me to." He thought it best to not answer her question. "But I suspect he has his mobile on voice mail because he doesn't want to be interrupted right now. Give him another hour, then try him again. I'll also call him, if that makes you feel better."

Dena confessed it would, apologized again for intruding, then rang off.

She closed her phone and laid it on her lap. The back of the bench seemed colder than it had been several minutes ago, but she leaned against it, needing the support for her plummeting exuberance. She tried angling her body away from the breeze but it seemed to swirl around her. The answer was to get up and walk, perhaps completing her errands. But she stared at the phone in her hand, her fingers tracing its cold surface. It tempted her to contact McLaren one more time. As she flipped it open she saw a young woman walking up the High Street, carrying a guitar case. Dena drew a deep breath, got up and crossed the road, and approached the woman.

"Pardon me." She stood to the side of the woman, hoping she posed no threat.

The woman stopped abruptly, looking at Dena with a mixture of curiosity and apprehension. She brought the case closer to her body, angling it across her waist, as though it were body armor. "Yes? Do you need something?"

"This may be a daft question, but did you know Luke Barber?"

The question caught her by surprise. She blinked rapidly and stammered she did. "Why do you want to know? If you were a friend of his, it's kind of late to be showing up to pay condolences to Luke's dad."

"Sorry. No, I didn't know Luke. I'm just looking for someone who did."

"And since I have my guitar, you thought I might have done."

"Do you know a man named Michael McLaren? He's looking into Luke's disappearance." She added quickly when the woman started to walk on, "I'm a friend of his. Of Michael McLaren's, I mean. My name's Dena Ellison. I'm looking for him and thought he might be here."

Bethany eyed Dena with open skepticism, nodding at the mobile she held. "Why don't you phone him?"

Dena lifted her phone and looked at it as though she'd just seen it. "I tried. Several times. It goes to his voice mail." She looked around, hoping to see a constable strolling his beat. "Look. If you're uncomfortable with this, ring up the Derbyshire Constabulary and ask for Detective-Constable Jamie Kydd. He knows Mr. McLaren and he can vouch for me." She stopped abruptly, aware she was babbling, that she was looking foolish. She smiled, hoping to appear calm and repair any damage she may have done.

"What's so urgent that you have to find Mr. McLaren now? Why can't you leave him a voice message?"

"I could, but it may be some time before he picks up his messages. I have some important information pertaining to the case. I—He should have it as soon as possible."

Bethany screwed up the corners of her mouth and studied Dena's face. A burst of laughter from the schoolyard broke Bethany's contemplation. "He could be talking to John Evans."

"Who's he?"

"A music teacher. Luke went to him for a while. I take an occasional lesson. I'm headed there now, in fact." She hefted the guitar case, as if to prove her point. "I have no idea, of course, if Mr. McLaren is there, but maybe John saw him this morning. Wouldn't hurt to ask. You want to come with me? His house is just there." She pointed to the house cattycorner to the news agent. "My house is across the street from him." She smiled sheepishly as Dena walked along side her. "You probably wonder why I've got my guitar with me, walking along the High Street, if I live opposite him. It was being repaired—the bridge was pulling away from the body. I just picked it up." She half turned, looking over her shoulder, as if indicating the repair shop.

"I won't take up much of your lesson time, I promise. Just a quick word with Mr. Evans. Thanks."

They walked the short distance to John's house in silence—Bethany concerned about the truth of Dena's narrative, and Dena concerned about McLaren's inaccessibility. She'd never known him to ignore a phone call, but she'd never really called him much during the day, just because she didn't want to bother him. If he was in the middle of talking to a reluctant witness or, worse yet, physically persuading someone to cooperate… She glanced around her, hoping she'd see him. For the first time since they'd become a serious twosome, she felt a prickling in her blood. Not fear—that was too strong a word. More like apprehension. A disquieting sensation that she couldn't describe or understand. She knew no reason why this uneasiness claimed her. Their last conversation had been about Friday's dance date. He'd given her no cause to be anxious.

"This is it." Bethany's voice broke through Dena's thoughts.

"Sorry?" Dena jerked her head up from her gaze at the pavement.

"John's house. This is it." She repeated the statement as she opened the front garden gate. "It's all right, you know," she added as Dena hesitated on the pavement.

Dena nodded, shoved the whisperings to the back of her mind, and followed Bethany to the front door.

Chapter Twelve

"On second thought, I don't think I'll go in." Dena stopped abruptly at the bottom step and gazed up at the front door. It was large and black, like the entrance to a cave, and seemed to bar any anticipated help.

"But it's no trouble at all." Bethany held out her free hand as if to guide Dena up the steps. "If you're worried about taking up my lesson time, well, you said it'd just take a moment."

"Thank you all the same, but I've reconsidered, and I doubt Mr. McLaren is there. I don't see his car around—"

"Does your friend want to come in?" John Evans stood in the open doorway, removing his coat and smiling at Bethany. "We're just home," he called toward the back of the house. "No need to disturb you. Bethany's come for her lesson." He turned back to Bethany. "It's no bother if she wants to come in and talk."

"I'm not sure if she does." Bethany walked into the house, leaving John to invite Dena inside.

John frowned, looking concerned. "I understand you're hunting for someone, Miss."

He held the door open, a mute invitation to enter the house. Dena remained on the front path. The sounds of traffic, children playing, and birds underscored her explanation.

"No, Mr. McLaren isn't here." The sunlight

filtering into the foyer nearly turned his gray hair silver. He glanced at Bethany as she unpacked her guitar, told her to tune up, then concentrated again on Dena. "I spoke with him prior to today, but I haven't seen him since. I'm sorry I can't provide you with further information. This appears to be important."

Dena smiled and said she needed to give McLaren some information. "It could help him with Luke Barber's case."

"And you've not been able to raise him." He nodded toward her mobile phone, which she realized she still clutched in her right hand.

"He has it on voice mail."

"That's quite frustrating, I know."

The repeated thumping of the guitar strings bore into the silence as Dena debated about repeating the information to John. He remained where he stood, silent, his attention on Dena. Bethany draped her arm over the guitar's neck, ready for her lesson, and looked at John. The guitar case lay open on the floor beside her purse, the plush yellow lining a vivid echo of the sunlight haloing her form.

"Well, if I can be of any help, let me know." He placed his hand on the doorknob and began to close the door.

She thanked him and the door closed as John turned to Bethany and said, "Are you ready, dear?"

****

McLaren ate breakfast while half listening to the radio news. When he'd downed a glass of orange juice he loaded the breakfast dishes into the dishwasher, made notes of whom he would speak to that day, and grabbed his mobile phone, keys and jacket. Locking the kitchen door behind him, he stepped outside.

The world was white and momentarily dazzling with the morning sun glancing off the snowpack and ice. The air still held the night's cold, but it would soon warm, McLaren thought as he glanced at the cloudless sky. Some snow blanketed the smoother surfaces like the front walk and road, and had accumulated in small drifts against the bases of trees and the stone wall running along his property. The branches of the willow in the front garden held a light dusting, as did the cap of the wind chime. Still, there were many bare patches that remained snow free, especially beneath the canopy of massive tree boughs.

He stepped onto the front walk. The soles of his boots bit into the thin snow covering, exposing the flagstone surface and leaving dark gaps in the whiteness. Like musical notes sprinkled across a sheet of paper, he thought, glancing back at his trail. He hoped the car park had been spared a major onslaught, for Jamie's sake.

On the rougher or vertical surfaces the snow had not collected. Freezing temperatures claimed those regions and left their argentine declaration. Frost fringed the edges of the ornamental grass and the rim of the bird bath. It feathered into intricate swirls and fern-like fronds on the windowpanes and roof tiles. It lay in lacey plumes along the stony edges of his walkway.

Dry leaves had turned ghostly white under the frigid coating, their veins looking more like bleached rib bones of a once-living thing. They crunched under his feet as he made his way down the walk.

He stopped short, still several steps from his car. A white cloth, barely visible beneath its snowy powdering, lay bunched up on the ground by the car's left rear wing.

He picked it up gingerly, not knowing if anything was secreted in the cloth. As he shook it carefully he noted it was a torn T-shirt. No logo or other graphic adorned the shirt, so identifying its owner was just about impossible. He shook off the snow, folded it up and laid it on the back seat, then walked around the car's exterior. A fragment of cloth similar in color and texture to the shirt was caught between the rear bumper and the car body, a frozen clue.

A slow smile crept over his face, then erupted into a bark of laughter. His assailant had remembered leaving his telltale fingerprints during the fight, and had wiped the car down with the shirt.

The man's got guts, McLaren thought as he opened the driver's door. Found out where I live, polished my car for me in the dead of night…

He shook his head, amused at the event, then grabbed the scraper from the glove compartment. After clearing the frost from the glass, he started the engine. It idled for a minute as it and the car's interior warmed up. Moments later he was driving to Langheath, still chuckling.

****

He found Bethany at her home, lingering over a second cup of tea before she had to leave for her music lesson. She stacked the morning newspaper, fashion magazine, picture book and current best-selling novel at the far end of the kitchen table before offering him a seat. He declined the tea offer, and instead asked about Ashley.

"I had no real feelings about her one way or the

other." Bethany traced the pattern of the spoon handle with her fingertip. "She and Luke were a couple and of course I'd been married for a year before Luke and I ever became a musical duo." She shrugged and looked at McLaren. "What are you suggesting I should feel?"

"Jealousy, perhaps. Or antagonism."

"Luke grew up in Langheath, Mr. McLaren. So did I. We had all those years to fall in love with each other, become a serious couple, and to get married. We never did. Oh, we liked each other. We would do, or we'd never even considered forming the singing group. But neither of us felt a passionate spark toward the other one. I married Nathan, and Luke became engaged to Ashley. Why would I be jealous of Ashley, or she of me? I never even considered marriage to Luke and he never even made the first hint of asking me. It's as simple as that."

"How about the time spent together?"

"What? Like, did I pine for him when we weren't rehearsing or playing someplace?"

"All those hours doing something like music, which demanded reliance on the other person, must have sparked some feeling between you."

"It did. Friendship." She bit off the word angrily, glaring at him. "I didn't love Luke and he didn't love me. I don't know if Ashley resented the rehearsal and performance time away from her, but I certainly didn't feel that when I went home to my husband. If you don't believe me, I suggest you speak to Ashley."

"I'm merely trying to understand feelings in the case, Bethany. After all, there has to be a motive for Luke's disappearance."

"Granted. And you believe either Ashley or I was

insanely jealous of the other and wanted exclusive rights to Luke. Well, I can't speak for her, but I can speak for myself and tell you that's absurd. As I just stated, I had plenty of time to make a play for Luke—all during school—before I married Nathan."

"Fine. I don't want anyone to be unhappy." He gave her a smile and leaned back, giving her a bit of distance.

"You should clone yourself, Mr. McLaren. Most people couldn't care less about anyone else. Or were you being facetious?"

McLaren gazed around the kitchen: a modern room for a serious cook, he thought, with its white cupboards, brown slate floor, brown marble work tops, and restaurant-quality stainless steel appliances. "What about the night Luke went missing?"

"You mean, did Ashley join in the search?"

"No. You told me Gary Barber, Doc Tipton, John Evans and Callum Fox did the physical search while you remained at Gary's. Do I remember that correctly?"

"Yes. I stayed behind to act as a kind of command center, I guess. I thought someone needed to be by the phone."

"Right. Did anyone come by?"

Bethany frowned, looking puzzled. "Come by…?"

"For whatever reason. To ask about Luke, to offer a suggestion on where to look, to say he last saw Luke at a specific place…"

"No. Just the police, but that was later, of course, and that was in response to the phone call."

McLaren nodded and in the brief silence the sounds of traffic filled the room. "Did Luke express any preference to you about whether he wanted to go into music or tennis as a profession?"

"I know he loved both. And I believe he was getting conflicting opinions from his dad as well as Doc and John. But he never really said a thing to me about it, though if I had to guess I'd say he was leaning toward music. He did mention to me once that the pro tennis route was grueling, and there'd be no love lost if he quit it."

"That surprises me."

"You assumed he would turn pro, then?"

"I have no opinion one way or the other, but I heard about his remarkable skill at serving. Target accuracy, if that makes sense."

"Oh, yes. His ball hitting the that hole in the wall. Luke was good, there's no doubt of that. Perhaps even exceptional. I'm really no judge about tennis. But I believe he loved music more."

"Maybe his mother's influence."

Bethany murmured she didn't know, then added that the tennis term love fit rather well at timcs.

"Because he loved the game?" McLaren ignored the chiming of the village church bell and concentrated on Bethany.

"Quite the opposite. At least around the time Luke went missing. Love in tennis means zero, nothing. And that's how he scored his tennis career."

"How about you? What do you score your music career now that you're a solo?"

"It's a bit of a struggle. I won't lie. Luke was my path to a good living. We were just starting to get the bigger venues interested in us."

"And now?"

Bethany screwed up the corners of her mouth and

shrugged. "It's been a set-back, of course. You go from being a duo that a lot of folks and festival managers have heard and are familiar with, and you're suddenly reduced to a solo act who's developing her own material. It— I lost a lot when Luke disappeared."

"What does Nathan think of your career? He works as a physical trainer, I believe."

"I don't know what his occupation has to do with mine, but he supports me one hundred percent. He couldn't be more pleased with my music."

"Did he feel that way when you were with Luke?"

****

McLaren listened to the messages Dena left on his mobile before stopping at the bakery. His late night and the morning cold were slowing him down. A cup of coffee would combat both.

The aroma of fresh-baked scones, bread and bath buns tempted him to stay inside, but he left the shop before he could invent an excuse to stay.

He crossed the street, marveling at the amount of traffic flowing through the village. The three wooden benches bordering the swath of park on the High Street's western side were either coated with ice or occupied with people. He hesitated momentarily, debating whether to sit in his car or go back to the bakery, when someone vacated his seat. McLaren hurried over and sat down before he noticed his bench mate was Tom Yardley.

Tom was concentrating on braiding three pieces of wire together and didn't look up. McLaren watched Tom for several seconds before commenting that the wire looked like guitar strings.

Tom turned his head, clearly surprised to see

McLaren. He angled his body slightly, wanting to shut out McLaren but not wanting to antagonize him. "Yeah, that's what I thought." He seemed to think it diplomatic to converse civilly. "Silk and steel. I've seen the same color ones on Phil's guitar."

"Are these old ones he had?"

"Naw. I found 'em when I was workin' this mornin'."

"They don't look broken." McLaren maneuvered so he could judge the strings' lengths. "Daft someone would just ditch them."

"I wouldn't know. I find all kinds of stuff."

"A perk of the job. Where'd you find these?"

One of the strings sprung loose of the braid. Tom grabbed it and bent it back in place. "Across from the car park at The Split Oak in Somerley. You know it?"

McLaren nodded, feeling his hands grow cold. He kept his voice steady. "And you found it this morning? You were out early, especially so far from Langheath."

"I was there at four-thirty. It's my normal time for stuff like this. I was going to shovel the car park and the pavement for the pub, but they were roped off. Some police scene. I guess the owner knows about it." He snorted and shook his head. "As usual, I'm out of a job even if it did snow last night." His voice held a tinge of sarcasm but he added quickly so McLaren wouldn't get mad, "I think it'll make a great bracelet if I can braid the strings together."

"Seems to be working." McLaren took a sip of his coffee, then said the strings didn't look as though the snow had stained the wires' silk wrappings.

"They don't seem to've been there that long. Maybe last night before it snowed, don't ya think?"

"Very likely." He took another swallow and stood up. "Well, it'll be nice when you're finished." He walked back to his car, thinking Tom had just ruined Jamie's morning.

****

McLaren took the A6 back north to Buxton, singing along to Kate Rusby's *Underneath the Stars* CD. He parked along the High Street, then consulted his notebook for the address of the fitness center before he got out.

The road was streaked with water from the melting snow, and he averted his glance as the sunlight glanced off a large watery patch. Sparrows hopped along the puddles as they bathed or took sips, chirping their territory. Melting snow dripped from the overhead storefronts or canvas awnings, plopping onto the pavement or someone's head. A dog tied to a bicycle rack yapped at McLaren as he passed the butcher's, but the woman inside the shop continued her unhurried shopping.

A three-minute walk took him to Spring Gardens shopping complex, an area of shops and small restaurants at the bottom of the High Street. He entered the enclosed mall, which housed a dozen or so shops, and soon found the fitness center.

A wall of plate glass windows comprised the gym's shop front, presumably to nag guilty parties into keeping their muttered resolutions about getting into better shape. He entered the gym and was confronted by a row of treadmills and stair steppers on his left and reception desk on his right. The music pouring out of the ceiling speakers, he noted, was upbeat and rhythmic.

After asking at the desk for Nathan, he was directed to a man standing beside an exercise bicycle. He was speaking to a woman who straddled the bike seat and pedaled leisurely. The woman's excess weight showed itself in her double chin and in her stomach, which spilled over the top of her nylon shorts. The outfit appeared to address the woman's hopes more than her current situation, for it stretched taut in various places and seemed to groan against the fleshy pressure. The man appeared more appropriately dressed. His blue sweatpants and sleeveless T-shirt not only sported the logo of the Step Into Health Fitness Center but also hung loosely from his muscular body.

He turned as McLaren walked up, his brown eyes sparkling at the hope of another client.

"Nathan Watson?" McLaren paused several feet from the bike, not wishing to interrupt.

"Yes." Nathan smiled and nodded. The dampness of his brown hair glistened in the light from the clerestory windows. "Are you wanting to join the center?" He glanced at McLaren's obvious inappropriate dress, yet recovered quickly with a handshake. "Can I help you?"

"If this is a bad time to talk…" McLaren nodded toward the woman, who had stopped to take a breather.

"Keep going, Jackie. You're doing fine." Nathan walked a few feet from the bike, then asked again if he could help.

"I spoke with your wife this morning."

"Yes?" The word came cautiously, as if he were expecting bad news.

"My name's Michael McLaren. I'm looking into the disappearance of Luke Barber."

"That was a while ago."

"I realize that, but his father wants a new investigation."

"And he asked you." It was more of a question than a statement, laced with skepticism and surprise.

It could be my souvenir bruises that makes Nate rather distrustful, McLaren thought. Perhaps these badges of honor aren't the most convincing certificate I could show him. "Yes, despite what you think. Is there some place we could talk?"

"Over there." He walked over to a corner of the large room. "Now, then. What's going on?" he asked when McLaren came up to him.

"Simple enough. Gary Barber wants the case reopened on Luke. The man wants to know what happened to his son."

Nathan agreed he'd do the same thing if he ever was in Gary's situation.

"You've no children, then."

"No." He pressed his lips together and jammed his hands into the pockets of his sweatpants. His biceps glistened with sweat.

"You seem upset by my question."

"Not upset, really. It's just none of your business."

"I apologize. I didn't know it was that personal."

"Well, now you know. I thought you were here to discuss Luke's disappearance. Why all the interest in my fatherhood…or lack of?" He noted the time on the large wall clock above the door to the shower rooms.

"I was just curious. I like to know the people I speak to."

"Is that right? Well, how about you? Are you married? Do you have kids? Were you always nosing around in other folks' lives? What's your annual income? Do you go to church?"

The muscles in McLaren's jaw tightened. "I'm not here to play games, Mr. Watson."

"Just giving you a taste of your own medicine, mate."

"Not really. My questions have a very real significance to Luke Barber. Your questions bordered on the intrusive and were insulting to Luke's case. Now, are we ready to talk in a more friendly fashion?"

"I've got to get back to work, McLaren. It's been smashing talking to you."

"I don't see why you're antagonistic, Mr. Watson. I'm merely wanting some information so I can investigate Luke's disappearance. Gary Barber's a friend of yours. Why don't you want to help him?"

"Look." Nathan took a step toward McLaren and pointed his index finger at McLaren's chest. "I liked Luke. He was a super lad and he had a great singing voice. Besides that, he could play tennis like a man possessed. He was good to his dad and helped little old ladies across the street on Sundays. What else do you want me to say?"

"How about something useful? Did you talk to him on the day he disappeared?"

"No."

"Did you see him that day?"

"No."

"Did you hear anything from anyone about him leaving the village, perhaps going on a trip?"

"No."

"How about problems…did he have any trouble with a specific person or was he worried about his health or his career choice?"

"In spite of sounding tedious, no."

McLaren exhaled sharply and laid his hand on Nate's shoulder. "I realize this has been a tiring conversation, Mr. Watson, and I realize you need all your energy for your job, here. But while you're being a smart ass I'm losing daylight and my patience." His fingers curled into a fist, tightening on Nate's T-shirt and pulling it forward. The fabric stretched across the man's shoulder, threatening to rip at the seams. "Now, if you want to start again and show off those manners your mum tried so hard to instill in you, we can play nice. If not…" He gave one tug to the shirt and a sharp tearing sound broke into the quiet.

Nate nodded and smiled weakly as McLaren relaxed his grip. "Sure. Okay. I didn't mean anything by it." He smoothed the T-shirt flat against his chest and glanced at Jackie. She was taking another rest period on the bike. "I get defensive about a few subjects, sorry."

"And which one hit a nerve?"

"Luke."

"Oh yes?" McLaren's right eyebrow rose to match his rising voice tone. "Why so defensive? You just said you liked him."

"I'm not going to tell you I hated his guts, which is slightly stronger than I actually felt. If you discover that he's dead, well, that'd put me right on top of your suspect list, wouldn't it?"

"Why didn't you like Luke? Were you jealous of the time he spent with Bethany?"

"It's absurd, I realize, but it still doesn't stop the feelings. Luke Barber, despite living on a farm, seemed gifted and lucky. He led a charmed life. He was a brilliant musician and tennis player. He could choose which path to follow and he'd still be on top of the world and make money hand over fist. While I…" He broke off and stared at the floor.

"You've had to struggle," McLaren supplied.

Nate stared frankly at McLaren. His gaze had softened since his initial burst of anger. Now he appeared almost contrite. "It's the same, worn out story that thousands of blokes know. My dad left my mum when I was fifteen years old. I had a job after school and on weekends to help with the family income. After I left school I had a handful of jobs, lost two due to downsizing."

"That's a lot to happen to someone our age. What are you…in your mid twenties?"

"Twenty-eight. I married Bethany seven years ago."

"Before she and Luke began singing together."

"Yeah. I was working at two jobs at that time and the thought of her making the big time in music, bringing in a substantial wad of cash, well, it bolstered my spirits. I was pretty low at that time and couldn't see much exciting in my future."

"So, Bethany's music could still help out."

"In other ways than just swelling our bank account. I'd like to have a kid around the house, but right now it'd be a terrible strain on our wallets. We can't afford a child. Perhaps if Bethany starts bringing in real money…" He shrugged and looked slightly less worried.

"Do you know…or do you think…Luke had been pressured by anyone?"

"About his career?"

"Was there anything else that could've bothered him?" McLaren looked startled.

"Oh, lord, no. Not that I know of. I just thought… Well, I don't think anyone was really giving him a hard time about his music or tennis other than John Evans and Doc Tipton. There wasn't a criminal element lurking about or pressuring him, if you mean. He wasn't that famous yet."

"Was there someone he didn't get along with in the village?"

"He wasn't on good terms with Phil Moss or Tom Yardley, but not many people are. Phil appears tougher than he is, but he could still be very unpleasant. I don't know *if* anything happened between them, but Phil's been around long enough and has had a slight history of pestering Luke, so he might know something. Or be involved."

"I heard rumors of drugs."

"Nothing would surprise me if it was connected with Phil. He's a nasty piece of work."

"So you don't know why Luke would've gone missing, if he did it of his own choice."

"No. I saw Tom Yardley give Luke a lift that day, but there's nothing much odd in that. They occasionally went places together."

"What, like pubs?"

"I guess. I don't know for sure. But his disappearance has bothered me. It's all so strange. I could see if he had a brother and they got into a fight about wanting the same girl, or if they were in rival musical groups or tennis tournaments, but there was nothing like that. Nothing from anyone he knew, as far as I ever heard."

"So even if there was something troubling him, he wouldn't have confided in you, for instance, since he had no brother or sister. I thought that since he sang with Bethany, you three might be close enough for Luke to talk about things that bothered him."

"No. And I always thought that too bad, 'cause Luke was the sort who would've liked a brother."

"But so many brothers don't get along."

Nate muttered that he'd heard stories from some of his mates about that. "About the best example of brothers who really were best mates were the Tiptons."

"Doc Tipton?"

"Yeah. His twin, Alan, and he did most everything together. They played tennis, though Doc ended up pursuing his career and Alan thought of it more as a hobby. Still, they rarely let more than a few days go by without ringing each other up or doing something together."

"Too bad more families can't get on like that."

"Yeah. I think it started when they were younger. The family'd go to New Zealand periodically. To visit Doc's great uncle. Doc and Alan loved it there. Well, the whole family did. I think that's where they developed that bond. Their uncle had a large sheep station and the boys could roam wherever they wished. Perhaps that's also why Doc was so terribly broken up by Alan's death. It was like half of him died." He stopped and glanced at McLaren, perhaps to see if he understood.

"We're always saying goodbye to someone we love. It *is* heart breaking, but the alternative isn't very good."

"What?"

"Steeling your heart against love and friendship."

"Well, I'm hanging on to Bethany with every fiber of my being. I'm blessed to have her. Double blessed because she's going to be a star someday and then we can start our family."

"Did John Evans encourage her with her music, or did she always know she wanted to do that?"

"She was always musical, playing the fiddle or guitar in school. She also dabbled in song writing. But making a career of it… Well, it kind of came about when we got married. My job situation nudged her in that direction, although she didn't need much nudging. She loved music and I think this was just a good excuse to try it and see how far she could get."

"And you're okay with the life on the road, if it comes to that."

Nathan glanced at the wall clock and called to Jackie that he'd be right there. Turning back to McLaren, he said, "No. I like a quiet home. I like to come in at the end of the work day and have my tea and watch the telly and know that Bethany is there, safe. I don't want her traveling about. Too many things can happen when you're by yourself." He returned to his client, leaving McLaren to wonder if that same thing had happened to Luke when he was by himself.

****

McLaren drove to Chesterfield and parked down the street from the car dealership owned by Darren Fraser. He was prepared to wait until Sharon Fraser took her lunch break and then speak to whomever filled in, but he didn't have to wait. When he glanced inside the showroom, another woman sat at the receptionist desk.

The woman, a twenty-two-year-old blonde who might've been at home wearing a thong swimsuit and red lipstick, and posing on the bonnet of a car, looked up from the romance novel she was reading and smiled. She rattled off her question with practiced polish.

When McLaren asked if he could speak to Sharon, the girl frowned and apologized. "She's at lunch. But she'll be back in an hour. You could wait, I suppose." The sentence drifted off as she looked around for some place McLaren could sit in the interim. "Or I could give her a message, if you care to leave one." She set down the book and picked up a biro. "Of course, if I could help you in any way..."

McLaren exhaled heavily and shook his head. "I always seem to miss her. I've been trying to talk to her for over a week."

"How vexing for you, sir. Could I have her phone you?"

"I'm trying to return an earring I found."

"Recently?" She opened a desk drawer and took out an envelope.

"Yes. I was looking through the papers from the car I'd bought here three years ago and I noticed the earring at the bottom of the manila envelope. I assumed Sharon had dropped it and didn't realize it when she put together the papers and brochures for my car. I had never noticed it because I never took everything out. You know," he added, hoping to make his story sound authentic. "You just reach in and grab the paper you need at the moment."

"Yes, sir."

"Well, anyway, I couldn't for the life of me think

where this earring came from other than here. So I rang up the dealership and spoke to Sharon and she said it probably was hers and I said I'd drop it by." He hesitated, smiling and staring at the envelope the blonde held. "No offense, but it *is* a diamond earring and I wouldn't want it mislaid. I'd like to give it to her personally, just to be certain she got it."

"Certainly."

"Just to make sure…since I see you also work here…would you know if it *is* Sharon's and not some other person's?"

"If she said she lost an earring—"

"Yes. And I'm not hinting at all that she's lying, but she could be mistaken. Especially if someone else was filling in for her, as you are so capably doing."

"Thank you, sir."

"Just to confirm that it could be hers… I know Sharon doesn't work every day, so I wonder if you could look up on your personnel files to see if she did indeed work that Friday in January. It'd save me making an embarrassing mistake and save her from having to return it to me in case it isn't hers." He smiled and leaned closer. "It'd be most helpful."

"Certainly. I understand." She clicked on the computer and the mouse cursor hovered over the personnel file folder. "What date was that, do you remember?"

"January. The twentieth. Three years ago. A Friday, if I remember correctly." He waited while the woman clicked and scrolled through the file.

"Here's the schedule." She put her finger on the monitor and read aloud. "Sharon had been scheduled to work but she rang in ill. She was home." She looked up from the monitor. "I'm so sorry. It doesn't seem to be hers."

"And as much as I'd like to reunite the jewelry with its owner, I know it's not yours. I wouldn't have forgotten you if you'd been working that day." He flashed a grin, said he'd try again, and left whistling the theme song from "New Tricks."

****

It was just going onto four o'clock. Plenty of time to turn over a rock and see if bad boy Philip Moss had anything to add to the discussion. Especially since he wasn't far from Philip's home.

McLaren took the back streets, avoiding the early rush hour traffic, and parked in front of Philip's flat. The five-storey building at 61 Charington Garden had been built in the last half of the previous century and showed its age in the faded door, windowsill paint and the stained concrete foundation. Landscaping consisted of a few scraggly bushes planted several feet from the wall, and a large metal tub that housed a spindly tree. He had no idea what kind it was—bare branches and bark never were strong identifying marks for him. The bushes, he assumed, were fairly new and were replacing the original overgrown ones. Someone had done a half-hearted job of cleaning the pavement, for there were still spots of thick ice, but he stepped around them and entered the building.

The foyer was nearly square, with two doors staring at each other at right angles to the entrance. Wall sconces sporadically illuminated the treads of the brown-painted metal stairway that angled upward from the middle of the far wall. The first landing, McLaren noticed, wallowed in late afternoon shadow, for the fixture's light bulb had burnt out. Worn coconut fiber mats hugged the thresholds of their respective doors, their frayed edges and wisps of castoff fiber more off-putting than welcoming. Scuffmarks of innumerable shoes patterned the dark tan linoleum floor, adding another layer of design to the dull checks.

McLaren walked over to the row of metal-front letterboxes. He was keenly aware of his footsteps echoing against the hard concrete walls and spiraling upward in the stairwell. It sounded like a dozen men scampering after him.

Light from an overhead fixture angled down onto the face of the boxes so he could read the names of the flats' occupants. Philip's name was hand printed on a less than white slip of paper jammed into the name holder of the letterbox. McLaren noted the flat number and jogged up the steps. Philip's flat, A, was the first door on the right at the top of the landing.

The door jerked open on McLaren's second knock, and he stared into a pair of serious dark eyes. They complimented the equally dark hair that rose short and spiky on the man's head. A muscular arm stretched across the half open doorway, barring McLaren's entrance and signaling that the man was in no mood to be interrupted.

"Yeah?" Philip's voice, barely hospitable, grunted the question and his irritation.

"Philip Moss?" McLaren flashed a smile and stood with his legs apart.

"Yeah?"

"My name's McLaren. I understand you knew Luke Barber."

"Yeah. What of it? You handin' out prizes for the

correct answer?"

"I'd like to talk to you about Luke for a few minutes."

"Why? Am I mentioned in the bloke's will or somethin'?"

"That I wouldn't know."

"Then shove off, mate." Philip started to shut the door but McLaren shoved his knee into the open space and grabbed the edge of the door. He pushed it open as Philip stumbled backward. "Mind if I come in?" Without waiting for an answer, he strolled into the flat.

The room seemed to be made of empty pizza boxes, crushed beer cans, music magazines, and CD cases. An inexpensive acoustic guitar leaned against the wall and snuggled up to a tired-looking rucksack. McLaren moved a stack of used food cartons from the sofa and gestured to Philip to sit down. He did so reluctantly.

"So much better when we can relax and chat as friends, don't you think?" McLaren perched on the sofa's arm, enjoying the height advantage, and smiled at Philip.

"Yeah. Sure. What about Luke? I've got things to do and you're holdin' me up."

"This'll take just a few minutes…if I get straight answers. If you want to play games and waste my time, well, I'll waste yours until you tell me the truth. Got it?"

"Yeah. Sure."

"I see you have a guitar." McLaren nodded toward the instrument, wanting to establish some rapport and break the ice.

"Right."

"How long have you been playing?"

"About three and a half years. It was actually Luke's."

"Really?"

"Yeah. His first one, he said. But he got better so he got a better guitar. He gave that one to me when I said one day I'd like to learn."

"Nice that you have something that meant a lot to him. Sort of continues the friendship, I expect."

"Whatever you want. Sure." Philip glanced at his watch and sighed loudly. "Get on with it."

McLaren picked up a guitar pick on the sofa and ran his thumb across the hard plastic edges. "You know, Phil, if everyone were as compassionate as you are, there'd be no need for hell. You'd make life a living one and no one'd have to go anywhere." He shifted slightly, bending closer to Philip.

"I don't know a thing about Luke's disappearance, if that's where you're steerin' this. The coppers asked me back then and now you're messin' with me. I wish to God everyone'd lay off."

"I will. As soon as we have a decent conversation between two gentlemen. Right." He smiled again and crossed his arms over his chest. "I heard a nasty rumor that you asked Luke for drugs. What about it?"

Philip tilted his head to one side and smirked. "If that's all that's botherin' you, you don't know what's happenin' in our society, mate. That's nothin' at all. You make it sound like I killed him."

"Maybe you did."

"You can say anythin' you like but it don't make it so. Grow up."

"Why did you approach Luke for drugs? Your

usual source dry up?"

"You're even stupider than the coppers, mate. Everybody knows athletes and musicians float on drugs. It's their world. They can get anything they want at any time. They've got connections."

"You think everyone's as dirty and pathetic as you are, obviously."

"I'm lookin' at a good example, aren't I?" Philip grinned and slumped back into the sofa.

"Did Luke come through for you?"

Philip snorted and screwed up his mouth. "I never said I asked him. You hard of hearin' in your old age? All I said was that athletes and musicians live in that world and they can get what they want. I just had a nice chat with Luke one day. I wanted to give him some big brother-type advice. I was older than him by two years. I felt a kind of…oh, an obligation…to keep him clean and on the right path. I didn't want him strayin' into the drug scene 'cause no matter how he went—music or sports—he'd run into the bloke who wasn't as upstandin' as he was."

"You go to church daily, do you?"

Philip looked at the time and leaned forward, his forearms on his thighs.

"You're a real concerned citizen, Phil. Maybe you should lecture in schools about the evils of drug use. Has this come about from experience or have you ever been arrested for drug possession?"

"Are you stupid?"

"Meaning what? You don't use or you've never been nicked?"

"What do you think? I don't make mistakes."

"You still haven't answered my question about

your own drug use or about approaching Luke."

"I told you I never said I asked him. How much plainer do I have to make it?"

"But you do use."

Philip crossed his arms on his chest and frowned. "Look. I've had it with you and with this conversation. You're not a copper and you can't nick me for anythin', so bugger off before I phone the rozzers to have you hauled off."

McLaren shrugged and looked around the room.

"Pardon the mess. Good help is so hard to find."

"Just so you don't find yourself up to your arse in my investigation, you'll be all right."

"Is that a threat, McLaren?"

"Just big brother advice, Phil. I'd hate for you to make a big mistake."

"Looks like you made a few mistakes yourself, mate. You get those bruises and that bloody eye shakin' hands with a snowman?" He laughed and snuggled into the corner of the sofa.

"I'd say you should see the other bloke, but you wouldn't believe me."

"You're damned right." Philip angled his wrist so he could see his watch. "You're beginnin' to bore me. You about finished?"

"Just about."

A knock on the door interrupted him. Philip called, "Come on in," but remained seated. "You know, McLaren," he said, keeping McLaren's attention on him, "you just might be right. Maybe I've been too hasty about all this. Maybe I should tell you the whole thing. Don't they say confession is good for the soul?" He smiled, laying his arms along the top of the sofa, and spoke very slowly. "You see, it was like this, McLaren. Luke and I—"

That was the last thing McLaren remembered before waking up in the dark, the feeling of cold and the panic of imprisonment in a small space nearly crippling him.

Chapter Thirteen

It was the aroma that saved his sanity, he thought later, telling it to Jamie. They sat in McLaren's living room, two tableside lamps on, a pot of coffee on the low wooden table, and the black sky outside the multi-paned windows hinting at an eternity of time.

Jamie set his coffee cup on the table and tilted the lampshade so the light shone on McLaren's face. "You don't look any different than when I last saw you, although your bruises have started to fade a bit. I don't think your eye is as red as it was. Where'd you get hit?" He leaned closer, trying to discern the wound site.

"Back of my head. Yeah, there. Ouch, damn it!" He pushed Jamie's hand away and turned his head. "Get that blasted light out of my eyes."

"You're all right. Your temper hasn't suffered any." He repositioned the shade and sat back. "And you've no idea as to who slugged you."

"I told you. I was having a friendly chat with Philip Moss—"

"I can imagine how friendly that was."

"—and all of a sudden I wake up in my car."

"In the car park at Philip's flat?"

McLaren touched the sore spot on his head and winced. "No. He or the git who slugged me must've driven me to the river and left me. The other one—whether Philip or his chum—probably followed in one of their cars and then they drove back to the flat."

"Or to chummy's place. You've no idea who the bloke was."

"No. But it had to be a mate of Philip's. When this guy knocked on the door, Philip didn't seem surprised. In fact, I think he was expecting this guy, because he kept looking at his watch all the while I was there. He yelled for the guy to come in, smiled at me, and all of a sudden I wake up in my car."

"Not the best conversational ending you've ever had."

McLaren reached for his coffee cup and took a sip. "When I came to, I didn't know where I was. It was pitch black and bloody cold. I realized I was in a small space but I didn't know…" He broke off, suddenly conscious he was going to relate the story again of his childhood terror. He had no reason to recount it. Jamie knew about his overnight imprisonment in a cellar, the terror of the dark and the small mouse-infested area, the rustlings in the black space, the feel of tiny claws and hairless tails running over his legs. He had yelled for help until he had no voice, pounded on the door until his hands were numb and raw. No one had known he was missing. And might not have known for many more hours. The search had been extensive, McLaren's parents asking Jamie and other friends where McLaren might have gone. In the end, Jamie had supplied the clue that led to McLaren's rescue. After that, the deserted house had been torn down, but he still carried the emotional scars of the event. He was still that terrified ten-year-old boy when confronted with absolute dark, confined small spaces, and mice.

"At least Philip and his mate didn't really harm you, Mike." Jamie smiled, trying to look cheerful to soothe McLaren's fears. "He could've killed you."

"I realize that. Either the git who knocked me out could've ended my life then and there, or they could've done it at the river." He paused, envisioning his drowning in the wintry stream, his burial in a snowy bank. It might be spring before his body would be found… "Evidently, they were sending me a message."

"Stay away?" Jamie glanced at his friend as he swallowed another mouthful of coffee. "I thought that's what email was for."

McLaren ignored the attempted joke. "Either 'Stay away' or 'See what we can do to you if we wish?' It's not a pleasant thought whichever message you prefer. I know they could've killed me."

"No love lost between you, then."

McLaren snorted and filled his cup. The hot coffee didn't do a thing for his throbbing head but it kept him awake. And he had to think through this now while it was fresh in his mind. "The other thing I realized—other than the dark and small space—" He paused and swallowed, the old panic simmering in his blood. "The other thing I remember was the smell."

"You said that. What was it, specifically?"

"The odor in that place kept me sane until I was fully cognizant of where I was, that I was in my car and in the wood. Not back in—" He broke off, embarrassed that he was about to talk about his childhood adventure again. He took a slow sip of coffee, willing his racing heart to slow down, and held the cup in both hands. It was the tactile realization that planted him in the moment and in his house. "I saw the moonlight shining through the pine boughs and on a patch of river ice. I saw the stretch of snow among the trees and could hear the faint ripple of water over stone. But that was after the odor jarred me into full consciousness." He glanced outside, measuring the hue of the night sky with the canopy in the wood. "It was the smell of oil."

"*Oil?* Like cooking or motor?"

"Motor oil. That petroleum base is instantly recognizable."

"Did you smell that on Philip when you were at his flat?"

McLaren shook his head. "He works in the car repair department at Frasers' dealership, though. Still, he smelled fresh as a daisy."

"At least he's a break from some of the usual yobos you deal with."

"The only other thing that sticks in my mind is the impression of dirty fingernails."

"Not Philip's, though."

"No. He was clean. It may be a flash I saw out of the corner of my eye. I can't quite remember."

"But it could connect with the motor oil smell. If this mate of Philip's was also a car mechanic, it would make sense."

McLaren nodded and drained the last of the hot liquid. The cup scraped across the china saucer, disturbing the sudden quiet.

"At least it's not connected to your last assault. At the pub," Jamie reminded his friend. "You said that bloke smelled of fresh laundry."

"I don't know if that's particularly reassuring. *Two* blokes out to get me?"

"Do you want me to have Philip's car searched for your DNA?"

McLaren sighed heavily and said that wouldn't

help. "They probably used my car, and Philip or his pal drove it. But even if they hauled me in one of their cars, it doesn't bring me closer to solving Luke's disappearance. And I don't want to go off on a tangent with this assault. I need to focus on Luke right now."

"What about the little break-in tonight?"

"Before I got here?"

"How many more are there? Of *course* before you got here." Jamie glanced at the overturned chairs near the fireplace and the papers strewn around McLaren's office.

"I'd make a hell of a witness. The bloke was running away when I drove up. All I remember is a not-too-tall dark figure. Not any different from my car park friend."

"You arrived in time, yet too late to do any good. Do you have any thought on who ransacked your house? *Why* he did it is fairly obvious if it's the same bastard who broke into your car." He shook his head and bent over to pick up a book from the floor. "What's he after?"

"I hope it's not money. I'd hate to see what he'd do when he realizes this is all there is."

"Be serious, Mike. The house break-in following on the heels of friend Phil's parting shot is awfully obvious. What's he want?"

"Tom could be the culprit. It doesn't have to be Phil. I kinda upset him a little the other day."

"Phil or Tom. Great. Whomever. You still haven't told me what they're looking for."

"Hell if I know. Are case notes too mundane?"

Jamie stopped running his thumb along the corner of the book and fanning the pages. He set it on the coffee table. "Not if those yobos are worried you have something on them. They'd want to stop you and destroy any evidence you might have."

"*What* evidence? I can't even identify the car park attacker, let alone discern where Luke is."

"But Chummy doesn't know that. You're driving around, asking a lot of embarrassing questions, the sound of jingling handcuffs not far behind you. They're probably scared spitless and wondering what the hell you know."

McLaren swallowed the last of his coffee and stretched. An owl called urgently from a tree near the front door, then quiet descended once more. "You could be right. It makes sense."

"You're damned right."

"The other thing that makes sense is that Tom IDed the weapon my attacker used in the car park."

Jamie choked on his coffee and let McLaren slap his back before he expressed his surprise in several choice words.

"I'm serious, Jamie. Did you ever find anything when you searched the pub's car park?"

"Not a thing, as I told you earlier on the phone. When the officers and I got there, the cupboard was bare, metaphorically speaking. Why ask me again?"

"Just making sure. Tom found three guitar strings across the street, very close to the pub. New, unbroken."

"Guitar strings…"

"Wire, not nylon. Do anything for you?"

"I don't play, as you know, but I bet three strings twisted together into a thicker mass would make a nice ligature."

"Hard for the victim to break and it quickly cuts into the throat, yes."

Jamie nodded, his gaze on the carpet, envisioning the scene of the attack. "And Tom found these the following day?"

"Yeah. Before you returned that morning." McLaren explained about Tom's job and early morning start.

"Four-thirty is a bit before we started work," Jamie admitted. "You think he's telling the truth?"

"Why should he lie about that? If he attacked me, he could've said he bought the strings. He wouldn't point me to the scene of the crime by sitting outside and plaiting strings together, either. He'd not want me to see he retrieved the weapon."

"That's true."

"No, Jamie, those strings have to be the weapon. My attacker dropped them when he fled."

"Well, if Tom hadn't found them, we would have. Do the strings suggest anyone?"

"Not really. It hints at Bethany or John, but a man jumped me. And a young one."

"So those two are eliminated."

"Phil has a guitar, but he knows I've seen it. He wouldn't be so stupid to use a weapon that would direct me to him."

Jamie muttered that they rarely had that much good luck in a case. "So where does that leave you?"

"Besides my sore throat?" McLaren shook his head and said it was just another loose string at the moment.

"Mike, even if Tom and Phil wouldn't wave a red flag at you, they're still a threat."

"So is Luke's killer."

"This isn't funny. You want me to take over? I can poke around on my day off. It's this Saturday."

"Gary didn't turn to you. No offense, Jamie."

"No, but maybe if our two wide boys hear that it's once again an official police investigation that could land them in the nick—"

"I'll be all right. I'll tread softly."

"And I'll be the new Chief Constable. Fine. It's your poor bruised body. Just swear that you'll proceed slowly and cautiously. I've got used to having you around. I hate to drink alone."

Quiet welled between them. Jamie glanced at his friend. McLaren hadn't changed his expression. Jamie sighed, trying to cover his outburst and hoping he hadn't sounded maudlin. "Well…" He glanced at his watch. "Anything else? You sure you don't want to go somewhere to be seen to? You could be concussed from that knock on your head."

"I'm fine. Just sore."

"All right. If you're sure…" He got up. "Good thing I'm on evening shift today. At least I'll get a few hours of sleep. Which is probably more than you'll get, if I know you. You'll sit up, trying to piece things together."

McLaren snapped his fingers and Jamie groaned. "Mike, enough for now. You need to get some rest."

"I'll get some rest when I've got it figured out. Jamie, please, just another minute. How about this…" He sat down and gestured for Jamie to reclaim his seat. "I'm just thinking…"

"God help us."

"They must've driven me out to the river quite soon after they knocked me out. When I woke up, it was just more than ninety minutes after Philip last looked at the time."

"Which was…?"

"I got to his flat at four o'clock. We talked for maybe ten minutes and then I see stars."

"So, assuming they lugged you into a vehicle right away, that'd take them, oh, five minutes to do. And they drove you to the River Lathkill and dropped you just outside the Dale. They were taking a chance, moving you at that hour. Sure, it's January and it gets dark a bit past four-thirty, but it's not exactly three in the morning. They were probably holding their breath the whole time."

"They probably weren't taking too great a risk carting me out the door. It took five minutes, like you said. From the look of Philip's block of flats, most people were probably inside, asleep and resting up for their nighttime fun. Not too many witnesses."

Jamie paused, considering the scenario. "Well, thank God you were still in your car instead of on the moor. At least you could drive home."

"After I knew where I was." McLaren shook his head, remembering the area. "Thank God for that old pump house. It took me a minute to place it, but once I did, well, I knew where I was. It only took me slightly more than a half hour to get home at that time of night."

"Why there, I wonder. Why not just dump you some place in Chesterfield, if that's where Philip lives?"

"Two reasons, the way I read it. First, they dumped me in a fairly desolate spot so they wouldn't run the risk of being spotted. It's less populated with potential witnesses, instead of the traffic-choked A6, for example. Second, it goes back to that message again, I think. This is what we can do with you, McLaren. We had you in our power, and we could've killed you any number of ways."

"Nice, warming thought."

"Anyway, getting back to the question of transportation… I think Luke had to have been driven off some place. The police did a thorough search of all buses and trains in the area. They did appeals on radio and television and came up with nothing. Which doesn't preclude Luke's helpful driver from keeping his mouth shut, but it gets me to thinking."

"About whom, in particular?"

"Philip."

"You think he drove Luke someplace?"

"I've heard a few rumors about Luke being seen with Tom Yardley or given a lift by Callum, but I can't prove it."

"And they're not going to admit it if they want to stay free of any entanglements in the case."

"Right. But about Philip… I don't think he necessarily drove Luke anyplace. I'm thinking more of the transportation tonight."

"Using your own car. Sure."

McLaren's forefinger tapped against his lips and he frowned. He spoke slowly, thinking through the scenario. "Philip works in a car repair department. He has access to them because the owners leave them there overnight, many times, to be worked on." He looked at Jamie, waiting for the connection.

Jamie nodded. "Sure. Who'd be the wiser of a few extra miles on the mileometer? The mileage is recorded when the owners bring them in, but what owner looks at the car's mileage when he picks up his car? Would he notice the car's been driven a few extra miles?" He looked at McLaren, his eyes shining in the lamplight. "We don't have any proof. We'll never get any proof after three years. All that mileage has…"

"Gone by the wayside?" McLaren leaned back and rubbed his forehead. "Does it make sense?"

"Sure, but like I said, we can't prove it."

"Pity. It's rather brilliant, that. Borrowing a car, using it for a job, then returning it. There's no way it'd be traced back to you if you didn't get into a traffic accident."

Jamie looked thoughtful and his gaze became serious. "We know friend Philip belongs to a gang."

"Yeah. He's the leader of what there is. There are two and a half of them, unless there are a few more under stones that I haven't turned over."

"Could this be an initiation?"

"What? Carting me out of the way?"

"Yeah. Or Luke's disappearance. Whichever you like."

"I don't like either, but I doubt it. Philip's just a small yobo who wants to be Crime Boss someday but doesn't know how to go about it. He's really nothing more than a bully and he manages his subordinates with fear. Why?"

"I'm just hoping the next initiation or job isn't to top someone. If you got up his nose, next time you may wind up in the morgue."

McLaren nodded, then looked at Jamie and smiled. "The morgue isn't my idea of a good time, no. So I feel the need to get even."

"Get even? How?"

"Did you read that police report you emailed to me?"

"Not lately. Why?"

"Oh, something in it just sprang to mind. Harry Rooney mentioned Philip having a set time to pick up drugs." He paused, watching Jamie's expression.

"You think that's connected to all that time-consultation he did while you were in his flat?"

McLaren shrugged. "Could be. You want to find out?"

"Sure. I may as well get some points with the Super by nabbing a dealer. When?"

McLaren outlined his plan, and Jamie whistled cheerfully.

****

McLaren slept fitfully, the hours alternating between dreams of drowning in a locked room and bouts of sleeplessness. The dark of open space usually held comfort for him, wrapping him in rest and the pleasure of star gazing or listening for owls. But that night it magnified the fear that lurked constantly at the back of his mind, that waited for a chink in his resolve to keep it at bay so it could flood his memory and reduce him to a sobbing child again. Some time during his wakeful hours, he turned onto his side and gazed out the window. The moon sat like a huge egg on the top most branch of the willow in the front garden. No breath of air stirred the bare branches, and the moon seemed as though it could happily remain there forever. Yet, the next time he looked, it had glided southward and now peeked at him as a sliver of silver at the frame of the window. He must have fallen asleep without realizing, for when he looked again, the sky was black and starless.

The ringing alarm clock pulled him from an encounter with Philip, and his palm smacked the top of the clock. The sudden quiet was nearly as abrupt as the insistent beep. He struggled to a sitting position, his legs dangling over the edge of the bed, and ran his hand over his chest. He wasn't dreaming; he was alive.

He blinked himself awake and moved slightly so he sat in the sunlight. It crept around the edge of the curtain, angling into the dark corners and chasing away the bogeymen. He thought he'd never in all his life been so glad to hear the alarm ring.

His head throbbed, but he had expected that. It would probably hurt for another day or two. He looked at his face in the bathroom mirror and noticed that the bruising was changing from purple to yellow or indigo. Good. Those would be gone in a few days. His bloodied eye still held traces of redness but it, too, was healing. He whistled as he showered, shaved and dressed.

He found the watch among the socks in the dresser drawer. Though not a Rolex, it was still an expensive make, but the leather strap was worn. The buckle was missing the metal tongue. Probably why the watch fell from the wearer's wrist, he thought. He stuffed the watch into his trousers pocket. It'd be gone if the owner returned to do further searches.

After a quick meal of baked porridge and pears, he did the washing up, then grabbed his guitar from its case. He took it to the back room and sat on the sofa, his slippered feet propped up on the coffee table. He tuned the guitar, taking his time and getting each string exactly in pitch. Some days he didn't care if the string was slightly flat or sharp, but this morning it mattered.

He was in a strange mood, wanting perfection. Perhaps it stemmed from the progress he'd made yesterday, zeroing in on the solution to Luke's disappearance. Perhaps he was hyper about Friday and his date with Dena. Which didn't quite make sense. He was no seventeen-year-old out with a girl for the first time. It was Dena, whom he loved and would soon marry. If he felt anxious about her now, what would their married life be like?

Which might explain why he was hesitant to begin his day.

He fingered some chords and idly ran his right thumb over the strings. It sounded in pitch. All he had to do was decide on a song.

He was halfway through "The Swans' Song" when a fragment of Nathan Watson's conversation nudged into his mind. He set the guitar on the sofa and leaned forward, rubbing his head. Nathan had said he and Bethany couldn't afford to have children yet, but a photo of an infant sat in their living room. And he'd seen a picture book that morning on the kitchen table.

McLaren went into his office and got a sheet of paper and a pen from the desk drawer. He listed the people who could be considered as having parented Ashley's child. A child, he reminded himself, whose birth date preceded Ashley's wedding date, if the nursery school enrollment was correct.

It took only a minute, if that. There weren't that many people that he knew:

Ashley
Callum
Luke
Bethany

Nathan

Harry

He hesitated as he considered adding Philip and Tom to the list, then wrote them in before he changed his mind. Just because he thought them to be non-starters and little more than vermin didn't mean some woman had avoided a sexual fling. Also, there were John Evans, Gary Barber, Darren Fraser and Doc Tipton. They were older than the men in his first list by twenty or thirty years. Still…

He set the list aside, not sure what it told him. Maybe he needed a woman's viewpoint.

Dena answered her phone with a cheery "Morning, Michael."

"Morning, sweets." He sank against the back of the chair, grinning. Hearing her voice, knowing she was safe, eased his headache more than any medication could. He angled the phone against his ear. "You had me worried yesterday. I tried calling you several times but got no answer."

"I tried calling you several times, too."

"I know. I picked up your messages a bit later. I had the phone off. I didn't want to be interrupted while I was talking to someone."

"That's what I assumed. I hope you won't be mad, Michael, but I rang up Jamie and gave him a message for you, in case you and he spoke before I could get you."

"I was going to phone you this morning, to see what you wanted. What did you want?"

Dena told him about researching the birth and burial records. "I just thought you should know, Michael. Please don't be mad at me."

He let out his breath in a slow, silent sigh.

"Michael, you're cross."

He closed his eyes and rubbed his forehead.

"Michael, talk to me."

"Dena, I wish you wouldn't do this."

"Do what? Help you?"

"Not that I expect a repeat of last year's episode, but if you remember what happened the previous time you played Sherlock—"

"I knew you'd be cross."

"If you knew, then why did you meddle?"

"I thought you needed some help. You're doing all this alone, Michael. Surely a little bit of time at the library, to find things out for you—"

"I appreciate the thought, Dena, but I can handle this myself. I don't want to jeopardize your safety."

Dena pulled in her bottom lip and pressed her fingertips against it. "You sound like Jamie, when I told him yesterday."

"Then you should know it's not a smart thing to do."

"I was hoping you'd want the information."

"I do. I'm glad to have it, but I would've got to looking at those matters today." He stared at her photo. It looked at him from across the room. "Will you promise me you won't help me anymore?"

"Michael—"

"Please, Dena. I won't be able to trust you with anything if I know you're going to traipse around the country. Did anyone overhear you when you spoke to Jamie?"

"I doubt it."

"What does that mean?"

"There were three people sitting on a bench next to me, but I turned my back to them. I doubt if they heard anything. Besides, they were older and were talking about shopping and the weather and such. They weren't interested."

McLaren sighed loudly and sat up. "I hope not."

"So, what are you going to do about that, about what I told you? Why would Gary Barber lie about his wife's burial? What does that mean?"

He hesitated, amazed that she'd jumped to the conclusion that he would've seen if he weren't so methodical. He stared at the list, then tossed it into the waste can as he tried to recall his talk with Nathan. The sound of a motorcycle roaring up the road broke the quiet. "I wish I knew."

"Why do you think Bethany gave up her child?" She paused, hoping that would get him to talk to her and forgive her. "That's what you think, isn't it? Because she has that photo in her front room, and that picture book? They're keepsakes from her child, not something recent, like a niece she might have."

McLaren sighed, the question prodding him from his contemplation of her photograph. "Yeah, that's what I think. The discrepancy of Ashley's marriage and the age of her daughter matches with what you found. Although it could be a coincidence. People do have affairs or have the honeymoon before the wedding."

"Ashley and Callum, you mean. You think it's really their child?"

"It doesn't matter what I think. None of this is illegal. But no, I don't think it's their daughter. I still think it's Bethany and Nathan's. Doesn't that birth certificate prove it?"

"Just from those dates? Is that what makes you believe this?"

"That, yes, but Nathan said he didn't want any children yet."

"So Bethany gets pregnant and they give it up for adoption." Dena sighed sharply and gripped the phone tighter. "That's horrible. It must've been a terribly difficult thing for her to do. She obviously still loves her daughter if she's kept the photo and book."

McLaren nodded, images of Bethany and Ashley flitting through his mind.

"So, what about Margaret?" Dena spoke hesitantly, unsure if she should change the subject. "Don't you think it's incredibly strange that I can't find anything about her death or burial?"

"I wouldn't if she died some other place, but from Gary's account, and other people I've talked to, she died there. So, yes, I'd have expected some mention in the local newspaper."

"I even looked up notices in Liverpool, and she wasn't mentioned."

"For a specific year?"

"No. I padded it. Five years on either side."

"You should've found something in a ten-year range, then." He sank back against the chair and sighed loudly. "I don't know, Dena. I don't understand."

"Me neither. It's so silly. Why lie about the date of his wife's death?"

"Maybe it'll come to me in a flash of inspiration. But thanks for the help."

"Even though I shouldn't have meddled." She said it light-heartedly, trying to win his forgiveness.

"Even though." The resignation in his voice told

her he was grateful even if he was slightly annoyed.

"What have you got planned for today?"

McLaren glanced at the notes he'd scribbled. Many names were crossed off; some had memos beside them; some had question marks or were underlined. "I want to speak to Sharon Fraser, for starters."

"You think she knows about Margaret's death?"

"I'm not worried about that right now, though that is needling me and I want to find out. She lied about working on the day Luke disappeared and I need to know why."

"Speaking of lies…I found an interesting photo in one of the newspapers I looked at yesterday. No, Michael, don't groan like that. I'm going to email it to you. You'll forget all about Sharon when you see this." There was a moment's silence before Dena exclaimed, "There! It's sent. Look at it and tell me what you think."

"What is it? Does it have to do with this case, or just some interesting titbit you uncovered regarding tigers or something?"

"Don't get cute. It's a photo of your Doc Tipton and his brother."

"Are you going to tell me or is this Twenty Questions?"

"If you're going to make fun—"

"I just got it. Hold on." He opened the email and clicked on the attachment. The photo showed Alan and Albert Tipton. "I know about the brothers. Is there something more to this?"

"Oh, Michael, I have to go. Just read the article and we can talk about it tonight, if that's okay."

"Dena—"

“Really, Michael, I can’t talk any more. I’ll be late. We’ll talk later. I love you.” She rang off before he could say anything else.

He hung up and looked at the photograph. The two brothers grinned at the camera, though tennis champion Albert smiled the more widely, having accepted an award for volunteer recognition. Gary Barber stood between them, shaking hands with both.

McLaren leaned toward the computer screen, frowning. He enlarged the photo and stared. He remembered seeing a photo of the other brother, Alan, at Doc’s house, but now that he saw it close up he saw they were identical twins. Except that Albert was clean-shaven and Alan sported a modest moustache that nearly touched the mole at the corner of his mouth. Gary Barber had more hair on his head and less wrinkles, but the photo was twenty-five years old, and people certainly aged in that length of time. He smiled, made a notation in his notebook, and closed the email.

He got up and was heading for the dining room where his jacket hung over the back of a chair when the phone rang. He returned to his office and picked up the receiver. “Jamie. You’re out and about early. Not working today?”

“Such a wag. Comedy isn’t your style this early in the day, Mike. I do roll out of bed in time for roll call, you know.”

“Your unblemished record is something all the lads hope to attain, I know. So, what’s going on?”

“I had a message from Dena yesterday. She couldn’t get you and she had some message for you.”

“I just spoke to her, thanks. I got her phone messages, too. You at the station already?”

"I'm not going there today. Why? You need something? If it's more rifling through old files or postmortem reports—"

"I thought you said you were working."

"Not all police work occurs at the station, Mike. You of all people should know that."

"I'll refrain from replying how I'd like to and merely ask where you are."

"Just about fifteen minutes from Manchester."

"Manchester…? Why? What's going on?"

"I'm on a committee. It's a bi-annual thing. We're meeting today."

"Something stimulating like new requisition procedures for paperclips?"

"New provisions relating to mentally disordered and mentally handicapped people," Jamie said, mechanically rattling off the committee name. "Why? Do you need something? I won't be back until tonight, but if that's too late—"

"Will you be able to look something up for me?"

A silence filled the phone while McLaren imagined Jamie glancing heavenward and praying.

"Jamie?"

"Yeah?" His voice sounded wary.

"You okay?"

"Just wondering if Manchester's nick is more luxuriant than ours."

"It's nothing illegal. I'm not asking you to get on their computer system."

"That's a relief. I told Paula I'd be back for dinner."

"Are you going to listen or just think up smart replies?"

"What do you want, then?"

"You know that case I'm working on…"

"I've heard something about it, Mike."

"Can you find out something for me?"

"In person?"

McLaren stared at his computer screen. "No. Make a few phone calls."

"Make a few… When? Now? I've got to be at the station—"

"No, Not now. Whenever you have a break, or at lunch, if you have a minute."

"How many calls? Where to?"

"I'll email you the info. Not many, though. However many cemeteries there are in Liverpool."

Jamie hadn't expected that. He blinked rapidly and stammered. "C-cemeteries? What the hell is going on?"

"Just something to do with Gary's wife."

"Margaret? What about her?"

"I have an idea and I need to follow it."

"So the calls are to the cemeteries inquiring about Margaret, then." He didn't sound thrilled.

"*You* can't do it?"

"You're closer, Jamie. Besides, you're always asking if you can help me."

Jamie slowed down to let a car pass. "Sure. But something easy, like running after bad guys. Phone calls, however—"

"It'd be better if you could go to each one and talk to the superintendent or whomever, but a phone call will do."

"Thanks. You're so considerate."

"Give me a minute to email you the list. I'll look up the cemeteries and phone numbers and then you can take it from there."

"I repeat. You're so considerate."

"If you don't want to do it—"

"No, no. I'll do it. I'm in this far, so I may as well make your calls. You need it all done today?"

"It'd be nice, yeah."

"It's not necessarily urgent, then."

"Not life or death, no. Another day or two won't hurt."

"Good. I have this odd quirk. I'd rather not do anything to hurt my career." He rang off, promising McLaren he'd ring him up that evening when he returned home.

McLaren spent several minutes looking up and typing the names of the cemeteries in and around Liverpool. He debated about actually sending them, considering he might be wasting Jamie's time and trying his patience. But Jamie had the advantage of police authority, whereas McLaren was just a nosey citizen, as many people reminded him. So if anyone balked at looking into cemetery records, Jamie would have the needed legal muscle to handle it.

He hit the computer's SEND button and waited for the 'ding' to announce that the email had gone off before he slipped into his jacket, grabbed his keys, and left the house.

****

The weather hadn't changed much from yesterday; a hint of approaching snow laced the cold morning air. Frost painted the concrete path and cracked beneath his shoes. He whistled "The Swans' Song," picking up where he'd stopped playing it a half hour ago, got into his car, and drove to Chesterfield.

The B6057 was crowded, having picked up many drivers around Newbold, a village north of Chesterfield. As he passed the sign indicating the turnoff, he remembered the story of the underground tunnel said to link the village's Eyre's chapel with Chesterfield's crooked spire church. He smiled, briefly wondering if there was substance to the tale. But wouldn't there have to be if the predominantly Catholic Eyre family was on the wrong side during any of England's religious upheavals? And with the family's history winding back to their arrival in Britain with William the Conqueror in 1066… McLaren shook his head, wanting to believe the romantic tale.

A lorry passed him, its mud flaps swaying and curling in the breeze. He slowed as he entered the town and waited through several traffic signals before turning onto the street he wanted. The noise of traffic filled the car's interior even with the windows up, and he turned the volume up on Handel's *Royal Fireworks Suite*. He glanced around him as he parked outside the Frasers' car dealership. The road looked to be a solid mass of slowly moving cars. Whether everyone was hurrying to Chesterfield itself, or merely passing through on their way to eastern destinations, the town quickly swelled with workday cars and pedestrians.

McLaren glanced at his watch and waited for a few minutes before leaving his car. He'd arrived exactly at opening time, yet wanted to give Sharon a few minutes to settle behind the reception desk.

He entered the showroom, aware of the recorded doorbell-like sound announcing his presence. The floor glared in the morning sunlight and glanced off the highly waxed bodies of the vehicles sitting near the floor-to-ceiling windows. He paused inside the door, allowing his sight to adjust to the brightness, then walked over to the reception desk. Sharon looked up, smiling. The smile quickly faded as she realized who stood before her.

"Mr. McLaren." Her tone was cordial yet held no warmth. "Good morning."

McLaren flashed a grin, looking around the showroom. Two salesmen sat at a small table, sipping coffee. A third man stood behind a small glass-walled partition. Satisfied, McLaren placed his hand on the edge of the desk and leaned forward slightly. "Would you be able to give me a minute, Mrs. Fraser?"

Sharon glanced over her shoulder, perhaps looking for her husband. Or the cavalry. Seeing no customer, she turned back to McLaren and nodded. "What is it?"

"I just have a question or two."

"Why, uh, sure. What do you need to know?"

"You stated you were here on the day of Luke Barber's disappearance. Is that correct?"

She nodded, not wanting to trust her voice.

"Yet, I know for certain that you were not here working. You were home ill."

"How did you learn that?"

"Does it make any difference? We can consult your company personnel file and see that you were home ill, if you can't recall."

"I *was* ill. I stayed home. I don't see why that's so significant."

"Did you see a doctor?"

"No. There was no need to."

"If you were ill…"

"It was a sore throat and cough. Nothing to worry

the doctor about."

"Sounds uncomfortable. Did you stop at a chemist's for some medication?"

"No."

"Perhaps a neighbor came in with…chicken soup?" He tilted his head, looking concerned.

"The neighbors didn't know I was home. They assumed I was at work, as usual."

"You know for certain they thought that?"

Sharon narrowed her eyes and glared at him. "Your sarcasm isn't appreciated. I was ill that day. I don't see why you're questioning me. It's none of your business."

"So you've no witness or other documentation, such as a receipt for medicine, of your illness that day."

"I don't need to prove it to you or anyone else. The police didn't seem to think it warranted investigation, so why you're sticking your nose—"

"Just trying to be thorough, Mrs. Fraser."

"Your thoroughness is bordering on rudeness, in my opinion."

"I had no intention of being rude. Sorry if you feel that way. Now, without being rude or nosy, I ask you again why you told me you worked the day Luke went missing. You seem quite adamant now that you were home. Such a strong opinion must speak well for your memory. So, why do you recall this now and not a few days ago when I spoke to you?"

Sharon busied herself with rearranging a stack of papers on her desk.

"The longer you keep quiet, the more you raise my curiosity, Mrs. Fraser. And a whole lot of people—not all of them my friends—can attest to the fact that when I get curious, sometimes not so pleasant things happen."

He stood with his arms across his chest. A hint of a smile showed on his lips as he glanced around the showroom. He seemed to be resolved to staying there all day.

Sharon laid her hand on top of the papers and looked up at McLaren. Her voice lost some of its defiant tone as she spoke. “Perhaps I was wrong about the date. That was what…three years ago? Can you remember where you were on a particular date three years ago?”

“Usually not. But if it was tied in with the disappearance of a person I knew, I think I’d remember.”

Sharon shrugged, her eyes looking dull under the brilliant overhead lights. She toyed with the ring on her finger. “So what if I got it mixed up? What’s the difference?”

“The difference is that it casts doubt on your innocence. If you were home, without an alibi…” He let the significance suggest itself.

She raised her gaze from her finger to his eyes. Fright replaced the dull, bored expression, making her eyes shine in the light. She clutched her hands, the strength of her grip forcing the blood from her fingertips and leaving them white. “You can’t believe that! How could I induce Luke to leave Langheath?”

“Oh, I wouldn’t know specifically, but there are several incentives I can think of. Money is always good as a starter. If that doesn’t appeal to you, how about getting Callum to use a little muscle?”

“Callum! Are you round the twist? Why drag him into this?”

“If he were in love with your daughter and wanted

Luke out of the way, Callum might very readily agree to helping Luke leave town."

"That's nonsense. Callum had nothing to do with Luke's disappearance. And neither did I. You're completely clutching at straws, wanting to see your name in the papers, scoring where the police have failed." She sat up a bit straighter, the color returning to her cheeks. Now that she seemed to feel confident, her voice grew stronger. "I think you better leave now."

"Were you really ill that day, or was it just an excuse to stay home?"

Sharon stood up, her neck tightening. "I'll give you thirty seconds to vacate our property."

McLaren smiled and held up his hands in surrender. "Round Two goes to you, but the war's not over."

Chapter Fourteen

McLaren rounded out the morning by talking to Harry Rooney and Callum Fox again. Neither man had anything to add to their original statements and neither could remember seeing Sharon Fraser at home or in Langheath the afternoon of Luke's disappearance.

Back in his car, McLaren turned on his iPad and spent several minutes looking at photos of Alan and Albert Tipton. Then he logged off and drove to Gary Barber's farm.

Gary took McLaren's request to look around Luke's room with the nonchalance typical of Derbyshire country folk—neither surprised nor agitated, at least on the surface. Gary escorted McLaren into Luke's bedroom, yet remained outside the door, as he had during McLaren's first visit.

"What are ye lookin' to find, then?" Gary leaned against the doorjamb, his gaze on McLaren's movements. The collie padded up to the man and sat beside him.

"I don't know exactly. Something out of place. Something that will point me in another direction."

"Ye're not gettin' on well with yer investigation?"

"Oh, I'm doing all right, but I just thought I may have overlooked something."

"I've not moved a thing since…that night. I always thought Luke would be back, and I wanted him to find his room as he left it." He bowed his head, looking at the floor. "It gave me a bit o' hope to leave it that way, too. To live in the belief he'd be back."

"I'd have done the same thing, Mr. Barber."

"Oh?" Gary repositioned his pipe to the corner of his mouth and looked pleased. Several puffs of pale gray smoke drifted into the air.

"Certainly. Where would we be without hope?"

Gary nodded. "Well, take all the time ye need. I'm in no rush. The house'll be here for quite a while yet. Come, Toby." He patted the side of his thigh and the dog got up. He followed Gary down the hallway, and McLaren listened as the outside door shut behind them.

McLaren started at the dresser near the door and slowly, painstakingly, made his way around the room. Although he had looked through Luke's belongings before, he did so again, hoping he had overlooked something. He checked through the bed linen and under the mattress and pillow, in all the drawers of the dresser and desk, in every box, shoe and garment in the wardrobe, in the guitar case and the can of tennis balls. He fanned through the books of music and 3-ring binder of notes and event schedules, turned on Luke's computer and tablet and looked through the files, read the stray papers on the desk. He was about to admit there was nothing there when he looked again at the desk diary. The page was flipped to the day prior to the disappearance. He hadn't remembered the discrepancy before, so he turned to 20th January. McLaren paused with his hand above the page. Gary had indeed kept the room as Luke had left it. McLaren picked up the diary and angled the page toward the light. A penciled entry on the memo sheet was barely visible. He clicked on the desk lamp, held the page under the light, and read the entry.

3:30 PM

He turned to the front of the diary, thinking there might be a list of abbreviations. When he found nothing, he flipped through the month, but there were no other similar notes. The back of the diary held no clue to the appointment, so he replaced the diary and left the room. He found Gary inside the barn.

"Ye're empty-handed." Gary took the pipe from his mouth and eyed McLaren. "Didn't find anything useful?"

"I found a note to meet someone, but I don't know what the appointment was or where he was to go. Do you recall Luke mentioning he had a meeting or appointment at three-thirty the day he disappeared?"

Gary shook his head and jammed the pipe between his teeth. He took a puff before saying Luke wasn't due for his dental exam for another four months. "And he wasn't ill, so that rules out the doctor's surgery."

"Did he have an on-going date with someone? Perhaps it was weekly or monthly, but it was so regular that he didn't need to remind himself what it was?"

"Nothin' that I knew, sorry. And I'd know if he always left the house each Friday at half past three."

McLaren nodded, saying it was the only thing he could think of. "And that day he went missing…he didn't say he had to leave early to go anywhere or see someone? He was going to leave at the normal time, for all you know."

"Aye. That's why Bethany thought it so queer when he didn't show up a' her place. She expected him." Gary cleared the ground next to him with the toe of his boot, shoving aside the stray wisps of straw and dry leaves. He knocked his pipe against the fence and watched the spent tobacco drift to the ground. “I don’t know what to tell you other than that. But if he had a meetin’, it would’ve had to be close by and very quick if he was to be at Bethany’s by four.”

McLaren thanked Gary for his help and left, trying to remember who lived the nearest to the Barber farm.

****

Bethany had no idea where Luke would’ve gone at three-thirty, but agreed it had to have been in the village. For, as she reminded him, “to go anywhere in the village and be able to pick me up at four o’clock means he would’ve needed his car. And it’s still at the farm. So it wasn’t some appointment like for a hair cut or the doctor’s. It was a meeting with a person, and the man had to come to the farm.”

Which threw the suspicion on Gary Barber. Would he not have heard a car arrive or seen Luke talking to someone? Even without the sharp crunch of ice under foot, just walking across the graveled farmyard was as good as any alarm. Unless Gary had been in a field or doing some noisy work… McLaren sat in his car, his head against the headrest, and closed his eyes. What had Gary said about that afternoon? And that raised the question of motive; why would Gary kill his own son?

McLaren had also asked Bethany again about the men who had searched for Luke, about the areas where they had been stationed. Gary had been in the village looking around, but that was after Luke’s mysterious rendezvous, so that didn’t help. John had searched the fields, farm and outbuildings. Granted, the farm could include the house, which might give him plenty of time to wander into Luke's room and scribble the appointment on the desk diary. But it made no sense. If John wanted to incriminate someone, why not just write down a name? Plus, that would suggest he knew Luke was gone for good. Did his behavior or history with the boy warrant that?

Besides, Bethany sat by the phone, acting as the command center. She would've known if John had taken an inordinate time in Luke's room.

But Gary had assigned everyone to specific posts. Maybe he took the village on purpose, knowing where to find Luke and help him out of town.

Again, it made no sense. Again it meant that Gary was connected with the entire vanishing act. Did Luke need to get away from someone, perhaps due to a personal problem? What problems did he have besides choosing between tennis and music, deciding to marry Ashley, and leaving his dad alone on the farm?

McLaren rubbed his eyes and noted the time. Dusk was well advanced, throwing the land into hues of gray and deep indigo. The school neighboring Bethany's place had let its charges go hours ago, the rooms and halls now empty and quiet. The shadows would be creeping across the floors and coloring the air; the darkening light would soon hide everything from sight and throw a restful mantle on the day.

He turned the key in the ignition and roared away from the curb, suddenly anxious to get home and confer with Jamie.

****

He'd begun compiling a list of motive and people when he heard the crunch of car tires on gravel. He walked to the front door and waited on the porch as

Jamie parked and came up the walkway. The light from the lamppost stretched his shadow behind him and illuminated his face.

"You look knackered," McLaren said as he closed the door behind them. "Rough committee meeting?"

"Rough list you gave me." He tossed his jacket and car key onto the sofa and looked at the dining room table. "You got anything for a tired old man who's given his last ounce of energy for his mate?" He headed for the sofa but McLaren guided him to a chair around the dining room table.

"Look at my list while I rummage around for something to take your mind off your troubles."

"I considered stopping at the off-license in the village, but I figured you'd have a fridge stocked with all necessities."

"I do. I expected you." McLaren's voice floated out of the kitchen, followed by the sound of the fridge door opening and closing, a metal cap popping and falling to the worktop, and liquid pouring into a glass. "First aid." He came into the dining room and handed the glass mug of beer to his friend. "You want something to eat?"

"What've you got?"

"Plenty of stuff for sandwiches."

"Say no more. Sit still. I'll do the cooking. You need to sit and heal." He wandered into the kitchen, pulled plates from the cupboard, and minutes later returned with four roast beef, tomato and cheese sandwiches. As he set the plates on the table he smiled. "I think I can think, now. I rushed right here from Manchester. Traffic's murder."

"How'd you come?"

"The A57 and then south. Why?"

"Just wondering. There are probably no great routes at this time of day."

"Speaking of routes…Did you have any luck with friend Philip?"

"I learned he goes to a drop off place to get his supply. He never meets anyone, so I don't have the supplier's name. I persuaded his chum Tom Yardley to tell me when and where the next purchase is made. I implied that I was interested only in that, so he wouldn't feel as though he was completely betraying Phil."

"And he was all right with that?"

McLaren flashed a smile. "I don't know, but he seemed relieved that I didn't slug him. He somehow got the idea I wanted in on the deals and wouldn't say anything to the police if I got a percentage of the profit."

"He could readily believe that, I've no doubt."

"Funny what a bit of previous muscle flexing will do to color a bloke's perception."

"So when do you want me?"

"Tonight. It's in Chesterfield, in a not too desirable section. Are you up for it?"

"Are you kidding? Nothing like a shot of good news to revive the body."

"Good. I was hoping that would be the case." He outlined his plan and visibly relaxed when Jamie said he couldn't see any holes in it.

"You're not doing this solely for revenge, are you, Mike?" Jamie raised his eyebrow, giving McLaren a look mixed with suspicion and anxiety.

"Me? You're joking."

"Vengeance is best served cold, you know, if that's where you're heading."

"It's cold enough outside, Jamie. We've got snow on the ground, remember?"

"You know what I mean. I don't mind a bit of pay back to a toe rag like Phil Moss, but I don't want your emotions to take over." He refrained from bringing up the Charlie Harvester episode that happened last month in Scotland.

McLaren snorted and waved away Jamie's concern. "I'm not that angry, for God's sake. I just want to teach him a bit of humility and manners."

"And if you get to compound that with a touch of score settling, you won't complain, right?"

"I see nothing remotely wrong with combining that with the removal of a drug dealer. So no, I'm not complaining."

"That's *if* Phil Moss caves in and talks to you tonight. Which, I admit, he probably will."

"I *can* be very persuasive, can't I?" McLaren smiled and picked up his drink.

Jamie took a bite of his sandwich and sagged against the chair back. "Fine. Since you're not going to change your mind we've got an hour before we have to leave." He looked again at the table. "Do we have to sit here?"

"Why? What's wrong with the chair?"

"Nothing if you want to keep awake. How about the sofa? It's more comfortable."

"I need you awake. That's why you're here, remember? The cemeteries will haunt you if you don't give me the information."

Jamie carried the plates into the living room,

returned for his beer, and wedged the sheets of paper and pen under his arm. He deposited them on the coffee table before plopping onto the sofa. He patted the cushion next to him. "There's room for you, Mike. We can work here just as well as at the table."

McLaren sighed loudly and sat next to Jamie. "You better."

"Besides, comfort stimulates my brain. You don't want me to get a headache and forget what I found out today, do you?"

"So you did learn something." He rubbed his hands together and swallowed a mouthful of sandwich before reaching for the pen and paper. "Go ahead. Shoot."

"Strange expression for a peace-loving man."

"You'll see how peaceful I am in a minute if you don't tell me what you found out."

"Rough day?" He grinned as he pulled his notebook from his trousers pocket. "I rang up every cemetery on your list. I talked to the caretaker of each one. He consulted his files in each instance."

"Let me guess. No Margaret Barber."

"There were a handful of names that could pass if you were desperate, like Margo Barker, Marge Berber, Marjory Burber—"

"But Margaret Barber doesn't exist. Wonderful." He took a sip of coffee before asking, "How about the death date? Any luck there?"

"Nothing. Again, in every instance, there were burials that day, but the names were completely different. And I don't think she was buried under her maiden name."

"Why would she be? She was still wed to Gary at the time of her death. From what you and he told me, there wasn't a suggestion of a divorce. And Gary was certainly in love with her, so he wouldn't have wanted her buried with any other name. Damn."

"It looks pretty odd, I admit. But Gary wouldn't do that. He loved Margaret. He'd want her remembered as his wife."

"Then where is she?" McLaren sank against the back cushions and frowned.

"Gary's a friend of mine, Mike. Has been for decades. I might consider a cremation and her ashes scattered, but I've always heard Margaret was buried in Liverpool. I'm just astonished Gary would lie about something so trivial. There's no reason to do it."

"There *is* a reason, though."

Jamie stared at McLaren as though his friend had grown another head. "What the hell is it? I can't think of any."

"There could be another one, but the only reason I can think of is that Gary obviously doesn't want Margaret found."

"You're joking."

"I'm afraid not."

"But why? What's the motive?"

"Because she's not dead." McLaren said it so softly that he thought Jamie hadn't heard, for the man didn't move. But seconds later Jamie squeaked out his question.

"Then where could she be, if you're right about that?"

"Probably just about anywhere. Manchester, Liverpool, York… Take your pick of any large metropolis. Cities are brilliant places to hide. What are the chances of someone you know from Langheath spotting you on the street or in a shop?"

Jamie nodded as he slowly visualized Margaret in a Manchester flat. "But what's the point of it? What does Gary gain from the lie?"

"He hasn't collected on her life insurance or gained control of a family business, unless you know something I don't."

"Okay, so monetary gain is out. What else?"

"The only other thing I can come up with is that he's saving his reputation in the village."

"Are you serious?"

McLaren shrugged and grabbed his coffee. He took a sip before continuing. "He's a proud man—and I don't mean that in a negative way. He reared Luke single-handedly, which is no small accomplishment. He keeps his farm running and his head above water with minimum staff. He's held out against the modern farming conglomerates, feeling it's his duty as well as his passion to keep the local lads employed on his farm. He's helping himself by sticking with the way of life he loves and he's helping the local economy. I don't know, of course, but I'd think there would be a good chance that these huge mega farms have staff brought in. Specialists, perhaps, with the newest farming methods so they can squeeze every last kernel of grain from an acre or ounce from a pig. From what little I know of your friend, he hates that. So if Margaret leaves him, maybe deciding the farmer's wife role doesn't fit her, he's too proud to let it be known around the village. He wants to save face and do it in such a way that people won't continually come back to him to ask how she is, if she's enjoying her new life."

"So he kills her…figuratively."

"That's how I see it." McLaren angled his head back and stretched. "Unless you have some other idea."

Jamie shrugged and grabbed his glass. He stared at the amber-colored liquid as though it were a crystal ball. "It just seems so…I don't know…"

"Far-fetched? Why else lie about her burial site? What's so bloody embarrassing about someone dying? It happens every day, every minute. It's a natural thing. But keeping her burial plot a secret guarantees no one will discover she's really living somewhere else."

"All right. I grant you your conclusion. But why did Margaret leave?"

McLaren drained the last of his coffee in one long swallow. "Now, that's a bit more complicated. What motivates people to pull up roots or leave a marriage? Jealousy, a separate goal than your spouse, fed up with something in the marriage, irritating habits, different life style, money problems, differing opinions on how to rear the children, in-law problems…" He set the mug on the coaster and screwed up the corner of his lip. "Pick one. They're all pretty devastating if they happen to you."

"You forgot one, Mike. Fallen out of love."

McLaren nodded, images of Dena filling his mind. He drew in his breath quickly, determined not to wallow in guilt or sentiment. "See how impossible it is for an outsider to know? Any of those reasons could have spurred Margaret into leaving."

"She had a tremendous musical talent. Maybe she felt it was being wasted on the farm."

"There you are. It all comes to a head one day, she makes her statement or demand, Gary can't or won't accommodate her…" He grimaced and stretched out his legs. "I hate to see families broken up, but it happens."

"Could've happened to them, I suppose."

"Still, this gets us no closer to the actual truth. We won't know until we find her or the registration of her burial."

Jamie propped his feet on table. "Are you sure Dena looked up the correct name and dates when she did that bit of research the other day?"

"*Gary* was the one who told me he buried his wife in Liverpool."

"She might as well be in London or Seattle or the antipodes for all the good I've done."

"Well, you tried, Jamie. Thanks."

"I wish I could've— What?"

McLaren snapped his fingers and sat up. He turned toward Jamie, his eyes bright with excitement. "What'd you say?"

"About what? Wishing I could've helped?"

"No. Before that."

"Oh. Just that for all the good I've done with this, she could be buried in China and we'd never know."

"Actually, you said the antipodes."

"Did I?" Jamie frowned, picked up his glass and strode into the kitchen. He returned a minute later with his glass refilled. "What's the difference?"

"The *antipodes*. Australia and New Zealand, *not* China. Do anything for you?"

"Besides make me hungry for kiwi fruit and wanting to see the All Blacks play, no. Why?"

"Doc Tipton's family used to holiday in New Zealand."

"Congratulations. There's just one problem."

"What?"

"Doc Tipton wasn't married to Margaret Barber, if that's where you're headed with this."

"I realize that. But I might have a link." He went into his office and brought back his iPad. Turning it on, he said, "Dena emailed me a newspaper article she found. It's twenty-five years old and has a photo with it."

"Marvelous."

"It *is*, actually." McLaren brought up the email and angled the iPad toward Jamie so he could see the photo. "See anyone you know?"

Jamie leaned forward slightly and peered at the tablet's screen. His expression changed from amusement to astonishment. He looked up from the screen and found McLaren's gaze on him. "Bloody hell."

"At least."

Jamie looked at the photo once more before handing the tablet back. "I don't believe in ghosts, no matter how you try to convince me."

"Dena found it. That's what she wanted to let me know."

"What's it mean, besides the two Tipton brothers were alive and well and in Derbyshire a year after Alan supposedly died?"

"I'd accuse Doc of getting his dates mixed, but he told me quite definitely his brother died twenty-five years ago. In Australia, although this article places him here twenty-four years ago."

"Nice trick, reappearing a year after your death."

The room plunged into silence as each man considered the reason behind Doc Tipton's lie.

"You don't think he just got muddled, then." Jamie

leaned forward, his forearms on his thighs, and gazed again at the screen.

"The man's…what? Sixty-five? Would you get muddled about significant dates of your brother?"

"He could have the beginnings of dementia, I guess."

"He could have a lot of things, but he sounded rational when I spoke to him."

"Why would he tell a story like that, then? Why lie about Alan's death? It's such a meaningless thing to do."

"Everything we do or say has a reason. You know that, Jamie. We do or say certain things because there's a motive behind it, either a reward or to save us from some sort of punishment."

"What's the motive behind Doc's lie, then?"

"Well, I guess he could've done it for the same reason we assume Gary did."

"To save face? What's he got to protect? He's a tennis pro. He's never married, so he has no wife who left him."

"Maybe he hadn't."

"Hadn't the wife, you mean?" Jamie blinked, unsure of where the conversation was headed.

"See anything else besides the date discrepancy in the photo?" McLaren handed the tablet back to Jamie, who stared at the three men's faces.

"Other than Alan having a moustache, which he hadn't when I knew him, I don't see anything odd."

"It's difficult to see, I realize, but look again."

Jamie looked again at the faces in the photo and slowly turned his head toward McLaren. "The mole?"

"Exactly."

"Did the reporter get the names mixed?"

"I doubt it. Look who's holding the award." He tapped on the tablet's screen, directing Jamie's attention back to the photo.

"It says *Alan* Tipton." He let the iPad sink slowly to his lap, his sandwich forgotten. "But that's wrong! Doc—*Albert*—is the tennis champion."

"You think so?"

Jamie stood up and strode across to the window. "Hell, yes! He's got all those trophies and awards and scrapbooks from his tennis days. He's been in the village forever. We all knew about Albert and Alan. They were always around, always playing tennis or going to matches or spending time in New Zealand..." He turned from gazing out the window, his passion spent. "I hung around Gary enough to know the Tiptons well. The only way I could tell them apart was..." He grimaced and looked at McLaren.

"By the mole on *Alan* Tipton's face."

"I've known many people who have had moles removed, but never a mole that suddenly appeared in the exact spot on another person. As this seems to have done with Doc."

"So Doc's been living a lie all these years. He's really Alan." Jamie's voice was flat, tired from the speculative session. He sat on the arm of the sofa, his hands on his right thigh, and leaned forward. "*Why?* They evidently traded identities, as the photo suggests, but why?"

"I can't explain that one as readily. Maybe it's nothing more than the real Albert getting tired of the tennis world and wanting to quit. Maybe he tried before but the media kept hounding him, so he and his brother decided to switch identities."

"Even if they did, *Doc* was still around for the media to pester."

"Agreed." McLaren poured himself another cup of coffee and downed part of it. "But maybe it's as simple as personalities. Maybe Doc could tell the media where to get off and was firm about it. Maybe he made his brother a proposition, perhaps giving him money if the brother would disappear and let Doc be the tennis pro in the world's eye."

"Could've been the other way, though, Mike. Maybe the real Albert, the tennis pro, sustained an injury and had to give up tennis. Don't a lot of athletes get injuries?" He asked it not so much of McLaren but from thinking aloud. "Sure. He couldn't bear to be reminded of his glory days so he persuaded Doc to keep his trophies and things. Maybe he never thought Doc would switch identities with him."

"We have no way of knowing when that started, unfortunately."

"No, but it probably doesn't matter. The fact is, they obviously did. This photo proves it."

"Nice theory." McLaren finished his coffee in one long swallow.

Jamie held up his hand, shaking his head. "Hold on. If the brothers traded places, and Doc told everyone his brother was dead, why would the *real* Albert come back to the village? That defeats everything."

"But that was just a year after the real Albert left. Maybe Doc hadn't started the story yet. Maybe they hadn't even traded identities, so that came later. If they hadn't thought of switching, there was no reason to be nervous that the real Albert returned for a brief visit."

He ran his fingers through his hair and sighed. "I don't know. I wasn't here. Did you hear anything at that time, either from Gary or general village talk?"

"No. Sorry."

"Well, if Doc started and perpetuated the lie about his brother's death, it was probably right after this visit." He nodded toward the tablet. "He couldn't have got away with the lie if he told his sob story about the real Albert's demise and here the chap shows up walking and talking."

"So what's this photo give us, then?"

"It still substantiates that Doc is lying about his brother, that Doc claims to be tennis champ Albert Tipton."

Jamie snapped his fingers, leaning forward. "Besides the mole, there's another way to tell them apart."

"I'm all ears."

"Alan—the *real* Alan, I mean…who's now the phony Doc—has a scar. Nothing big and showy. It's small but obviously visible. A satiny patch of skin, maybe a half inch long, on the right side of his nose. He got jabbed by a piece of glass."

"Ouch."

"I remember when he got it. He'd bought a bottle of juice or something and was running home. He tripped and fell and broke the bottle. His shoulder and head took the brunt of his fall and his face slammed into a few pieces of broken glass."

"He's damned lucky he didn't put his eye out."

"Yeah. It was a near miss. Anyway, the scar's visible, especially if he turns his head and it catches the light." Jamie peered at the photo. "Not detailed enough.

You can't see it."

"Next time I see Doc I'll look for the scar."

"Luckily it's not on his upper lip or side of his head where he could camouflage it with a moustache or sideburns."

"I just happened to think…" McLaren eyed Jamie and smiled.

"God, *now* what?"

"Can you look up passport information tomorrow without getting caught?"

"I doubt if it's visible on his passport photo, Mike, if that's what you're thinking. What is it?"

"Well, we have two people who have more or less disappeared."

"Margaret Barber and the real Albert Tipton."

"Do you recall if they were particularly chummy when they lived in Langheath?"

Jamie scratched his chin and did some mental calculations. "They could've been. I didn't live here, remember, and there's our age discrepancy. I'm about twenty-eight years younger than the brothers, which made me thirteen at the time of Albert's supposed death. And eighteen when Margaret died or left five years after his departure. And I wasn't particularly zeroed in on adults' love lives at my age. I had no reason to observe them to see how they acted around each other. So I guess she and Albert could have loved each other secretly. Why?"

"If Margaret vanished from the village—by death or of her own volition—twenty years ago, and if Doc's brother vanished twenty-five years ago…" His right eyebrow shot up and he smiled at Jamie.

"She could've joined him in New Zealand, you're

suggesting."

"She could've done. We don't know anything to the contrary."

"So you want me to look at passport dates tomorrow."

"That'll give us an answer, I bet."

Jamie nodded and stood up. "I have to admit it all fits, Mike. They both go missing and are conveniently out of the vicinity so we can't locate them. The mole on Doc's face, the retreat in New Zealand…"

"Do you know where they stayed in New Zealand? Not that brother Albert is there now, necessarily, but if the Tipton house is still standing, why wouldn't he move in?"

"They stayed on Stewart Island, I think."

McLaren grinned and walked over to Jamie. "New Zealand's third major island. Down at the end of South Island. Right. Doc told me but he could've thrown up a smoke screen." He rubbed his hands together, obviously pleased. "Stewart Island is remote, rugged, partially inhabited, fairly inaccessible, and probably still has limited mobile phone service as well as infrequent ferry and airline connections."

"Sort of a perfect hideaway, isn't it?"

"I wonder if Margaret knew about it, or if he sent her a letter asking her to come."

Jamie commented on the time as they shrugged into their jackets and picked up their keys. "Doesn't really matter if that's where they are."

McLaren opened the front door and inhaled sharply as the cold night wind whipped into the room. "At least they have their privacy. Much better than London or Liverpool if you want to get away from it all."

"And not too many people to ask embarrassing tennis questions." Jamie paused, his mouth open, frowning. He said slowly, "My school geography lesson just came back to me. Isn't there a Liverpool in Australia?"

"Now you're thinking like a detective!"

Chapter Fifteen

They drove separately to the meeting place, a particularly grim spot in a derelict area of the town. The lengthy stretch of deserted roads between Somerley and Chesterfield brought them there earlier than they'd planned, so they waited for several minutes south of the rendezvous. Wind and biting cold seeped between the plastic wrap and doorframe of McLaren's car, and he stamped his feet. He angled his body as far from the makeshift window as he could and stared at his watch. The sweep of the second hand ticked loudly, booming into the quiet of the car interior, prodding his heartbeat into overdrive. One minute…two minutes…three minutes. After eight minutes' wait he flashed his headlights, and he and Jamie drove on. Four blocks from the designated spot he slowed and watched Jamie's car fall farther behind. Saying a silent prayer, he turned onto a side street.

Facades of buildings shone in the light of his headlights, looming beside him like menacing mountains and throwing ink-black shadows behind him as he passed. Litter dotted the pavement and street gutters; scraps of newspapers, cigarette packs and fast food cartons tumbled off before the gusts of wind whipping between the dilapidated buildings. A discarded soft drink can banged along the curbstones, eventually halting at a drain covering. Graffiti and broken glass seemed to be the area's main architectural element, for both were sprinkled liberally across the landscape. The night peeked through the broken windows, tiptoeing toward him. He turned the heater's fan on high and drove on.

As he came up to an empty church, he grinned. The stop sticks had worked well. In this dark area Philip Moss hadn't seen the narrow strip of spikes laid across the street. He now leaned against his car, talking on his mobile and cursing his punctured tires. McLaren parked opposite Philip, got out, and innocently walked up to him, asking if he needed help. The few working streetlamps farther down the road threw sporadic pools of amber light that glowed feebly against the night. Like lanterns in the fog. But this area that embraced the church and Philip wallowed in darkness. A bit unnerving most times, no doubt, but perfect for McLaren's purpose. He angled his approach to stay in the unlit section.

When he came within several feet of Philip, the man answered eagerly that he'd be grateful of a lift.

"I'd given up on anyone coming along." He kept his voice warm and friendly, anxious to get help from the stranger. He didn't ask why this man had appeared out of nowhere at midnight. It didn't do to ask questions when employed in illegal activities.

"Glad to find you." McLaren remained in the blackness for a moment longer, giving Jamie a chance to drive up. No dog yapped, no traffic or snatches of conversation sounded from the street. It was as though they were on a desert island.

"Would you mind giving me a lift?" Philip peered into the dark, trying to glimpse his rescuer.

"I'm always glad to help where I'm needed." He stepped out of the blackness, letting the beams of his headlights reveal his face.

"You!" Philip took a step toward McLaren. "You haven't had enough?"

"I have. That's just it, mate. I've had a stomach full of you and your kind."

Something in McLaren's voice alerted Philip. "What do you want? You can't be just driving around here at this time of night, just for a lark."

"I want some information."

"Like what? I'd have thought you would've learned your lesson already. I guess I'm going to have to give it to you again."

"I think this time *I'm* the teacher." He grabbed Philip's arm and slammed him against the side of his car. Philip groaned and tried to wriggle free of McLaren's grasp. McLaren smashed the left side of Philip's face against the window. "I want the name and address of your drug supplier."

Philip forced a laugh that he didn't feel. "You're obviously on something yourself, man. I don't know what you're talking about."

McLaren yanked a knife from his pocket, opened the blade and held it against Philip's neck. "Do you want to talk?"

"Man, you're loco! I don't know what you mean."

"I used to be a copper, Phil. Do you know that? Top of my class, but I was, shall we say, *asked* to leave due to my overenthusiasm for certain aspects of the job. But I was a cop long enough to learn a hell of a lot of things. Things that would make your skin crawl, give you nightmares. Do you know I can hide your body so no one will ever find it? Or I can keep you imprisoned and let you slowly starve to death. Your decision."

Philip groaned as McLaren bent his arm backwards.

"I don't think I heard your decision. Tell me again." He kicked Philip's shin. "What the bloody hell…" He turned slightly as the sweep of car headlights illuminated them.

Jamie braked his car several yards from McLaren and ran up to the two men. His voice boomed into the quiet. "What's going on?" He stared at Philip. "You want me to phone 999?"

McLaren pulled Philip around, the knife blade still against the man's neck. "Get the hell out of here if you value your life, mate."

Jamie looked from McLaren to Phil, as though sizing up the situation or his chance of doing any good. He held out his arms as he walked up to McLaren. "Hey, friend, I don't have a thing on me. Just cool down, take it easy. I don't know what's going on here, but if you've got a disagreement with this gentleman, fighting isn't the way to solve it."

"A damned lot you know." McLaren pointed his knife at Jamie. "I suggest you leave now, while you still can." He turned again to Phil. "The name, Phil."

"Come on, now. Let him alone. I'm warning you, mate, I'll call the police." Jamie started to draw his mobile phone from his pocket when McLaren lunged at him. He moved so quickly that Jamie was doubled over, grasping his stomach and staring at the blood seeping between his fingers, before Philip could move. A whimper escaped Jamie's lips and he sank to the pavement. A smear of red liquid seeped into the patch of snow beneath him.

McLaren tightened his grip on Philip and held the knife inches from Philip's eyes. The blade and hilt were stained red. McLaren's voice hissed low and threatening in the man's ear. "You'll never see it coming, Phil. Probably won't feel it till I've already finished. Now, you've got to the count of three. One…"

"*Comb!* His name is Comb. I-I don't know any more than that."

"That's a start. What else?"

"I don't know his first name, I tell you. I *swear!*"

"Address, Phil. I need his address. Where does he live?"

Philip rattled off the address, his voice cracking from fear. He stared at the ground, afraid to meet McLaren's gaze, but looked up as a police car braked opposite them. McLaren jammed the knife into Philip's hand and waved at the two officers coming toward them.

"Thank God you came along." McLaren spun Philip around and relinquished his hold.

"What happened?" One of the officers grabbed Philip's upper arm and the knife while the other officer walked over to Jamie. "He do this?" He inclined his head toward Philip.

McLaren nodded, his words coming quickly and emphatic. "Yes. I saw him arguing with this man. I ran up just as this gentleman was stabbed."

The officer spoke into his shoulder mike and asked for an ambulance. "Do you mind giving me your name, sir?"

McLaren gave the requested information and said he'd stay with the wounded man until the ambulance arrived.

The officers put Philip in the car's back seat, nodded to McLaren, and drove off.

McLaren remained where he was for several seconds, letting the car turn the corner and his heart rate return to normal.

"He'll be out in an hour."

"Doesn't really matter, does it? Phil gave us the name and address. You can act on it and nick the dealer. He'll be out of business so fast he won't know what happened."

"Due to a first rate bit of acting, yes. But those two coppers…actors they aren't."

"Good enough for this." McLaren grabbed Jamie's hand and helped him to his feet. "I've got some water and towels in my car."

"You don't happen to have a hot toddy or cup of coffee in there, do you? That pavement's damned cold."

McLaren's laugh bounced off the buildings, sounding hollow in the deserted surroundings. "I guess you earned it. The stop sticks were an inspiration, by the way."

"I couldn't think of any other way to hobble friend Phil."

"Well, I'm grateful the Chesterfield coppers went along with this. Do you know those two officers?"

"No, but they knew what we wanted them to do, obviously."

"Well, I'll thank the Super in the next day or two. We couldn't have done it without him." He helped Jamie clean his hands and wipe the theatrical blood from the front of his jacket. He opened his car door but stood with his hand on the frame. "Thanks again,

Jamie."

"Any time, Mike. But maybe next time *you* can be the victim. I don't think I'll ever be warm again."

****

They followed the A625 to Castleton, where Jamie lived. McLaren slowed to watch the taillights of Jamie's car until they vanished around the turn in the road. When the dense forest swallowed them and reclaimed the darkness he traveled on for another minute past Castleton, then turned north. His village appeared moments later.

Once inside his house, he gathered up the mugs and plates from dinner and took them into the kitchen, running water onto them before loading them into the dishwasher. Then he walked back to the living room and sat down. He grabbed his sheet of notes and re-read it.

The time element on Luke's desk diary still bothered him. Three-thirty was an odd time to meet someone if he was to pick up Bethany at four. He realized he'd thought through it before Jamie came, but he couldn't go to bed. The puzzle needled him too sharply.

The problem, of course, was why Luke had thought it necessary to write down pm. Three-thirty am made no sense. Why meet in the dead of night…unless it was something illegal?

McLaren slumped back in his chair, his mind whirling. The only thing illegal he'd found at all surrounding Luke was the mention of him supplying drugs. And that was only a suspicion.

Which brought him back to the pm designation. Why remind himself it was an afternoon meeting if he wasn't connected to anything illicit? And although McLaren had yet to prove it, from what he knew of the lad, Luke hardly seemed the type to risk anything illicit that would ruin his career. Therefore, the pm didn't refer to time but to a person. PM were initials.

His fingers tightened around his pen as the name whispered to him. His friend from that evening, Philip Moss.

But that brought him back again to the supposition that Luke got drugs for Phil. Why else would he be meeting Phil? To tell him to leave him alone, that he wouldn't be a drug dealer? Would he need a formal appointment for that? Why not just wait until he ran into Phil to tell him? Which wouldn't be all that long, from what McLaren knew of the two.

But if Luke wasn't meeting Phil, that brought the question back to the beginning. What was the appointment and with whom? If not for a drug sale, did it have to do with Luke's disappearance? He went missing around that time: Bethany was waiting for him to pick her up, Gary didn't realize anything was out of the ordinary that afternoon despite the fact that Luke's guitar and car still remained at the house.

Or had they?

Could the car have been driven somewhere, perhaps to the three-thirty meeting, which could've taken a minute or less if it was a drug pay off? Could Luke have driven straight home to get his guitar, only he never left the house?

But that would mean Gary, or someone who waited at the house, was involved in Luke's disappearance. They'd have to be if Luke kept the three-thirty appointment and returned home before picking up

Bethany.

Again, the nagging questions crowded McLaren's mind. What was the point? Who would've been at the house? Why didn't Gary know someone waited for Luke?

Had Gary been lying all along? If he didn't have a hand in Luke's disappearance, did he know who did, perhaps even know who met Luke that afternoon? And if so, why was it necessary to get rid of Luke, and why didn't he try to prevent it? Wouldn't most parents fight to their death to defend their child?

Despite the lateness of the hour, McLaren tore the top sheet off the pad of paper and started a new list, writing Suspects in one column and Motives in the second column. The moonlight slid across the room as he thought through the case, writing down his impressions. When he finally left off and went to bed, he had a substantial list.

Suspects Motives

Gary Barber: Disappointed Luke won't continue the family farm

Disappointed Luke's head has been turned by Bethany and Doc toward another career

Phil Moss: Angry Luke won't supply the drugs he wants

"Doc" Tipton: Wants Luke to succeed so he can keep his prestige in the village and tennis world, perhaps gain more students

John Evans: Ditto Doc—music world

Nathan Watson: Wants a settled life, not a touring musician wife

If Luke follows tennis, Bethany might stay home

Eliminate Luke to keep Bethany home?

Callum Fox: Luke's tennis doubles partner.

Would he be happier if Luke was eliminated or went into music?

He could shine in the tennis world if competition from Luke was gone

Sharon Fraser: Wants Ashley to have a secure future by marriage.

If Luke pursues either a music or tennis career and is gone from home a lot, Ashley might not have the companionship and love she wants

Ashley Fox: Jealous of Luke's time with Bethany?

Jealous of Luke's time spent on tennis or music?

Bethany Watson: Ditto Ashley—jealousy?

****

He woke Tuesday morning still thinking of Luke and the three-thirty PM message. Sleep had come late when he'd gone to bed and when he did sleep he dreamt of the key players in the case. As he showered, shaved and dressed he'd convinced himself that the desk diary entry was a hoax, for either way he considered it, nothing made sense. Luke wouldn't sell drugs, therefore he had no reason to meet Phil Moss. And the person most likely to have written the fake message was John Evans or Bethany, both conveniently inside the farmhouse during the search for Luke.

Motive, again, whispered to McLaren, but it was a different motive. Why would Bethany or John pencil the message in the diary? If Luke wasn't meeting Philip Moss, why write it down to suggest he had? To shift obvious suspicion from the person responsible for Luke's disappearance and throw it on a known hoodlum? The police might readily believe Moss was guilty; his background suggested he'd be capable of it.

But would the investigation hold up?

McLaren scrambled some eggs and toasted several slices of bread, then brewed a small pot of tea and ate while he re-read the notations from the list. His reasoning still seemed correct, which cheered him—he was a veteran of evening enthusiasm and morning reality.

He logged onto the email again and studied the photo. Was he making too much of the Tipton brothers switching identities? What harm did it do if the real tennis playing Albert got sick of it all and chucked it, and Alan saw his chance to snatch a bit of fame and prestige through his brother's hard-won trophies?

But it could matter a great deal. It showed that Doc was capable of deception and living a twenty-five-year old lie without making any slip-ups. Could he do the same thing with kidnapping and murder?

The whisperings started immediately, reminding him he assumed Doc lived vicariously through Luke, and he would be devastated if Luke left the tennis world. Did the same thing pertain to anyone else on his list?

Just about everyone depended on Luke for one thing or another. His speculation did no good. He had no proof against anyone yet, but he vowed he'd get it before the day ended.

Yet, he couldn't avert his stare from one name on his list. John Evans. Had he heard about Luke's phenomenal tennis serve, hitting the ball into the hole of the old Wakebridge Engine House? McLaren brought up a map of the area around Crich Stand, southeast of Cromford. The computer monitor blinked into the half-light of his office and listed several old lead mines in the district. Imaginative names such as Bacchus' Pipe, Glory, Leather Ears, Wanton Legs, Merry Bird, Silver Eye, Pearson's Venture, Crooked Back. All were long ago abandoned, but their veins still gave mute evidence across the land, suggesting the vertical mine shafts and mazes of tunnels below. Crooked Back sat a little more than a mile northwest of the village of Crich. The whole area was dotted with these shafts or piles of rock known as beehives. Some level tunnels fanned out into the hillsides. Most all were dangerous now, either flooded from underground seepage, or infested with rotted support timbers.

The missing brick of the Engine House wall would beckon a superb tennis server such as Luke, McLaren thought, the temptation to lob a ball into the gap in the brickwork perhaps too strong to pass up.

And the area could prove a temptation for someone else…another type of hideaway for a body.

The suggestion washed over him, leaving him cold and shaken. It was a hell of a place to secret a body. With miles of shafts, the chances of finding Luke were nearly impossible.

But just because John might know about the mine tunnels and the Engine House didn't make him Luke's killer. Knowledge of the terrain and local history was common in the area, reaching far beyond Crich, Cromford and Langheath. No, there had to be a definite connection between the two men.

The distance bothered him. It was approximately eight miles from Langheath to the mine. Maybe more if the killer took the less-traveled roads. Would he be able to transport a body in the late afternoon, oblivious to the traffic and potential witnesses? It would probably be a good thirty-minute drive, so the killer had to be certain he'd not be missed in the village.

Could John Evans lure Luke to some meeting? It was probably possible. John gave Luke guitar lessons, had even given him one the morning of his disappearance. He could've restrained Luke then and there, or asked him to come back at a certain time on some pretext. It wouldn't take much to join up with Luke. They were friends.

McLaren was about to abandon his reasoning when a voice in his mind shouted that the killer didn't have to dispose of the body just then. He could keep Luke in the car's boot, for example, go on with the pretense of the search that evening, then deposit the body in the dead of night, when most people were asleep.

The phone rang, yanking him from wondering if Luke might be someplace closer to the village. Jamie's voice sailed into his ear.

"Mike! Are you awake?"

"This is live, Jamie, not an ansaphone recording."

"It was just a rhetorical question, Mike. I've got some info that will wake you, if you haven't had your cuppa yet."

"I have, but I can always stand to be more alert. What did you find out?"

"Margaret Barber and the real Albert Tipton both left the country."

McLaren smiled and settled back in his chair. "Brilliant. Where'd they go?"

"You want to guess?"

"How many chances do I get?"

"The usual—three."

"New Zealand."

"I should've said one."

"When did they leave?"

Jamie's voice faded slightly as he apparently turned his head. A rustle of paper was followed by a scraping sound before he spoke again. "Sorry. I jarred the teacup and the notebook page flipped over. As you probably suspect, Albert actually left twenty-*four* years ago, not twenty-five. After that little celebration in Langheath."

"*After?* He must've been in the village, then, that previous year, working on the fete. He wouldn't have received the volunteer award otherwise."

"Has to be, doesn't it? It would raise a few eyebrows from the residents otherwise."

"So he disappears permanently afterwards." McLaren jotted the dates down on the sheet of paper. "Right. You know where he is now in New Zealand, or *if* he's still there?"

"I don't know where he is now, but he entered the country at Auckland. And it definitely was Albert. That's the name on the passport."

"Auckland's a normal port of entry. Nothing sneaky there."

"I doubt if he had to do anything sneaky, Mike. He may not have known what Alan was doing back home. I don't think it makes any difference what Alan told everyone about his brother. The point is that Albert left, emigrated to New Zealand, and Margaret Barber flew there five years later."

"I wonder why she waited so long to join him. If they loved each other, wouldn't she have flown to his side almost immediately? No pun intended."

"Maybe she was trying to hold on to her marriage.

Maybe she thought having a child would make a difference."

"I give her credit for staying, if she wanted to patch up things with Gary."

"It might've been difficult for a long time, her feeling unfulfilled or unappreciated. But she finally reached her limit and left Gary and Luke."

"I assume she also landed at Auckland."

"Yeah, but as you said, Mike, that's the main jumping off spot."

"Sure." He grew silent, thinking of the tangle of lives and lies and broken hearts. Some things had been done for love; some things had been done for lack of love. No love. Zero love. Love—a tennis term. Did it mean there was no love at all between Ashley and her second choice of a husband, or between Nathan and his forsaken daughter, or between Gary and his son? Maybe it meant the opposite, that there was love, that Ashley still yearned for Luke, that Bethany regretted giving up her daughter, that Gary would've killed to protect his son.

McLaren sketched a heart on the sheet of paper and drew a musical note inside it. Love. A score of nothing. But there were the musical scores, the love songs that were so important to lovers. Maybe there were love songs in each person's life. He hoped so. Life was rough enough without the solace of love.

"Did you see if Albert is on the telephone? Can I phone him?"

"I wasn't able to look, Mike. Some of the lads came into the room and I had to log off."

"Sure. I don't want you getting caught looking up stuff. Thanks, Jamie."

"It doesn't do much for you, though, does it? I mean, so we know the real Albert and Margaret could be ensconced together happily on Stewart Island. What's that do for you?"

"Just shines the light a little brighter on Doc, that's all. I detest a liar."

"And there's no one else connected to your case who's any older, is there? No one who could give you personal insight or history between the brothers or between Gary and Margaret, I mean."

"John Evans is about it, but he's ten years the Tiptons' junior."

"He could know something. It's worth a try, isn't it? He might know something more."

"What I really need now, Jamie, is a solid motive for Luke's disappearance."

"I thought you sorted all that last night."

"Well, I compiled ideas, but they're just the results of what I've heard and found out. There's nothing definitive."

"You want someone to walk around with a smoking gun after three years?"

"Don't be daft. But it would be helpful if I had a rock solid motive."

"Talk to John, then. Or is he on your suspect list?"

"He is, but so is everyone else I've talked to."

"Well, unless Nature is tricking us, at least check out Doc's scar. Perhaps a mole can grow in the same places on twins, but I doubt very much if both brothers would have the same scar."

"Okay."

"And maybe talk to Bethany again."

"I've spoken with her twice already."

"I'm not saying she's involved, Mike, but singing partners tend to be close. She might remember something about the afternoon appointment that didn't occur to her when you asked her yesterday."

"It's worth a shot." He folded the sheet of paper and tucked it into his trousers pocket. "Thanks, Jamie. You've solved one little mystery, at least."

"You can repay me tonight at the local."

"I'll even give you a tip. Dinner."

"I would've suggested it, but I didn't want to have to buy my own meal." He rang off, agreeing to meeting up at six-thirty.

****

McLaren drove to Langheath and parked in front of John Evans' house. He knocked on the door when the doorbell failed to summon anyone. The hollow rap against the wood seemed to echo in the door and seep into the front room, but no one came to let him in. He walked to the large front window and cupped his hands around his eyes to stare into the room. No one was in sight; no sound issued from any room.

He glanced at his watch. Just after ten o'clock. Surely John wouldn't still be asleep. The man had music students. At the least, he would be running errands during his free time.

McLaren exhaled sharply and walked back to his car. He was on a fool's errand. To be certain of finding John, McLaren would have to return and interrupt a music lesson.

He sat in his car, staring at the house. Hadn't Dena found out something else, given Jamie another message? He shut his eyes, trying to remember. The list of names and motives whirled in his head, shutting out

Dena's information. He grabbed his mobile phone and punched in her number. After a dozen rings, he closed his phone. She would be at work and was probably busy giving a tour. He'd try her later.

He waited until ten-thirty. When John still hadn't come home, McLaren left. He had no idea where to go, but he assumed if he drove around the village often enough, he might see the man.

At the far end of the village, near the intersection of Twin Dales Road and the High Street, he saw John. They approached the crossroads at the same time. McLaren drew alongside John's car and rolled down his window. John nodded and spoke through his open window. Like two police officers chatting from their cars.

"Are you needing to talk to me again, Mr. McLaren?"

"Just a question or two, if you don't mind."

John motioned toward Bethany, sitting beside him in the passenger seat. "I'm afraid this is rather a bad moment. We're rather pressed for time. Can you come back this afternoon?"

McLaren leaned closer. The scar shone in the sunlight. "Nothing urgent. I'll catch you up later. What time would be convenient?"

"Three or three-thirty? Does that suit you?"

"Fine." He moved his head to speak to Bethany. "How are you today?"

Bethany glanced at John, then at McLaren. Her face was immobile although her eyes shone brightly. "I feel like an old man."

McLaren blinked. "Really? You look quite the opposite—a lovely young woman."

"I don't feel like it. I'm tired out, like an old man." She glanced at John. "Not like John, of course. Like a *really* old man."

John shook his head, patting her arm. "It's the musician's life. It catches you up when you're not prepared. The late hours, the long rehearsals, the stress of lining up bookings. It's all too much for most of us." He angled in his seat, his left arm along the seat back and supporting him as he turned his head partway to the car's rear. "But there are some who can remain perfectly unaffected by it all. They're the true superstars in the music industry. They're the ones who'll have the long distance careers and who will live forever in people's memories." He smiled and turned, patting Bethany's hand.

"Well, I hope you feel more yourself very quickly." McLaren nodded and eased away from John's car.

He drove slowly, keeping John's car in his rearview mirror. When John turned southwest onto the B5057, McLaren drove to The Two Ramblers and parked in the pub's car park. He sat there, the pale sunlight slanting through the windscreen, and considered what just happened.

Bethany's remark was unusual. Most people would've just said they felt tired. But her statement about an old man seemed to be a message. Why an old man, and a really old one, at that?

The only old man McLaren could think of was T'Owd Man, the ancient stone carving of a miner. It was a well known Derbyshire relic. But why link that to John unless there was something in John's house. Was that her hint?

McLaren gunned his car out of the pub's car park and less than a minute later arrived at the house. He walked around to the back garden and knocked on the door. He waited and glanced around him. It would've been more to his liking if it had been night time, but he couldn't wait another eight hours. Giving his surroundings one last look, he walked over to a window partially hidden by a large juniper. He picked up a palm-sized rock that bordered a flowerbed, then took off his left glove and laid it against the windowpane. He angled his face away from the window and brought the rock down with as much force as he could. The glass broke and fell into the house.

He remained statue-still as he listened for a voice, within or outside the house, raised in concern. Nobody challenged him; no police car siren or burglar alarm sounded. He counted to one hundred, making certain no delayed reaction came. After using the rock to brush the few remaining shards of upright glass from the window frame, he tossed it onto the flowerbed, shook his glove and put it on, and climbed inside the house.

The lounge, living room and main bedroom held nothing of importance that McLaren could see. Books were mainly about music, classic literature, and gardening. The desk held no incriminating letters or maps; the computer emails and search history were exonerating of wrong-doing. Yet, Bethany seemed insistent.

A second bedroom led off of the same hallway. It was a small room, barely ten feet by ten feet, jammed with a desk and chair, chest of drawers, several filing cabinets, and a bookcase. But pride of place went to a wooden table occupying the far wall. He wandered toward it, disbelieving what he saw.

A prei deux sat in front of the table. Blue and white satin fabric covered the cushion of the prayer bench and threw back the light shining onto it. The upright portion of the kneeler was painted in the same pale hues but had the added design of stars, musical notes and flowers curving across the background. A small rose sprawled across the cushion, as though it were a forgotten rosary, and a large flowerpot of lilies nestled up to one end of the bench.

A lace-edged tablecloth covered the tabletop, the linen starched white and stiff and bright in the light of the lamp sitting near the back. The rest of the room sat in darkness but for the lamp. Its stained glass shade glowed blue and white, and seemed to hover above the items on the cloth.

He stopped, his hand about to touch the framed photo of a boy with a guitar. Was it John's son? He'd mentioned the lad had died going to a music gig in Denmark…

The other items spread across the table appeared to stress McLaren's thought. Used guitar strings and flat picks, an old capo, a dog-eared poster of a folk concert, a used candle in a glass holder, a small index card on which a list of songs was handwritten and to which snippets of cellotape still clung. A classic musician's habit, taping the list to the side of the guitar for reference during a performance… A bundle of picture postcards, tied with a blue ribbon, sat next to the base of the lamp. McLaren picked it up and flipped through the stack, noting the postal marks: London, Edinburgh, Glasgow, Exeter, Whitby, Drogheda, Conwy, Inverness. Places around the country where the boy'd been singing, and getting experience and name recognition. He snorted at the injustice of it all: there'd been no address to which Gary Barber could've sent correspondence in the last three years of Luke's life… McLaren set the bundle down and patted it gently, as though giving both lads his blessing. Next to the postcards, a handful of dried roses filled a cut glass vase, looking like they'd not been changed in years. He fingered a fallen petal, dark brown and shriveled. It was brittle and it cracked as he felt its texture.

Several smaller photos of the boy were stuck to the back wall and formed the shape of a Christian cross above the table. Drawings from infant classes through higher school grades showed the boy's artistic development as he aged. Each sheet of paper had yellowed and curled at the bottom. They, too, were probably as stiff as the rose petals.

He remained there for another minute, letting the altar significance wash over him. That's what it was, a place for John to pray to his son as though he were a saint. Or God. A shrine to a life cut short. A manifestation of a father's obsession, for he still grieved over his son's death. Decades later, he hadn't been able to let go.

McLaren ran his hand over his stomach, feeling suddenly ill and intrusive. The quiet threatened to crush him, and the enclosed space held the odor of the dying flowers. The smell was thick and sickly, like cheap perfume sprayed on too liberally to hide something offensive. John's habit of talking over his shoulder or to the rear of the house, the second place setting at the table—did he believe his son was there? How far did his fantasy go?

McLaren left the room and wandered into the kitchen. It was long and narrow, a style most associated with boats. He pulled open the cupboard doors and drawers, not knowing what he looked for. In the back of the silverware drawer he found a wallet and a mobile phone.

He drew them out and opened the wallet. It was stuffed with Luke Barber's identification card, credit cards, and miscellaneous sales receipts. Change and pound notes were there, so robbery apparently hadn't been the object, if the wallet was stolen. He opened the mobile and turned it on, but the battery was dead. He dropped it and the wallet into a paper sack. He could feel his face flooding with heat. Luke's wallet and mobile had never been found.

He looked around the kitchen, making certain he hadn't missed anything. A sheet of paper seemed to be beckoning to him from the front of the refrigerator. He walked over and released it from the magnetic clip on the fridge door.

The paper looked to be ordinary computer printer paper. It appeared to have been exhibited for quite a while, for the edges were curled and cracked, the paper faded to a light tan where the morning sun rested on it year after year. A hand-drawn sketch took up two-thirds of the page. A hand-drawn heart was drawn beneath it.

McLaren stared at the sketch. He'd seen a photo of the actual stone carving before. It was famous, gracing many books on Derbyshire history and attractions.

The Old Man carving, probably done in the Dark Ages—400-1066 AD—portrayed a lead miner. He carried a basket and a pick, common tools of the medieval mining trade.

The carving had been discovered at Bonsall, a village about seven miles southwest of Langheath and deep in lead mining country. In the 1870s the carving had been moved to its present spot, a wall inside Wirksworth Church, much to many Bonsall residents' protests.

McLaren turned the paper over. The reverse side was empty.

He flipped back to the drawing. Fragments of folklore and superstition crept back to him as he stared at the sketch. Funny. He thought he'd forgotten about T'Owd Man, the name given to the carving and the lead mining legends in general. Some had said it was sacrilegious, moving the carving from Bonsall. Others declared nothing but bad luck would come to the community for shifting T'Owd Man's resting place from the mine. For that's where the old man dwelled. Dark passageways and abandoned veins were his realm, and he came to embody not only the mines, but also the miners themselves, past and present.

So great was this tie with the centuries of previous generations that T'Owd Man garnered great respect. The best chunks of ore sat at the foot of the carving on Christmas Eve, a burning candle illuminating the gift.

Perhaps it was nothing more than superstition; perhaps it was a form of worship or a way to honor their forefathers. But T'Owd Man was firmly entrenched in generations of miners' lives.

So why did John have this old sketch of the old man?

A niggling in McLaren's brain gave him an explanation. John came from a long line of lead miners and farmers, or so Doc Tipton said. The drawing of

T'Owd Man seemed to confirm that. Even if it wasn't true, the mines evidently held some fascination for John. Could he have hidden Luke's body there? It was more than a guess; he was ninety-nine percent certain. If John had Luke's wallet and mobile, probably taken from Luke's dead body…

McLaren felt his throat closing up. His cheeks flushed with heat. The two-faced smiler with the knife behind his back, friendly and helpful in public, murderous and lying in private.

He stared again at T'Owd Man, as though he could hear it talking to him. Could John be taking Bethany there? No other reason seemed plausible for her cryptic message. She'd looked scared, not tired, and John was in too much of a hurry for McLaren's comfort.

And too immersed in his fantasy that no one should best his son, and it might not matter how that rival should be eliminated.

The paper fluttered to the floor as he ran for his car.

Chapter Sixteen

Normally he would've stopped alongside the road and called Jamie, but time was essential, so he talked while he raced toward the old Wakebridge Engine House.

"John referred to himself as the old man of the village when I spoke to him that day at his house," McLaren said after he filled Jamie in about John and Bethany. "Of course, anyone can say he's an old man, but coupled with the other things and what Bethany called him today—"

"It adds up," Jamie ended.

"If it's true that John comes from a family of miners, he just might know the abandoned mines intimately in the area."

"And what better place to hide Luke, if he is guilty of killing the lad."

McLaren swerved around a slow-moving tractor. "He killed Luke, Jamie. And if I'm too late, he may kill Bethany, too. I can't explain now, but she's a threat to his son."

"His son? He's been dead for years."

"I know, but I don't think John knows."

"What are you talking about?"

"There's probably a medical name for it, but I think he's delusional. He's out to eliminate everyone who he feels is a threat to his son's career. And right now that's Bethany. Can you get to the Engine House, bring a few coppers with you?"

"I'm leaving right now. Don't do anything stupid, Mike. If all this is true, John Evans is very dangerous. He's cold and calculating and able to bluff his way out of anything. If he killed Luke and he feels cornered or threatened by you—"

"I'll try to wait till you arrive, but make it fast!" He rang off and concentrated on the drive. It made sense. Every bit of information fit like pieces of a jigsaw puzzle. Especially T'Owd Man. He occupied abandoned mine workings in particular. What better hiding place for a body than an unused mine tunnel or shaft…

McLaren continued on the B5057 on the other side of the A6 outside Matlock. He hadn't the patience to crawl through the town's traffic, and he didn't want to waste precious time. John had a good half hour start on him, and unless he was slowed by traffic, he'd reach the mine well before McLaren. His ride could be in vain.

He turned onto a minor road just south of the A6, driving east again, and eventually joined the A6 on Matlock's south side. The car screeched past a handful of lorries and tractors ambling down the two-lane road and braked hard as McLaren came upon the sign indicating the village of Crich. The Engine House was close now.

The road was vacant of cars, and McLaren raced toward the mining site. His car tires cracked through thin depressions of ice and threw up handfuls of snow that lingered in the ruts along the sides of the road. He leaned over the wheel, straining for a sight of John's car. He didn't know what he'd do if he had guessed wrong, didn't know anywhere else to look. He prayed aloud that he was right, that he'd be in time.

He passed the Tramway Museum but drove on, even though the main road had dissolved into a cart track. The actual quarry was ahead somewhere, as was the Engine House.

When he arrived at the quarry he realized there was no way around it, so he drove back past the Museum, cursing his frustration and stupidity. He turned right onto Cliffside Road, keeping the quarry on his right. When the road cut sharply to the left, he took the right hand spur leading to the Bacchus' Pipe and Crooked Back mines.

The road gave out adjacent to the Pipe and he slowed. John's car was not there. He slammed his fist against the steering wheel and drove on. His car bounced heavily on the roadless soil as he steered toward the footpath to his left. Several hundred feet farther on he spotted the car.

McLaren squealed to a stop. He grabbed the torch from the glove compartment and flung open the car door. He raced up to the car, but there was no need to peer inside. Both doors were open and the occupants were gone.

He dashed up the hill, following the packed earthen walking lane that threaded toward the northeast, the path that centuries of miners had taken to the mines dotting the area. He was northwest of the village, in the area between Crich Stand, Plaistow Green and Wakebridge Farm. The land muted into a palate of drab browns, grays and washed out greens, the vegetation dry and withered. Iron grates or stone beehives warned of dangerous open mining shafts, but he ran past them, knowing John was not there.

On the northern side of a small hill the terrain opened up in a broad expanse of moors, crumbling mining fragments and smelting chimneys, stone fences, and soil-worn footpaths. Lines of trees that had been planted along the edge of mining veins stretched across the land. Freshly broken ice and bent grass indicated that someone had taken this route before him, and he ran on.

Just past an old pile of metal rails he came upon an open mine entrance. It stretched horizontally before him, burrowing slightly downward into the hill, and threw back the smells of damp earth, rotted wood, and rust. He paused by the entrance, letting his eyes adjust to the interior gloom, and listened.

The drip of water sounded to his left, echoing off the hard rock walls, and he stepped into the tunnel.

The aroma of wet rock and packed earth filled his nostrils, and he stopped to cover his mouth as he coughed. As he listened again, he heard John's voice. It was ahead and to the right. He stepped outside, jogged a few dozen yards from the entrance, and punched Jamie's number into his mobile.

"Mike, I'm nearly at the turnoff to Crich. Where are you?" Jamie sounded as though he were standing next to McLaren.

"At Crooked Back Mine. You know where that is?"

"Somewhere north of Crich."

"Take Cliffside Road. Oxhay Wood and Gingler Shaft will be on your left. When you pass Gingler there'll be a turn off a bit farther ahead on your right. That will take you to the Pipe and the mine where we are. You'll be northwest of Cliff Quarry, if that helps you."

"Somewhat. I'm just coming toward Crich now."

"When you exit on Main Road, take the second left. That's Hindersitch Lane. Keep to your left because that eventually takes you to Leashaw Lane."

"*Eventually?* How far away is this place?"

"Not far. A few minutes. The right hand spur off Leashaw goes to Bacchus' Pipe."

"I've heard of it, yeah."

"You'll have to drive off-road a bit, toward your left. You'll see Crooked Back if you follow the footpath. John's and my cars are parked near it." He glanced toward the tunnel, his heart racing. "I've got to get back to the tunnel. John's in there and I think he's got Bethany."

"Mike!"

"Yeah?"

"I'm nearly there. The other coppers are following me. Don't do anything rash. Wait for us."

"If I wait, Bethany may end up dead. Hurry up!" He ended the call, jammed the mobile back into his jacket pocket, and entered the mine.

This time he wanted John to know he wasn't alone. McLaren jogged to the area where three tunnels converged and yelled. "John! I know you're here. Let Bethany go."

The talking that he'd heard before phoning Jamie stopped, and the steady drip of water filled the space.

"Who is it?" John's voice held a mixture of apprehension and anger.

"McLaren. I know you've got Bethany. Let her walk out—*ahead* of you."

John's laugh, bitter and defiant, bounced off the rock walls. "Go to hell."

"You're halfway there now, John, if you don't let her go."

A sound like a slap rolled over McLaren's reply. He shouted again. "If she's harmed, you'll personally answer to me. Understand?"

Another slap cracked into the brief silence. The sound of something heavy falling echoed through the tunnels.

McLaren snapped on his torch and ran down the tunnel, yelling John's name. A flash of light, as if someone had moved the beam of torchlight, skittered across the floor, then slanted back behind a wall, plunging the tunnel again into darkness. McLaren ran toward the vanished light and the sound, his own torchlight picking out small depressions and exposed rocks in the floor. Several puddles threw back the light of his torch, momentarily blinding him. When he shifted the beam, the darkness returned, nearly suffocating him. His old fear welled inside him, nearly paralyzing him. The sound of dripping water seemed to resonate with the voices of a million mice, all lurking in the blackness beyond the light. He gripped the torch tighter. What would he do if he dropped it and it broke? Could he feel his way along the wall back to the tunnel entrance? Would he make his way toward John's sanity-saving light but know forever that a killer had rescued him?

He inhaled deeply and moved ahead, willing the noise of gnawing rodents from his mind.

At a hollowed out area in the tunnel, hardly larger than a car body, he found John standing over Bethany's inert body.

John stepped back, angling the beam of his torch away from Bethany. He shone it on McLaren's face. "McLaren. You pop up at the oddest moments. And places."

"No more than you." McLaren moved his beam from Bethany to John's face. "What did you do to her?"

"Just hit her a few times to keep her quiet. Her crying got on my son's nerves." He smiled, his eyes sparkling in the light. "He's got such a sensitive ear. Many gifted musicians do. Do you know he has perfect pitch? That's why he couldn't bear to hear her cry—her voice kept changing pitch."

"John, let me take Bethany away. You and your son can—"

"She doesn't cry all the time. Not when she's taking lessons, of course, and not when she's at our home. My son's listened from the hallway. He never comes into the room. He knows what it's like to have people hovering about and staring at you when you've not got the song down pat. He's considerate, my Will is. That's what makes him a truly exceptional human being as well as a great musician."

"John—"

"He told me the other evening at dinner that he thinks her voice could be cultivated to lead quality in a few years, but that's about it. Still, maybe he could do something with her looks. He knows some people who could give her tips on hair and makeup." He shrugged and nudged her shoulder with the toe of his shoe.

"Leave her alone, John."

"She's not hurt. A few slaps and she folded like a concertina. Will can tell you I didn't hurt her very much. Did I?" He bent, addressing Bethany, and laughed, the sound filling the small chamber.

"John, why don't you and Will come with me? We can leave Bethany here for now, and when she becomes calmer, she can join us. I've got a few CDs in my car. We could listen to them and your son can let me know what he thinks of the musicians."

John frowned and glanced behind McLaren. His voice changed timbre as he addressed someone in the corridor. "What do you think, Will? Do you want to listen to music?" He paused, evidently hearing or considering something. Seconds later, he looked at McLaren. "You heard him, McLaren. He wants to stay here. So do I. We've both had enough of other singers. It's time for my boy to shine in the spotlight, time for the world to listen to him on CDs." He nudged Bethany again with the toe of his shoe. "That's why we're eliminating the competition. And anyone else who stands in his way. Including…" He ran his tongue over his bottom lip and screwed up his face.

"Including who?"

"Including snitches and no talents and anyone who tries to meddle in his career."

"How do people interfere in his career? Can we stop them somehow?"

"I'm stopping them when I find them. I get everyone out of my son's way. It doesn't matter who it is…friends or neighbors. Mine or…others."

McLaren exhaled, feeling the heat flood his face. Was John playing or did he believe his son was there? "If you let me know, we could work together to clear the path for your son. Talent like his should be shown to the world, John. If you let me work with you—"

John concentrated again on the area behind McLaren. He listened for several seconds, then nodded and glared at McLaren. "He says you're one of them."

"One of who?"

"Them who want to stop Will. So I have to stop you." He set his torch on a small ledge-like space chiseled into the wall and angled the beam so it shone against the far side of the tunnel. McLaren took a step forward, but John's warning shot into the air. "Don't move."

McLaren felt his anger building. If he was to help Bethany, he needed to put an end to this charade and get her medical attention. McLaren took a deep breath and curled his fingers into a fist. His frustration boiled over as he barked, "John, we've wasted enough time talking. Bethany needs help. I'm going to get her out of here right now. Get out of my way."

"And *you've* talked enough, too. You don't fool me. I know you're thinking you can walk out of here with her on your arm and then send the coppers after me. Well, surprise. I've got other plans. I'm going to kill you now and I'm going to enjoy it." Before McLaren could reply, John grabbed McLaren's shoulder and punched him in the jaw.

McLaren stumbled, falling against the wall. He shook his head, trying to clear his mind. John stepped across the floor and reached for McLaren's jacket. McLaren turned away and pulled John's arm toward him. He landed a punch to John's jaw, which sent him staggering backward. As he hit the wall, he bent down and picked up McLaren's torch. He came at McLaren, the torch aimed at his head. McLaren ducked, grabbed John's wrist, and jerked him around, slamming him into the rock face as the torch rolled to the opposite wall. His right foot smashed into John's groin and the man went down like a sack of potatoes. As McLaren twisted his grip on John's jacket, he half hoisted him off the ground and glared at him. The warning behind his growled words was unmistakable.

"And I'm fed up with your sick fantasy. You need to be held accountable. Where's Luke Barber?"

John closed his eyes, wincing in pain. His head listed to one side as he mumbled something incoherent.

McLaren slapped John's cheek, forcing the man's eyes open. The pain evidently gripped him again, for he groaned.

"I asked you were Luke Barber was." McLaren's voice cracked through John's hurt and he gazed at the man's face. "Tell me, Evans. Where's Luke?"

"I…I don't know. Can't remember."

"Really? Need a bit of a memory jog?" He dragged John over to the wall, held him half upright against it, and kicked him again.

John screamed in agony.

"Your memory any clearer now?"

"Please."

"Please…what?"

"I-I'll tell you. I'll tell. No more, please."

McLaren turned his fist so that his knuckles jammed into John's neck. "Where is he?"

John opened his mouth but didn't speak.

"You want another mental prod?"

"McLaren…"

"You think I'm bluffing, Evans?" He kicked John in the knee, and exhaled heavily as John cried out. "I'm losing my patience, Evans. I don't know how much longer my good manners will last. I'm playing nice for the moment. You don't want to be around when I get mad. Now, I'll ask you again…nicely. Where is Luke Barber?" To underscore his statement, he slapped John's face. "Tell me. You don't want your son to get hurt, do you?"

John's shriek of pain reverberated in the small area, sounding like a thousand souls in agony. He nodded and looked at McLaren. "I'll tell you. Please, don't hurt my boy. I-I remember. He…" John's head fell forward.

"TELL ME!" McLaren's anger filled the tunnel and he pulled John to his feet. "Where's Luke?"

John gestured feebly toward the tunnel. "Down there. Farther along. Other side of this shaft."

McLaren grabbed John's chin with his free hand and forced the man to look at McLaren. "You had damned well be telling me the truth."

"I swear. Down there. His body's down there."

"You'd better bloody well pray it is." McLaren loosened his grip and John slid to the ground.

In the sudden quiet McLaren heard Jamie's voice calling his name and the sound of many footsteps. McLaren nursed his fist, picked up his torch, and moved into the tunnel.

"Jamie, here!" He waved the torch beam on the floor and walls, and sagged against the wall as he caught his breath. His left arm draped across his chest and pressed against his ribs. They hurt like hell.

"Mike?"

"Here. Right hand tunnel." He waved the torchlight again and moments later Jamie and several uniformed police officers joined him, the light of a half dozen extra torches dotting the gloom.

"You all right?" Jamie asked as McLaren gestured toward the small chamber.

"Better than John Evans. He's in there. So is Bethany. I haven't had time to check, but I think she just fainted." He stepped back, giving Jamie and the officers room to work, and stumbled down the tunnel. Alone in the darkness, he played his torch beam along the walls as he turned around. As he approached a large boulder, he saw a man's boot.

He stopped, his fear forgotten, and peered behind the rock. The remains of a young man huddled on the mine floor, very dead and very decayed.

McLaren yelled for Jamie and rushed forward. He waited in the intersection of the tunnels, shouting repeatedly. When Jamie rushed up, McLaren pulled him back to the boulder. He pointed to the body as he angled the light on it.

"Bloody hell." Jamie glanced from the body to McLaren. "You think it's Luke?"

"I assume so. John said I'd find him here. Has to be him."

"Unless there are…" Jamie stopped. He trembled, as though a small pinprick of terror kept down his back.

"Other victims?" McLaren finished the sentence, anger threatening to consume what little restraint he still had.

"The boss'll have some of the lads search the mine, of course. We'll know."

"Has to be Luke. John told me Luke would be here."

Jamie nodded, unable to reply. The situation sickened him. "I-I'll get the CSI lads over right away. They'll have to photograph the scene and do some investigating before Luke can be removed. You all right? You look a bit grim."

"I'll be fine. I just need to get out of here."

"Sure. Wait for me outside."

While the officers tended to Bethany, seeing to first aid, McLaren left the tunnel. Once out in the open, the nightmare and fear lessened. He snapped off his torch, shoved it into the back pocket of his trousers, and scooped up a handful of snow hugging the base of the mine entrance. He smeared it over his head and face, needing the cold to shock him fully awake. His head hurt from one of John's punches…or where he'd slammed into the rock wall. When he'd finished, he opened his fingers and let the snow fall to the ground.

An officer emerged from the mine and dialed 999, requesting an ambulance and additional help. When he'd finished, he reentered the mine. McLaren considered running after him to ask about Bethany's condition, but thought the men probably wouldn't know. They weren't doctors.

Some time later police vehicles and a helicopter arrived. Crime Scene Investigators, officers and the Home Office Pathologist and Biologist filed into the mine. Ten minutes or so after that, two officers carried a stretcher outside. A thermal emergency blanket draped across Bethany, the shiny fabric painfully bright in the sunlight. McLaren watched as the officers carried her several hundred feet from the entrance, and placed her into the helicopter.

Jamie and the other two officers led John outside. He was handcuffed and stumbling, but he could walk. He avoided looking at McLaren and obediently accompanied the officers back to the police car. Jamie came over to McLaren, his frown showing his concern.

"You should've waited for us." Jamie stated it simply, without accusation. He looked at his friend. "Are you all right? Your jaw will probably swell."

"I put some cold on it. It'll be fine."

"Where'd you get—" He nodded as McLaren pointed to the snow.

"Do you have to stick around?"

"Stick around…"

"To do anything for…Luke."

"Oh." Jamie stepped away from the tunnel. "No. The pathologist and biologist are doing their bit, and the photos have been taken. There'll be a lot done tomorrow, when it's brighter and the rest of the teams are here, but I'm not involved with any of that. He…he's in good hands." He hesitated, as if wondering if it weren't all a bit too much for McLaren to handle at the moment.

"Come on. Let's get out of here. I can't stand the stench." He started walking and Jamie fell in step alongside him.

They walked in silence, letting the wind and birdsong wash over them.

When they got to the area where the cars were parked, Jamie told McLaren to remain there for a minute. "I want to check out John's car but I'll catch a ride back with you, if I can."

"Sure. The bastard won't need his car from now on." He watched John as he stood beside the police car, talking to the officers.

"His key's in the ignition," Jamie called, explaining why he walked over to the car.

McLaren nodded and leaned against the side of his

car. He couldn't avert his attention from John.

Minutes later, he turned to find Jamie standing beside him, his face drained of color. Something about his friend's expression intensified McLaren's heart rate. He stared at Jamie, afraid to ask the obvious question.

He didn't need to. Jamie laid his hand on McLaren's arm and spoke gently. "I looked through John's car."

"Yeah. I know. What—"

"Mike. I opened the boot of the car."

"Right. So?"

Jamie glanced at the ground, looking as though he were uncertain how to explain something.

"*What?*" McLaren's voice rose sharply, tinged with concern and apprehension. "What the hell's the matter?"

Jamie closed his eyes briefly. When he looked at McLaren again, he spoke quietly. "Mike, it's Dena."

"Dena?" McLaren looked back in the direction of the mine, confusion darkening his eyes. "What—"

"She's in the car. In the boot."

McLaren stood up, his mouth open. "You mean, John kidnapped her along with Bethany? Dena's tied up? Is she all right?" His gaze shifted from Jamie to the rear of John's car. He took a step forward and looked around for her. "I've got to see to her. Is she sitting in his car? She'll need looking after. She must be terrified." He started to run but Jamie grabbed his arm, pulling him up abruptly.

"Mike. Please don't—"

He spun around, glaring at Jamie. "She's hurt? Is that what you're saying? She needs medical attention? I'll kill that bastard if she's hurt—"

“Mike, listen. Dena’s…she’s dead.”

No sound or emotion came from McLaren. He stood there, staring at Jamie as if he were one of the stone carvings in the mine. The cold wind and smell of damp earth whipped around him, yet he remained where he was.

Jamie touched his friend’s arm; still there was no response.

Seconds later, the click of the remote car door opener pulled McLaren from his thoughts. He turned toward the police car. An officer held the door open while a second officer was about to help John inside the car.

With a roar of pain and anger McLaren rushed toward the car. He moved so fast that he pulled John from the car before the officers and Jamie could respond. McLaren screamed all the obscenities he could think of, reaching within him for words he had tried to bury. He screamed that he would kill John, that he would gladly go to prison for avenging Dena. His hands closed around John’s throat as other hands closed around his own wrists and arms. They tugged at him, trying to distance him from the target of his hatred, but McLaren seemed possessed of an inner strength. His knuckles turned white as his fingers tightened and John tried to claw at the life-destroying hands. But the handcuffs hindered him and he tried to escape into the car. As McLaren bent down, the officers pulled him off John, and Jamie stepped between them. He pushed McLaren away from the car and onto the ground. The car door slammed; the engine growled into life, and the car sped away.

Jamie looked down at McLaren. He half sat, half

lay on the ground, his face contorted. Tears coursed down his cheeks but he made no move to wipe them off. He let Jamie pull him to a sitting position but didn't speak. It wasn't time for words.

Jamie walked several dozen yards off and rang up the police station. After requesting a tow truck, he turned back to his friend. He stood there watching, as if wishing he could take away the hurt or turn back the clock.

"You want to go now?" Jamie spoke quietly, yet there was a force behind his words that suggested rather strongly that they leave, or hinted that Dena's death would not plunge McLaren back into the abyss of his near-hermit existence, the existence that had threatened him mentally and emotionally.

McLaren remained seated and mute.

"Mike, we need to go. The sun will be setting soon."

Faint noises issued from the mine: snatches of orders given and questions asked, a clang of metal against stone, the dull thumps of shoes on packed earth. The wind strengthened as it raced across the moor and it slammed a handful of sleet against McLaren. No sign of recognition or sound came from him.

At some point four crime scene technicians exited the mine. Their boots crunched on the sleet pellets and frozen soil, jarring Jamie from his silent debate about McLaren. One man in the group zipped up his jacket; another man pulled his cap down more firmly on his head and rubbed his ears. No one spoke. It was as if they had played these parts hundreds of times before and needed no light or direction to accomplish their jobs. They stopped at the back of the car, still silent—

either numb from the cold or out of respect for McLaren. As they waited, the fourth man opened the boot of the car. The photographer adjusted his camera and took a series of shots of Dena's body *in situ* from various angles.

As the men moved the body to the stretcher, Jamie coughed and shifted his seated position, leaning forward to screen McLaren's view of the scene. McLaren seemed not to notice the men, car or activity. He stared ahead into the wintry landscape, perhaps seeing Dena and himself, perhaps hearing an intimate conversation, perhaps reliving his fight with John. McLaren's gaze never wavered from the object or scene he saw; he sat mum and immobile, apparently oblivious to his surroundings and the bustle of police activity.

With the body removed, the tech photographed the boot's interior. When he finished, another technician labeled the spare tire, petrol can and other plain-sight items. Of course, the boot's carpeting would be pulled up, photographed and examined after the car was towed to the police garage. But for now, this was enough.

Jamie watched the men spread a tarp over the body and secure the straps across it. After snapping the buckles closed they carried it into the mine. The darkness of the tunnel obscured Jamie's view and the men's footsteps faded as they rejoined the other officers in the depths of the mine, leaving the wind whispering to McLaren.

Jamie lost track of time as they sat outside the mine. Eventually the tow truck lumbered up the track and stopped a dozen feet from them. Jamie got to his feet and, after John's car was loaded onto the flat deck, sealed the car and pocketed the key.

McLaren watched the procedure, aware of the awful content recently lodged in the car's boot, but didn't move, watching the tow truck return the way it had come, deepening the ruts it had made in the earth. The engine's growl grew more faint as it headed back toward the main road, until it faded altogether, leaving him and Jamie on the moor, with the January wind whistling through the spent clumps of heather and pushing the sun toward the western horizon.

"Mike." Jamie walked back to his friend and laid his hand on McLaren's shoulder. He shook him gently.

No response showed Jamie that McLaren had heard him.

"Mike." Jamie shook him again, more urgently. "Mike, we need to get going. It'll be dusk soon." He glanced at the clouds. Already they were tinged with a faint purple hue as the sunlight slanted upward to color their bellies. "Mike, we've got to go home. It's getting late."

A sharp breath of wind stirred a handful of dust from broken heather steams, pushing it into the air and peppering their jackets. McLaren seemed not to notice.

"Come on, Mike. Sitting here won't do you or Dena any good."

Her name must have stirred something in his mind, for he looked up, staring at Jamie's concerned face. "What?"

"It's nearly dusk, Mike. We've got to go home." He smiled, wanting to ease McLaren's pain, hoping to convince him to leave. He'd never be able to force him into the car.

McLaren glanced at the landscape, seemingly surprised they were alone. "We'll have rain or sleet tonight." He nodded toward the clouds piling in from the west, gray and hugging the horizon. "I don't think it's cold enough for snow."

Jamie nodded. Anything to get him into the car. He extracted the key from McLaren's pocket and helped him to his feet. When he got McLaren into the passenger's seat, he slid behind the steering wheel and snapped their seat belts closed. He gave the area one last look. It wallowed in the bleakness of winter and now the tragedy of Dena's death. The dreary hues of a dead landscape were tinted with the color of mourning. The gray bank of clouds had darkened in those few minutes and would soon blanket the sky. Jamie turned the key in the car's ignition, glanced toward the tunnel, then turned the car for Somerley.

Chapter Seventeen

Jamie finished his shift at the Buxton police station with John Evans' interview. He picked up dinner at a Chinese takeaway and headed for McLaren's house. It wasn't an evening he looked forward to. Nor was the stretch of countless tomorrows. He prayed for a miracle that would keep McLaren sane and working. If he got a new case in the next week or so…

Jamie parked in the driveway behind McLaren's car and grabbed the sack of food. The aromas of Peking duck, Mu Shu pork, and stir fry green beans normally would tempt him to open the sack before he got it into the house, but he had no appetite. And he doubted if McLaren did. Still, it was a way to share the grief and nudge McLaren into talking.

Paula, Jamie's wife, had wanted to come along and pay her respects, and now that Jamie was here, staring at the old house, he was sorry he hadn't agreed to her request. He had convinced her it wasn't the time for the politeness and forced smiles of gratitude for condolences. Besides, McLaren needed to get past the shock first. Then he might be ready to receive visitors. Not that he was tonight, but Jamie's visit was born of necessity.

He reached across to the passenger's seat and slid the carton of beer under his arm. Gripping the food sack tighter, he locked the car, then walked up to the front door.

McLaren murmured that it was open and Jamie hurried inside, closing the door against the wind and the rain that had just started. He put the beer and food on the coffee table, slid out of his jacket, and got plates, silverware and glass pints from the kitchen. When he had dished out the food, he sat on the sofa, near McLaren, who slumped in his overstuffed chair.

"Where is she?" McLaren's plate and beer sat on the table, and he stared at Jamie. A lamp on the end table farthest from Jamie threw a pool of ochre-hued light onto the nearest sofa cushion and the table top. The only other lit lamp in the room was behind McLaren and plunged his face into shadow.

"Come on, Mike. Eat your dinner before it gets cold."

"I want to know where she is."

Jamie put down his fork. "You don't need me to tell you that. You know. I don't understand what kick you get out of your gruesome imagination—"

"*Gruesome!*"

"You know damned well what I mean and you know damned well about police procedure. So quit torturing yourself with questions and mental images. It's not doing you any good and it won't change anything."

McLaren leaned forward, his forearms on his thighs, his head bowed. "She died alone, Jamie. She died at the hands of a stranger, away from people she loved and who loved her." He wiped his forearm across his eyes, choking back his tears. "If I could've held her, even for one minute, giving her assurance that I loved her…"

"Mike—"

"But he took that comfort from her. I wasn't there and she died…who knows where."

"She knew you loved her, Mike. You were engaged to her."

McLaren seemed not to hear Jamie. "The last thing she said to me was that she loved me, Jamie. She was trying to help me with the case. With this bloody, God-awful case. And look what happened. I failed her."

"Mike—"

"I let her down. The love of my life, Jamie. I let her down! How can I ever…" He took a deep breath, willing his voice to stop shaking, "I-I wasn't there when she needed me, when that bastard…" He broke into body-shaking sobs and let his tears fall unheeded.

Jamie set his plate on the table and moved next to McLaren. He let his friend cry for several minutes. When the sobs slowed in their intensity, Jamie slid his arm around McLaren's shoulder. "You're playing the survivor's guilt game, Mike. If you really, honestly thought about it, you know you had no idea what was happening. You couldn't know John forced Bethany to phone Dena and get her over to Bethany's this morning. If you'd known, there's no doubt you wouldn't have let that happen. Right?" He smiled as McLaren raised his head.

"Is that how it happened?"

"Yeah. I interviewed John when I got back to the station. He's a pathetic git. He kept screaming that we had it all wrong, that we didn't understand."

"All wrong? With Bethany knocked out at his feet and…what you found…in the boot of his car?" He bit off the words, unwilling to speak Dena's name just then.

“Most of them do it. You should remember that, Mike. The great defense—deny it happened, deny you are responsible, and it’ll all go away. Or blame it on someone else.” Jamie reached for his beer and swallowed several mouthfuls. Despite the horrendous situation, it tasted good. He needed something good to hold on to. “But he finally confessed after two hours of my…water tight logic.”

“I wish I could’ve had two seconds with him.”

“There *are* times when I mourn the loss of the old ways. Sometimes a good threat or accident works miracles.”

“What did he say?” Despite his apparent interest in the carpet design, McLaren wanted to know. And Jamie thought it would help him heal.

“He admitted he killed Luke, though he claimed it was an accident, that his son just wanted Luke out of the way.”

“Where? Like in another town?”

“I don’t know. I couldn’t make much of his babbling. He saw Luke early that afternoon at the Engine House. A friend had dropped him off so he could practice serving balls at the missing brick hole. The friend was coming back for him—something about an appointment in Cromford—and John asked if he could see Luke serve. Luke obliged and John was duly impressed. He asked if that cemented Luke’s career decision to go into tennis. Luke said he’d made up his mind to pursue music and was looking forward to the tours and weeks on the road.”

“I’m no shrink, but that might’ve amplified his fantasy with his son.”

"You could be right. John cited the death of Will when he was traveling to his own music venue. I think John wavered between bouts of sanity and then believing his son was really here, slipping between the two worlds. But whatever he saw or thought, he honestly cared about Luke. He may've been really frightened now that Luke was adamant about a music career, or he may've been wallowing in his delusion with his own son. Whatever he thought at that moment, words became heated, with Luke basically saying it was his life, he loved music too much to give it up… You know the sort of thing. Anyway, John picked up a stone and bashed Luke's head in."

"Whether goaded by the son or not, yeah."

"He knew about the abandoned lead mines and shafts. His folk were miners, did you know?"

"Generations, it seems."

"Anyway, he figured the Crooked Back Mine was sufficiently desolate and off the beaten track, so he drops Luke's body in there."

"Did he choose that mine because it was handy, did he say?"

"Yeah, partly, but also because it was a fair distance from Langheath and the police might not think of looking there."

McLaren snorted and sank back into his chair. He reached for his beer and took a sip. "And…Bethany?"

"Merely a defense tactic on his part. As luck would have it, he was seated on a bench near Dena that day she…was trying to get you on the phone."

"Yesterday." McLaren's voice was so low Jamie barely heard it.

"Yes. He heard Dena telling me about the Tipton

brothers, that she suspected something but didn't know what it meant, and knew that someone in the village had something he didn't deserve."

"Had it under false pretenses, I think she said."

"She said that you needed to know, Mike, and evidently sounded serious enough for John to think she referred to him. Plus, Bethany brought her to John's house that morning, thinking you might be there or at least might know where you were. They'd been talking together when John opened the door."

"And, ever paranoid, he decided Dena had told Bethany her information."

"I suppose so."

"Or, as he said in the mine, Jamie, he was trying to…eliminate people who stood in Will's way."

"He could've assumed Dena's information was a roadblock to his son's career."

"Everything he did was for his son." McLaren tilted his head back and shut his eyes. He remained like that while Jamie continued.

"It makes sense in light of what happened. He got Bethany to meet up with Dena this morning so he could hear what she knew."

"And Dena, being loyal to me and remembering my scolding for getting involved in the case, thought she was protecting the information and kept quiet." McLaren lowered his head and wiped his eyes.

Jamie gave him a minute before he went on. "Either way, he took it as someone who stood in his or his son's way, so he had to…make sure she wouldn't talk." He took a sip of beer, feeling the thickening air. Setting the beer down, he said, "He didn't mean it personally, Mike. There really was no hatred in her death."

"Just another parental gesture for his child. Bloody hell." He leaned his head back and gritted his teeth. "I could kill him."

Jamie let the quiet build as he thought of the day's events. Would McLaren ever be the same caring man again? Jamie cleared his voice and spoke softly. "He went to the mine because he was going to kill and hide Bethany's body there."

"She's a…brave lady, Jamie. She gave me that hint about T'Owd Man, which she figured would point me to John."

"It was a lucky thing you met them." Jamie paused, glancing at the clock. Their food hadn't been touched but McLaren needed companionship and to be able to talk more than he needed the food.

"Dena…" McLaren took a gulp of air and looked at Jamie. "If I had had my mobile on yesterday and had talked to her, she'd be alive." He leaned forward, his eyes red.

He'd just started to heal, Jamie thought. From the emotional injury of leaving his police job, from the attack at the pub, from his mistrust of people. And now Dena's killed, and he's plunged right back into the anguish and suspicion he struggled to rid himself of.

"She'd be here with us, Jamie. But I had the damned phone off because I thought talking to Phil Moss was more important than talking to her." He muttered something under his breath. "If I only had had my phone on…"

Jamie leaned forward and pulled McLaren's shoulders around so that he faced him. "Look, Mike. You can say 'if' all day and it's not going to change a thing. It's no one's fault. Phil Moss is a real piece of work and you had to watch your step with him. He's this close to being a killer. You knew that. You also knew you needed to concentrate completely while you spoke to him."

"But Dena—"

"Wouldn't have wanted to visit you in the hospital, if things had got out of hand." He paused, refraining from mentioning that Phil Moss had still beaten and dumped McLaren in the forest, and that was why his mobile was off. "Playing 'if' isn't helping you. It doesn't help anyone. I know you feel damned awful about Dena and you blame yourself. I'm as sorry as hell and I grieve with you. But that doesn't change a thing. The sun will rise tomorrow and I'll deal with John Evans and you'll get calls for dry stone wall work. It's life, Mike. It keeps going, regardless of our insignificant lives that come and go. You will mourn for Dena and you will ache more than you ever thought possible, and you'll wonder how you can survive that pain. You'll remember it the rest of your life because you've never felt anything so strong and so terrible and so debilitating. It'll be with you every waking moment and in your dreams. But it will dull, given enough time. You'll never forget her, and you shouldn't, but you will be able to continue. And that's the day you need to keep in your sights and aim for." He finished quickly, thinking he had overstepped his friendship, hoping he hadn't alienated them. McLaren's grief was still new and growing, but Jamie needed to lecture his friend before the grief became a way of life.

McLaren sat quietly, the tears slipping from his eyes. He stared at Dena's photo cross the room. In the dim light the metal frame seemed to smile at them both.

Jamie looked at his friend. Six foot three and muscular, McLaren could handle most any situation he got into. But this one would not be smoothed over so easily, and McLaren would need a lot of help…if he would accept it.

McLaren walked to the door with Jamie and thanked him. He stood in the open doorway, oblivious to the biting wind and the sleet that pelted him and everything under heaven. The porch light cast an ethereal glow over him, as if he were removed from the scene, a wraith intruding upon the living.

It'll hit him later, Jamie thought as he walked to his car. Maybe tonight, maybe tomorrow, maybe not for a week or month, but it'll hit him. And he'll grieve for Dena in a desperation that we can't foresee. I just hope he can remember how much she loved him.

****

Darren Fraser came downstairs from folding and putting away his daughter's laundry. The clothes washing never seemed to end, nor did the aroma of fabric softener persistently clinging to him. Not too many years ago he'd smelled of Euphoria, been particular about the scents he used, especially the manlier fragrance of spice or forest. Those days felt long past. Now he lived enveloped in Comfort.

He fanned the edge of his shirt, trying to dispel the strawberry and lily scent, and stood in front of the television. The evening news had just begun, and he listened intently to the lead story. When it ended he turned off the set and poured himself a drink at the sideboard. His hands shook as he mixed the whiskey and soda, but he picked up the glass without spilling any. John Evans was in police custody for murdering some woman and under suspicion of killing Luke Barber. Bethany Watson had suffered minor abrasions and a concussion and was in hospital overnight for observation.

He walked to the fireplace and propped his arm against the mantel as he stared into the flames. Things were as twisted as a love knot, people doing things he never would have suspected. John Evans, for God's sake! That easy-going, music-loving milk sop.

Darren swallowed the whiskey in one quick gulp and banged the glass as he set it on the mantel. The body the police found in the mine was no doubt already formally identified, even if it wasn't on the television news. After all, Gary Barber would want to know. There was no reason to postpone it. It had to be Luke. Who else could it be, connected like that to John.

He lowered his head onto his arm and closed his eyes, trying to shut out the images of Sunday night. Should he ring up the police to tell them he assaulted that McLaren bloke outside the pub? They had ways of finding things out. Maybe they knew he'd bought the guitar strings in Chesterfield. That would link him to the assault no matter how much he'd tried to throw suspicion on someone else…anyone else.

Darren stared at his daughter's photo, suddenly terrified he had jeopardized everything he loved. He'd been so sure McLaren was going to try to pin Luke's murder on Callum. And that would be a catastrophe for his daughter. Ashley had lost Luke. How would she survive if Callum had been convicted? Wrongful arrests and prison sentences happened all the time.

He wiped his hand across his mouth, as though he

could taste his repulsive deed. Maybe he'd stir up more trouble if he confessed. He'd keep quiet. It wouldn't be the first time someone kept mum.

****

Phil Moss closed his mobile and leaned back in his chair. He and Tom had talked for a long time, sharing opinions about the news on the telly. Not that he was particularly surprised about the John Evans bloke topping Luke. Wasn't there an old saying that everyone was capable of murder if pushed hard enough?

He got up, grabbed his empty beer bottle, and padded into the kitchen. He dumped the bottle into the rubbish bin and glanced at his watch. His wrist was bare.

He walked back into the main room and rooted among the food cartons, tossed the sofa cushions onto the floor, shuffled through the magazines. No watch. It wasn't in his bed or in the dirty linen hamper or in his jacket pocket. He slammed his fist against the wall, leaving a dent in the plaster. He loved that watch. Where the hell was it?

****

Gary Barber hung up the phone and tried to understand what Jamie had told him. McLaren had found a body that afternoon and they believed it was Luke. There'd be a postmortem, of course. They also had the documentation of Luke's clothing the day of his disappearance and it matched what this lad was wearing. If he would make a formal identification…

He pulled out his checkbook and wrote a check. He'd mail it to McLaren tomorrow, along with a note of gratitude. He knew he didn't owe the man anything, for Jamie had asked McLaren to investigate. Still, Gary was grateful. He would have felt better if Luke had been buried, but that would come. He'd see to that.

Gary angled out the piano bench and sat down. Twilight crept across the fields and he could just distinguish the gate that Luke used to sit on, pretending it was a bucking horse. He watched until night swallowed up everything outside but he made no effort to switch on a lamp. The darkness suited his mood. Funny. He had prayed for this day, was even enthused to have McLaren look for Luke. He had assumed it would end like this, with Luke's body being found, but now that it was a reality, it felt surreal. He seemed to float above it all, looking down at himself.

He picked out "My Love Is Like a Red, Red Rose"—Luke's favorite tune—on the keyboard, his index finger missing a few notes or coming down too loudly on others. But the sentiment was there, as was the love. When it was over, he closed the keyboard cover and walked outside.

****

Later that evening, when McLaren had somehow cleaned up the dinner, he stumbled into the back room. The black sky seemed closer than it ever had, suffocating in its color and nearness. The sleet had stopped as he had put the food away, and now he stared at the clouds as they parted to reveal one silver star.

He wandered over to the stereo equipment and put in the CD of Handel arias. He turned up the volume for the first track and leaned his forehead against the windowpane. The cold glass cut through the dull ache of his body and mind, and he gazed at the star as the baritone in the recording sang.

I will not say it with my lips

Which have not that courage;
Perhaps the sparks
Of my burning eyes,
Revealing my passion,
My glance will speak.
Did you not hear My Lady
Go down the garden singing?
Blackbird and thrush were silent
To hear the alleys ringing.
Oh, saw you not My Lady
Out in the garden there,
Shaming the rose and lily
For she is twice as fair.
Though I am nothing to her,
Though she must rarely look at me,
And though I could never woo her
I love her till I die.
Surely you heard My Lady
Go down the garden singing,
Silencing all the songbirds
And setting the alleys ringing.
But surely you see My Lady
Out in the garden there,
Rivaling the glittering sunshine
With a glory of golden hair.

The song was written and sung for him. McLaren knew that as certain as he knew the sun would rise tomorrow and love was eternal. Handel had penned it for the centuries of lovers he would never know, and McLaren was one of them.

He hit the repeat button on the CD player and the music again filled the room. It seemed to wrap around his heart and sail up to the star.

He began singing with the baritone but quickly broke off and slumped against the glass, sobbing his love for Dena. He cried unashamed, desperate to understand her death and desperate to hold her one more time. His tears mingled with his grief for all the eons of lost loves and lost dreams, all the separations that would never be mended until Heaven called them together once more. He believed that with his entire being.

A word about the author…

Books, Girl Scouts, and music filled Jo A. Hiestand's childhood. She discovered the magic of words: mysteries, English medieval history, the natural world. She explored the joys of the outdoors through Girl Scout camping trips and summers as a canoeing instructor and camp counselor. Brought up on classical, big band and baroque music, she was groomed as a concert pianist until forsaking the piano for the harpsichord. She also plays a Martin guitar and has sung in a semi-professional folk group in the US and as a soloist in England.

A true Anglophile, Jo wanted to create a mystery series featuring a British police detective who left the Force over an injustice and now investigates cold cases on his own. The result is the McLaren Mysteries, featuring ex-police detective Michael McLaren.

Jo's insistence on accuracy—from police methods and location layout to the general "feel" of the area—has driven her innumerable times to Derbyshire. These explorations and conferences provide the detail filling the books.

She has employed her love of writing, board games and music by co-inventing a mystery-solving game, *P.I.R.A.T.E.S.,* which uses maps, graphics, song lyrics, and other clues to lead the players to the lost treasure.

Jo founded the Greater St. Louis Chapter of Sisters in Crime, serving as its first president. Besides her love of mysteries and early music, she also enjoys photography, reading, crewel embroidery, and her backyard wildlife.

Her cat, Tennyson, shares her St. Louis-area home.

www.johiestand.com